William Faulkner Manuscripts

General Editors

Joseph Blotner • Thomas L. McHaney
Michael Millgate • Noel Polk

Senior Consulting Editor

James B. Meriwether

A Garland Series

Contents of the Set

1. *Elmer* [1925]
2. *Father Abraham* [1926], bound with *The Wishing Tree* [1927]
3. *Soldiers' Pay* (1926). Two volumes
4. *Mosquitoes* (1927)
5. *Flags in the Dust* (*Sartoris*, 1929). Two volumes
6. *The Sound and the Fury* (1929). Two volumes
7. *As I Lay Dying* (1930)
8. *Sanctuary* (1931). Two volumes
9. *These 13* (1931)
10. *Light in August* (1932). Two volumes
11. *Doctor Martino and Other Stories* (1934)
12. *Pylon* (1935)
13. *Absalom, Absalom!* (1936)
14. *The Wild Palms* (1939). Two volumes
15. *The Hamlet* (1940). Two volumes
16. *Go Down, Moses* (1942). Two volumes
17. *Intruder in the Dust* (1948)
18. *Knight's Gambit* (1949)
19. *Requiem for a Nun* (1951). Four volumes
20. *A Fable* (1954). Four volumes
21. *The Town* (1957). Two volumes
22. *The Mansion* (1959). Four volumes
23. *The Reivers* (1962). Two volumes
24. Short Stories
25. "Unpublished" Stories

William Faulkner Manuscripts 19

Volume II

Requiem for a Nun
Miscellaneous Carbon Typescripts,
Galleys, and Page Proofs

Arranged by
Noel Polk

Garland Publishing, Inc.
New York and London   1987

Requiem for a Nun copyright © 1986 by W. W. Norton & Company, Inc.

Introduction copyright © 1987 by Noel Polk

The manuscripts in these volumes are housed in the Manuscripts Department of the University of Virginia Library, and permission to reproduce them has been granted by The Rector and Visitors of The University of Virginia on behalf of the Manuscripts Department.

The endpapers reproduce a holograph map of Yoknapatawpha County by William Faulkner, copyright © 1986 by Jill Faulkner Summers. It is reproduced here by permission of Mrs. Summers and The Rector and Visitors of The University of Virginia on behalf of the Manuscripts Department of the Alderman Library.

Library of Congress Cataloging-in-Publication Data

Faulkner, William, 1897–1962.
  Requiem for a nun.

  (William Faulkner manuscripts ; 19)
  Includes bibliographies.
  Contents: v. 1. Preliminary holograph and typescript materials—v. 2. Miscellaneous carbon typescripts, galleys, and page proofs—v. 3. Typescript setting copy—[etc.]
  1. Faulkner, William, 1897–1962—Manuscripts—Facsimiles. 2. Manuscripts, American—Facsimiles. I. Polk, Noel. II. Title. III. Series: Faulkner, William, 1897–1962. Works. 1986 ; 19.
  PS3511.A86   1986   vol. 19   813'.52 s   87-8741
                                  [813'. 52]
ISBN 0-8240-6825-4 (v. 1–2 : alk. paper)
ISBN 0-8240-6826-2 (v. 3 : alk. paper)
ISBN 0-8240-6827-0 (v. 4 : alk. paper)

The volumes in this series are printed on acid-free, 250-year-life paper.

Printed in the United States of America

Contents

Volume I

Introduction	vii
Outline of dramatic portions, Alderman Library 9817-b	1
Miscellaneous manuscript pages, Alderman Library IA:16a	3
Miscellaneous preliminary typescript pages, Alderman Library IA:16b	77
Ribbon typescript outlines of Acts II and III, Alderman Library 6271-x	183
Miscellaneous preliminary typescript pages, Alderman Library 6271-x	187

Volume II

Carbon typescript pages of Act I, Alderman Library 6271-x	1
Carbon and ribbon typescript pages of Acts II and III, Alderman Library 9817-a	51
Corrected galleys, Alderman Library IA:16	84
Corrected page proofs, Alderman Library IA:16f	215

Volume III

Typescript setting copy, Alderman Library IA:16c	1

Volume IV

Playscript drafts, Alderman Library IA:16b	1
Playscript drafts, Alderman Library 10124a	271
Composite playscript, Alderman Library 10124a	518

ACT I

THE COURTHOUSE

(A Name For The City)

~~REQUIEM FOR A NUN~~

~~ACT I~~

The courthouse is less old than the ~~jail~~ town, which began somewhere under the turn of the century as a Chickasaw Agency trading-post, and so continued for almost thirty years before it discovered, not that it lacked a depository for its records and certainly not that it needed one, but that only by ~~drunk~~ creating or anyway decreeing one, could it cope with a situation which otherwise was going to cost somebody money.

The settlement had the records; even the simple dispossession of Indians begot in time a ~~mi~~ minuscule of archive, let alone the normal litter of man's ramshackle confederation against environment---that time and that wilderness;---in this case, a meagre, fading, dogeared, uncorrelated, at times illiterate sheaf of land grants and patents and transfers and deeds, and tax- and militia-rolls, and bills of sale for slaves, and counting-house lists of spurious currency and exchange rates, and liens and mortgages, and listed rewards for escaped or stolen Negroes and other livestock, and diary-like annotations of births and marriages and deaths and public hangings and land-auctions, accumulating slowly for those ~~thirty years~~ three decades in a sort of iron pirate's chest in the back room of the

postoffice-tradingpost-store, until that day thirty years later
when, because of a jailbreak compounded by an ancient/iron monster
padlock transported a thousand miles by horseback from Carolina,
the box was removed to a small new leanto room like a
wood- or tool-shed built two days ago against one outside wall
of the morticed-log mud-chinked shake-down jail; and thus was
born the Yoknapatawpha County courthouse: by simple fortuity,
not only less old than even the jail, but come into existence
at all by chance and accident: the box containing the documents
not moved from any place, but simply to one; removed from the
trading-post back room not for any reason inherent in either
the back room or the box, but on the contrary: which----the box
----was not only in nobody's way in the back room, it was even
missed when gone since it had served as another seat or stool
among the powder- and whiskey-kegs and firkins of salt and lard
about the stove on winter nights; and was moved at all for the
simple reason that suddenly the settlement
(in time it would be a village; then a town; one day in about
a hundred years it would wake frantically from its communal
slumber into a rash of Rotary and Lion Clubs and Chambers of
Commerce and City Beautifuls: a furious beating of hollow
drums toward nowhere, but merely to sound louder than the next
little human clotting to its north or south or east or west,
dubbing itself city as Napoleon dubbed himself emperor and defending the expedient by padding its census rolls----a fever,
a delirium in which it would confound forever seething with

2.

REQUIEM FOR A NUN

ACT I:

The courthouse is less old than the town, which began as a Chickasaw Agency trading-post, and so flourished. But even the simple dispossession of Indians begot in time a certain minuscule of archive and record---a meagre fading dogeared uncorrelated at times illiterate sheaf of land grants and patents and transfers and deeds and tax- and militia-rolls and bills of sale for slaves and countinghouse lists of spurious currency and exchange rates and liens and mortgages and listed rewards for escaped or stolen Negroes and other livestock, and diary-like annotations of births and marriages and deaths and public hangings and land-auctions, accumulating slowly in a sort of iron pirate's chest in the back room of the postoffice-tradingpost-store, until one day inxthexmark somewhere in the early twenties it---the box---was removed to a small lean-to room like a wood- or tool-shed recently built against one outside wall of the morticed-log mud-chinked shake-roofed jail; thus was born the Yoknapatawpha County courthouse, cradle of justice and podium of judgment.

So even this first specific County office or at least storage-shed or anyway dumping-place of records, was even less old than

But they had it now, taken, as it were, by surprise, unawares, with no warning in advance to prepare and fend off: which was how the ~~lockxentered~~ padlock entered the business, putting the four ~~bandits~~---three---bandits into the log-and-mudchinking jail which until now had no lock since its clients so far had been amateurs---local brawlers and drunkards and an occasional runaway slave---for whom a single wooden beam falling across the outside of the door into two wooden slots like the door to a corncrib, had sufficed. But ~~thexexxxxxxxxxx~~ this was another kettle of fish; whether it like it or not, the settlement now held in custody what might be four---three---Dillingers or Jesse Jameses of the time, with rewards of money on their heads. So they contrived a lock on the jail door: a length of heavy chain passed through two auger holes, the ends clasped together by the monster padlock weighing almost fifteen pounds, with a key almost as long as a bayonet, not just the only lock in the settlement but the first lock in that cranny of the United States, having been brought into the country by one of the three white men who were what was to be Yoknapatawpha County's coeval pioneers and settlers: a man named Alexander Holston, who came as half groom and half bodyguard to Doctor Samuel Habersham, and half nurse and half tutor to the doctor's eight-year-old motherless son, the three of them riding horseback across Tennessee through the Cumberland Gap from Carolina along with Louis Grenier, the Huguenot younger son who brought the first slaves into the section and was granted the first big land patent and so became the first cotton planter, while Doctor Habersham with his worn black bag of pills and knives and his brawny taciturn

Even the jailbreak was fortuity again: a gang---three or four ---of Natchez Trace bandits (twenty-five years later legend began, and a hundred years after was still continuing, to affirm two of them to have been the Harpes themselves, Big Harpe anyway, because of the fact that the method of the break left behind it like a smell a kind of gargantuan and bizarre playfulness at once humorous and a little terrifying, as if the settlement had fallen, blundered into the notice of an idle and whimsical giant. Which was impossible, since the Harpes and even the last of Mason's ruffians were dead or scattered by this time, and the robbers would have had to belong to John Murrel's organization---if they needed any organization at all, other than the simple fraternity of rapine.) captured by chance by an incidental band of civilian more-or-less militia and brought in to the Jefferson jail since it was nearest, the military having gathered at Jefferson two days before for a Fourth of July muster and barbecue, which on the second day had degenerated---or had been refined by hardy elimination--- into a single general drunken brawling, until on the third morning when even the hardiest survivors were vulnerable enough for the people of the settlement to drive them out of town, the band in question having straggled and stumbled and been carried still comatose in an evicting wagon, four miles north of Jefferson to the Hurricane Bottoms, where they had made camp to regain their strength and legs, and where that night the four ~~or three bandits had stumbled onto their fire.~~ And here ~~report differed: some said that the sergeant of the~~

bodyguard and his half orphan child, was becoming the settlement itself (for a time, before it became Jefferson, it was known as Doctor Habersham's, then Habersham's, then simply 'Habersham'; a hundred years later, during a schism between two ladies' culture clubs over the naming of the streets in order to get ~~milxdelivery~~ house to house mail delivery, a movement was started, first, to change the name back to Habersham, then, failing that, to divide the town in two and call one half of it after the old pioneer doctor and founder)---friend of old Issetibbeha, the Chickasaw chief (the motherless Habersham boy, now a man of twenty-five, married one of Issetibbeha's granddaughters and in the thirties ~~was~~ emigrated to Oklahoma along with his wife's dispossessed people), first unofficial, then official Chickasaw agent until he resigned in a letter of furious denunciation addressed to the President of the United States himself; and---his charge ~~and pupil, a man now Alexander Holston became the settlement's first publican~~

5-A.

the four---or three---bandits, on their way across country to
their hideout from their latest foray on the Trace, stumbled
onto the campfire. And here report differed; some said that
the sergeant ~~of the militia~~ in command of the militia recognised one of the bandits as ~~being~~ being a deserter from his
corps, and others said that one of the bandits recognised the
sergeant as having once been a member of his, the bandit's,
group. Anyway, on the fourth morning all of them, captors and
captives, returned to Jefferson in a group, some said in confederation now seeking more drink, others said that the captors brought the prisoners back to the settlement in revenge
for having been evicted from it. Because Jefferson, ~~didn't want
any Natchez Trace bandits~~ being neither on the Trace nor the
River but lying about midway between the two, wanted no part
of the underworld of either. Because these were frontier, pioneer
~~are~~ times, where personal liberty and freedom were almost a
physical condition like fire or flood, and no community was
going to interfere with anyone's morals as long as the amoralist
practised somewhere else.

But Jefferson had the four bandits now. They put them in the
new log-and-mudchinking jail. It had no lock on it. Until now,
its inmates had been amateurs---local brawlers and drunkards
and an occasional runaway slave---for whom a simple wooden
beam dropped into wooden slots like the door to a corncrib
had sufficed. Now they contrived one: a length of heavy chain
passed through two auger-holes, the ends locked together by

4.

~~grammarian~~ and pupil a man now---Alexander Holston became the settlement's first publican, establishing the tavern still known as the Holston House, the original log walls and puncheon floors and hand-morticed joints and hand-wrought nails still buried somewhere beneath the pressed glass and brick veneer and neon tubes, the ancient giant of a padlock, fifteen pounds of useless iron lugged ~~fifteenhundredmiles~~ a thousand miles through a wilderness of precipices and swamps, of flood and drouth and wild beasts and wild Indians and even wilder white men, ~~brigands,~~ displacing that fifteen ~~poundsxx~~ pounds of weight and mass better given to food or seed to plant or even powder to defend themselves with, to become a fixture, a kind of landmark in the bar of a wilderness ordinary, locking and securing nothing because there was nothing behind Alexander Holston's heavy wooden bars and shutters needing further locking and securing, not even a paper-weight because the only papers in the Holston House were the twisted spills in an old powder horn above the hearth for lighting tobacco, always a little in the way since it had constantly to be moved: from bar to shelf to mantel then back to bar again: familiar, known, presently the oldest unchanged thing in the whole settlement, older than the people since Issetibbeha and Doctor Habersham were dead and Alexander Holston was an old man crippled with arthritis and Louis Grenier had a settlement of his own on his own vast plantation half of which was how even in the next county and Jefferson rarely saw him; older than the town since there were new names in it now even when the old blood ran in them---Sartoris and

6.

~~of his boots, men would murder a traveller and~~ ~~get him like~~
~~bear or a deer and fill the cavity with rocks~~ and sink it in
the nearest water;---not even trying to pass, ~~even~~ unseen
~~xxxxxxxxxxxxxxxxxxxxxxxxxxxxx prepared, through that~~ dark land
where other men, even though heavily armed and on the alert,
never travelled alone, ~~but actually announcing his military~~
    himself
~~coming as far in advance of him as the ringing of the~~ horn
~~would carry.~~

Stevens, Compson and McCaslin and Sutpen and Coldfield, and
you no longer shot a bear or a deer or a wild turkey simply
by standing for a while in your kitchen door, and now a pouch
of mail---letters and even newspapers---came regularly to the
settlement by means of a special horseman who did nothing else
and who was paid a salary by the Federal government: which---
the mail pouch---was the second phase of the monster Carolina
padlock's transubstatiation into the Yoknapatawpha County
courthouse.

The pouch didn't reach the settlement every week nor even
always every month. But sooner or later it did arrive, and
everybody knew it would, because it---the cowhide saddlebag
not even large enough to hold a full change of clothing, containing three or four or five letters and half that many badly-
printed one- and two-sheet newspapers already three or four
months out of date and usually half misinformed or even wholly
so to begin with---was the United States, the power and the
will to liberty, owning liegance to no man, bringing even into

7.

10 *Requiem for a Nun*, II, verso of preceding page

Sutpen, Compson and McCaslin and Stevens and Coldfield, and
you no longer shot a bear or a deer or a wild turkey simply
by standing for a while in your kitchen doorway, and now a
sack of mail and newspapers came into the town by means of a
special rider paid a salary by the Federal government: which
was how the ancient gargantuan lock came to ~~kxxk~~ in its iron
                                              cradle womb
vitals the seed of the Yoknapatawpha County courthouse.
                              itself

The sack of mail didn't always reach the settlement every week.
It didn't always do it even every month

that still almost pathless wilderness the thin peremptory
voice of the nation which had wrenched its freedom from one
of the most powerful peoples on earth and then again within
the same lifespan successfully defended it,---so much so that
the man who carried the pouch before him on the galloping horse
didn't even carry any other arms than a tin horn, month after
month traversing, blatantly, flagrantly, almost contemptuously,
a region where, for no more than the boots on his feet, men
would murder a traveller and gut him like a bear or deer or

fish and fill the body cavity with rocks and sink it in the
nearest water, not even deigning to pass quietly where other
men, even though armed and in parties or at least pairs, tried
to move secretly or at least without uproar, but instead announcing his own solitary approach as far ahead of himself
as the ring of the horn would carry. So it was not long before
Alexander Holston's lock had moved to the mail pouch, not that
the pouch needed one, having come already three hundred miles
~~from Nashville without a lock, less than ever there~~ in the
back ~~room of the trading post, surrounded and enclosed once
more by civilization, when it had not needed one during the~~
three hundred ~~miles of rapine-haunted wilderness, needing a
lock as little as it was equipped to receive one since it
been necessary to slit the leather with a knife just under each
law of the opening and insert the lock's iron mandible through
the two sides and clamp it home, so that any other hand with
a similar knife could have cut the whole lock from the pouch
as easily as it had been locked onto it; neither need nor oc-~~

8.

12 *Requiem for a Nun*, II, verso of preceding page

Stevens, Compson and McCaslin and Sutpen and Coldfield, and
you no longer shot a bear or a deer or a wild turkey simply
by standing for a while in your kitchen door, and now a sack
of mail and newspapers came to the settlement by means of a
special rider who did nothing else and was paid a salary by
the Federal government; and that was how the monster padlock
made the first step of its journey from xxxxxxxxxxxxxxxx
xxxxxxxxxxxxxxxxxx North Carolina to the door of
the Yoknapatawpha County jail.

The sack of mail didn't always reach the settlement every
week, it didn't always do it even every month. But sooner or
later, it did, and all knew it would, because it---the xxxxxx
cowhide saddlebag not large enough to xxxxxx hold a complete
change of clothing for one man, containing three or four
letters and as many badly-printed xxxxxx one-and-two-sheet
newspapers already three or four months out of date and usually
xxxxxxx half misinformed or even wholly misinformed to begin
with---was the United States, the power and the will to be
free, owning legence to no man, bringing even into that still
almost pathless wilderness the thin peremptory voice of the
nation which had wrenched its freedom from one of the most
powerful peoples on earth and then within the same lifespan
had successfully defended it;---so much so that the man who
carried the bag before him on the horse didn't even carry any
other arms with him than a tin horn, xx month after month
through a land where, for no more than xxxxxxx the possession

7.

from Nashville without a lock (at first it was projected that the lock remain on the pouch during the whole trip, each way between the settlement and Nashville and return. The rider refused, succinctly, in three words. His reason was the lock's weight. They pointed out to him that this reason would not hold water, since not only---the rider was a frail irascible little man weighing less than a hundred pounds---would the fifteen pounds of the lock even then fail to bring his weight up to that of a normal adult male, the added weight of the lock would barely match that of the pistols which his employer, the United States government, believed he carried and in a sense was actually paying him to carry, the rider's reply to this being succinct too though not so glib: that the lock weighed fifteen pounds either at the back door of the store in the settlement, or at that of the postoffice in Nashville, which his hearers admitted. But Nashville and the settlement were three hundred miles apart, so that by the time the horse had traversed that distance, the lock weighed not fifteen pounds but forty-five hundred. Which was manifest nonsense; no horse alive could carry forty-five hundred pounds. Yet indubitably fifteen pounds times three hundred miles was forty-give hundred somethings, either pounds or miles---expecially as while they were still trying to unravel it, the rider repeated his first three succint---two unprintable---words). So less than ever would it need one now in the back room of the trading-post, surrounded and enclosed once more by civilization,

where its very intactness, its presence to receive one, proved
its lack of that need during the three hundred miles of rapine-
haunted trace; needing a lock as little as it was equipped to
receive one since it had been necessary to slit the leather
with a knife just under each jaw of the opening and insert the
lock's iron mandible through the two slits and clash it home,
so that any other hand with a similar knife could have cut the
whole lock from the pouch as easily as it had been locked onto
it; neither need nor com-

pulsion but simply a gesture, of free men to free men, of civ-
~~ilization to civilization~~
ilization to civilization across not merely the three hundred
miles of wilderness to Nashville, but the fifteen hundred to
Washington: of respect without servility, allegiance without
abasement to the government which they had helped to found and
had accepted with pride but still as free men, still free to
withdraw from it at any moment when the two of them were no
longer compatible, the old lock meeting the pouch each time on
its arrival, to clasp it in iron and inviolable symbolism,
while Alexander Holston, ~~grew a little older~~ childless bachelor,
grew a little older and a little grayer, a little/ more arthrit-
        flesh
ic in ~~bones~~ and in temper too, ~~a little stiffer~~ a little stiffer
        bone
and more rigid in ~~gait~~ and in pride too since the lock was still
his, he had merely lent it, and so in a sense he was the grandfather of the inviolability not just of the government mail but
of a free government of free men too, so long as it remembered
to let men live free, not under it but beside it.

Then the ~~still~~ settlement had the four---three---bandits, any
        might have
one of whom, maybe all of whom, ~~had~~ a price on his head, so at
once they bored the auger wholes and found the piece of chain
and took the lock off the mail pouch and locked it on the
jail ~~~~ door. ~~They did it very quickly, not only not waiting~~
~~until he could have got back, but not even sending a messenger~~
~~across to the Holston House to ask old Alec's permission to~~
~~use the lock for the purpose---not that old Alec would have~~

9.

Stevens, Compson and McCaslin and Sutpen and Coldfield, and you no longer shot a bear or a deer or a wild turkey simply by standing for a while in your kitchen door, and now a pouch of mail ---letters and even newspapers---came to the ~~skxll~~ settlement by means of a special rider who did nothing else and was paid a salary by the federal government; that was how the monster padlock accomplished the second stage of its journey between North Carolina and the door of the Yoknapatawpha County jail.

The pouch didn't reach the settlement every week nor even always every month, but sooner or later it did arrive and everybody knew it would, because it---the cowhide saddlebag not even large enough to hold a full change of clothing, containing three or four or five letters and half that many badly-printed one- or two-sheet newspapers already three or four months out of date and usually half misinformed or even wholly so to begin with---was the United States, the power and the will to be free, owning liegance to no man, bringing even into that still almost pathless wilderness the thin peremptory voice of the nation which had wrenched its freedom from one of the most powerful peoples on earth and then within the same life-span had successfully defended it;---so much so that the man who carried the pouch behind him on the horse didn't even carry any other arms than a tin horn

jail door. They did it extremely quickly, not even waiting in until a messenger could have got back from the Holston House bar with old Alec's permission to use the lock for that purpose---not that he would have objected on principle nor refused his permission except by simple instinct; that is, he would probably have been first to suggest transferring the lock from the mail pouch to the jail if he had known in time or thought of it first, but he would have refused at once if he thought the thing was contemplated without consulting him; which everybody knew in the settlement knew, though this was not at all the reason why they didn't wait for the messenger. In fact, no messenger had ever been sent to old Alec; they didn't have time to send one, let alone wait for him to get back; they didn't even want the lock to keep the bandits in, since as was later prooved, the old lock would have been no more trouble for the bandits to pass than the heavy slotted wooden beam would have been; they didn't need the lock to protect the settlement from the bandits, but the bandits from the settlement, because the bandits had hardly reached the settlement when it developed that there was a faction or anyway a party determined to lynch them at once, which apparently had already tried and condemned them in advance and, it would seem, sight unseen too, since the first the settlement in general knew ℓ about it was when a small but determined gang moving by swift surprise almost succeeded in wresting the prisoners from their militia-captors before the militia could find any local authority to surrender them to, and would have succeeded except for a man named Comp-

10.

them to, and would have supposedly except for a man named Comp-
objected to his lock being transferred from the mail or used
son, who bought the pistols from Shell William-osboune
for that purpose
jail door. They did it extremely promptly, not even waiting
until a messenger could get back from the Holston House bar
with old Alec's permission to use, transfer, the lock; not that
he would have objected, except on principle; that is, he would
                          1
probably have been the first to suggest using the lock for that
purpose, if he had known in time or thought about it; he would
have refused his permission only if it had not been asked first.
And everybody knew this, though this was not at all the reason
why they didn't wait for the messenger. In fact, no messenger
was even sent to him; they didn't have time; as was later proved,
the old lock would have been no more trouble for the bandits to
pass than the heavy slotted wooden beam; they put the lock and
chain on to stop not egress but ingress because the bandits
                      settlement
had hardly reached the jail when it developed that there was a
faction or anyway a party in the settlement determined to lynch
them at once, apparently had already tried and condemned them
in advance

son who came to the settlement a few years ago with a ~~splendid~~ race horse which he swapped to Ikkemotubbe, old Issetibbeha's successor, for/ a square mile ~~xx~~ of what was to be the most valuable land in the future town of Jefferson, who, legend said, drew a pistol ~~xxxxxxxx~~ and held the ravishers at bay until the bandits could be got into the jail and someone sent to the trading-post back room for old Alec Holston's lock. Because there were indeed new names and faces too in the settlement now---faces so new as to have (to the settlement) ~~xxxxxxx~~ no discern*ib*~~i~~ble antecedents other than indubitable mammalinity ~~xxx~~ nor past other than the simple years which had scored them, and names so new as to have no discernible(nor discoverable either)antecedents or past ~~either~~ *at all,* as though they had been invented yesterday, report differing again to the effect that there were more people in the settlement that day that the militia sergeant whom one or all of the bandits might recognise.

So Compson locked the jail, and a courier, armed and with the two best horses in the settlement, riding one and leading one, cut through the woods to the Trace to ride the hundred-odd miles to Natchez with news of the capture and the settlement~~s~~'s authority to dicker for the reward; ~~and***Compson*xpresiding***~~ and that evening in the Holston House public room there was held the settlement's first municipal meeting---prototype not only of the town council when Jefferson would begin to consider itself a town, but of the chamber of commerce when it would be-

11.

jail door. They did it extremely quickly, not even waiting until a messenger could have got back from the Holston House bar
with old Alec's permission to use the lock for that purpose----
not that he would have objected, except on principle; that is,
he would probably have been the first to suggest or even command
the transfer of the lock from the mail pouch to the jail door
if he had known in time or thought about it; he would have refused his permission only if he had not been consulted first.
(which everybody in the ~~staff~~ settlement knew, though this was
not at all the reason why they didn't wait for the messenger.
In fact, no messenger had ever been sent to old Alec; they
didn't have time to send one; they had not even needed the lock
at all
for the sake of the bandits since, as was later proved, the
old lock would have been no ~~more~~ trouble for the bandits to
pass than the heavy ~~want~~ slotted wooden beam would have been

gin to proclaim itself a city---with Compson presiding: not
Alec, who was quite old now, grim, taciturn, crippled, sitting
even on a hot July night before a smoldering log in his vast
chimney, his back even turned to the conference table (he
was not interested in the deliberation; the prisoners were his
already since his lock retained them; whatever the conclave decided would have to be submitted to him for ratification anyway before anyone could touch his lock to remove it) around
which the progenitors of the Jefferson city fathers sat in what
was almost a council of war, not only discussing how they would
acquire the reward, but how they would defend it when they had
it. Because there were two factions of opposition now: not
only the group bent on hanging the bandits out of hand, but the
militia band too, who now claimed that as prisoners the bandits
might be in temporary custody of the settlement but as prizes
they still belonged to their original captors, who had surrendered nothing but the custody and had relinquished nothing
whatever of the reward: on the prospects of which, or anyway
on the strength of something, the militia band had got more
whiskey from the trading-post store and had built a tremendous
bonfire in the road in front of the jail, around which---the
fire and the keg----they and the lynching faction had
now confederated in a council of their own, if anything that
loud could have been called by any name implying medita-
tion: which was one version of it, and the only one then,
since Doctor Peabody, old Doctor Habersham's successor, never
told the other one until fifty years later when he himself was
an old man too: which was, that Compson had made formal demand

12.

on his, Peabody's, professional bag in the name of the public
peace and welfare, and the three of them----Compson, Peabody,
and the ~~storekeeper~~ post trader, had added the ~~xxxxxxxx~~
laudanum to the whiskey and sent the keg as a gift ~~of the~~ from
the settlement to the astonished militia sergeant, and then returned to the Holston House ~~public~~ kitchen to wait until the
uproar had died, whereupon the law and order party made a quick
sortie and gathered up the opposition, ~~like so much cord wood
and dumped them all~~ militia and lynchers too, and dumped them
~~all~~ like so much cord wood into the jail with the bandits and
relocked the door on all of them, and went home to bed until the
next morning, when the first arrivals saw a scene resembling
an outdoor stage setting: which was how the legend of the mad
Harpes started: a thing not just fantastical but incomprehensible. not just whimsical but a little terrifying, though at least
                         wanton and
there was no/smoking blood in it, which the Harpes would have
left: not just the lock gone from the door nor even just the
door gone from the jail, but the entire wall was gone, the
mud-chinked axe-morticed logs unjointed neatly and quietly in
the night and stacked as neatly to one side, leaving the jail
open to the ~~settlement~~ street like a stage, in which ~~xxxx~~
the last evening's insurgents still lay variously in deathlike
slumber, the whole settlement gathered now to watch Compson
trying to kick at least one of them awake, until one of the
Holston House slaves----the cook's husband, the waiter---~~xxxx~~
ran across the way and into the crowd, shouting, 'Whar ~~xxxx~~
~~the xxxxxxxxx xx xxxx, old boss say whar xx look.~~

13.

~~It was gone (as were the horses belonging to three of the opposition lynching faction)~~

de lock, whar de lock, ole Boss say whar de lock.'

It was gone (as were three horses belonging to three of the lynching faction). They couldn't even find the heavy door with its auger hole and chain, and at first they were almost betrayed into believing that the bandits had had to take the door/~~with~~
                                                                                                steal
~~them~~ in order to ~~keep~~ the lock, catching themselves back from the very brink as it were, from this wanton accusation of rationality. But the lock was gone, nor did it take the settlement ~~long to realise that not the bandits nor the reward, but the escaped bandits nor the aborted reward, but the dark missing lock was not even the situation which they faced, but the problem which threatened them~~ long to discover that it was not the escaped bandits and the aborted reward, but the lock, and not a simple situation which faced them, but a problem which threatened, the slave presently departing back to the Holston House at a dead run and then reappearing at the dead run almost before the door had had time to hide him, darting among the crowd up to Compson himself now, saying, 'Ole Boss say bring de lock'--- not send the lock, but bring the lock: so that soon Compson and his lieutenants---among them, Doctor Peabody and the proprietor of the store (and this was where the mail ~~carrier~~ rider began
                                                        the
to appear, or rather to emerge---/ fragile wisp of a man ageless hairless and toothless, who looked too frail even to approach a horse, let alone ride one six hundred miles every two weeks,

14.

yet did so, and not only that but had wind enough left to not only to announce and precede but even follow his passing with the jeering musical triumph of the horn----a contempt for possible---probable---despoilers matched only by that for the official dross of which he might be despoiled, and which agreed to remain in civilised bounds only so long as the despoilers had the taste to refrain)---repaired to the Holston House kitchen where old Alec still sat before his smoldering log, his back still to the room and still not turning it this time either. And that was all. He ordered the immediate return of his lock. It was not even an ultimatum, it was a simple instruction, a decree, uninterested, even inattentive, the mail rider now well into the fringe of the group, saying nothing and missing nothing, like a weightless dessiccated or fossil bird, not a vulture of course nor even quite a hawk, but say a pterodactyl chick arrested just out of the egg ten glaciers ago and so old in simple infancy as to be worn and weary ancestor to all subsequent life. They pointed out to old Alec that the only reason the lock could be missing was that the bandits had not had time or been able to cut it free of the door, and that even three fleeing madmen on stolen horses would not carry a six foot oak door very far and that a party of Ikkemotubbe's young men were even now trailing the horses westward toward the River and that without doubt the door and the missing lock would be found at any moment, probably under the first bush at the edge of the settlement: knowing better, knwoing that there was no limit to the fantas-

15.

tic the terrifying and the bizarre of which the men were capable who already, just to escape from a log jail, had quietly removed one entire wall and stacked it in neat piecemeal at the roadside, and that they nor old Alec neither would ever see his lock again.

Nor did they; the rest of that afternoon and most of the next day too, while old Alec still sat smoking his pipe in front of his smoldering log, the ~~grimxxeldersxnfxthe~~ settlement's sheepish and raging elders hunted for it, with (by this time: the next afternoon) Ikkemotubbe's Chickasaws helping too, or anyway watching: the wild men, the wilderness's tameless evictant children looking only the more wild for white man's butternut and denim and felt and straw which they wore, standing or squatting or following, grave attentive and interested, while the white people cursed and sweated among the bordering thickets of ~~thexperiens~~ their punily-clawed foothold; and always the rider, Pettigrew, ubiquitous, everywhere, not helping search himself and never in anyone's way, but always present, inscrutable, saturnine, missing nothing: until at last, toward sundown, Compson crashed savagely out of the last bramble-brake and ~~saidxxGodxdamnxit~~, ~~wellxpayxhimxforxhisxdamnedxlockxt~~ flung the sweat from his face with a full-armed sweep sufficient to repudiate a kingdom with, and said, ~~Godxdamnxitxwexllxbuyxhisxdamnedxlockxthen~~' 'All right, God damn it, let's pay him for it then.' Because they had already considered that possibilty; they had already realised its seriousness from the very fact that Peabody had tried to make a joke on the subject, which everyone realised *i*

16.

was not a joke after all; he----Peabody----had said, 'Yes---and quick, before he has time to advise with Pettigrew and ~~we~~ price it by the pound.'

'By the pound?' Compson said.

'Pettigrew just weighed it by the three hundred miles from Nashville. Old man Alec brought it from Carolina. That's fifteen thousand pounds.'

'Oh,' Compson said. So Compson called in his men, rallyingby blowing a foxhorn which one of the Chickasaws wore on a thong around his neck, though even then they paused for one last quick conference; again it was Peabody who stopped them.

'Who'll pay him for it?' he said. 'It would be just like him to want a dollar a pound for it even if, by Pettigrew's scale, it hadn't ever left Carolina.' They---Compson anyway----had probably already thought of that; that, as much as Pettigrew's presence, was doubtless why ~~Compson~~ he had essayed to rush his civic congeries ~~in~~ to old Alec with the offer so quickly that none would have the face to renege on his pro rata. But Peabody had torn it now. Compson looked about at them, sweating, grimly enraged.

'That means Peabody will maybe pay one dollar,' he said. 'Who pays the other fourteen? Me?' Then Ratcliffe (he was the trader, the store's proprietor; a hundred years later his name would still exist in the county, but by then it would have lost the *c* and the final *fe* both) solved it--- a solution so simple, so limitless in retroact that they didn't

17.

even wonder why nobody had thought of it before, which not only solved the problem but abolished it, and not just that one but all Problem, from now on into perpetuity, opening to their vision like the rending of a veil, like a glorious prophecy, the vast splendid limitless panorama of America: that land of limitless opportunity, that bourne, created not by nor of government, but <u>for</u> government: a government not of the people nor by the people but for the people as was/the heavenly manna of old, ~~illimitable,~~ ~~vast,~~ ~~without~~ ~~beginning~~ ~~nor~~ ~~end~~ with no demand on man save the chewing and the swallowing since out of its own Allgood it would produce create and support a race/of laborers dedicated to the/single purpose of picking up the manna and ~~even~~ putting it into his lax hand or even between his jaws,---illimitable, vast, without beginning nor end, not even a trade or a craft but a beneficence as sunlight or rain or air are beneficence, inalienable and immutable.

'Put it on the Book,' Ratcliffe said---the Book, not a ledger but the ledger since it was probably the only thing of its kind between Nashville and Natchez, unless there might happen to be a similar one ~~sixthe~~ a few miles south at the ~~next~~ first Chocktaw agency at Yalo Busha---a ruled, paper-backed copybook such as might have come out of a school room, in which accrued, with the United States as debtor, in Mo Ha Taha's name (the/Chickasaw matriarch, Ikkemotubbe's mother and old Issetibbeha's sister, who---she could write her name, or at least make something which was agreed to be, or anyway accepted as, a valid signature---signed all the deeds and patents as

18.

her son's kingdom passed to the white people, regularising it anyway), the crawling tedious list of calico and gunpowder, whiskey and salt and snuff and denim pants and osseous candy drawn from Ratcliffe's shelves by her descendants and subjects and Negro slaves. That was all the settlement had to do: add the lock to the list. It wouldn't even matter at what price they entered it. They could have priced it on Pettigrew's scale of fifteen pounds times one thousand miles, and nobody would ever have noticed it probably; they could have charged the United States with fifteen thousand dollars worth of the fossilised and indestructible candy, and none would ever read the entry. Thus it was done, finished. They didn't even have to discuss it. They didn't even think about it any more, unless perhaps here and there to marvel (a little speculatively probably) at their own moderation, since they wanted nothing---least of all, to escape any blame---but a fair and decent adjustment of the lock. They went back to where old Alec still sat with his pipe in front of his dim hearth. Only, they had underestimated him; he didn't want any money at all, he wanted his lock. Whereupon what little was left of Compson's patience now went completely.

'Your lock's gone,' he said harshly. 'You'll take fifteen dollars for it,' he said, his voice already fading, because even that rage could recognise impasse when it saw it, nevertheless---the rage, the impotence, the sweating, the too much---whatever it was---forcing the voice on for one more word anyway: 'Or-----' then stopping for good, until Peabody filled the gap:

19.

'Or else?' Peabody said. 'Or else what?'
Then Ratcliffe saved that too.

'Wait,' he said. 'Uncle Alec/'s going to
take fifty dollars for his lock. A garntee. He'll give us the
name of that blacksmith back in Cal'lina that made the other
one for him, and we'll send back there and have a new one made.
Going and coming and all'll cost about fifty dollars. We'll
give him the fifty dollars in cash to hold as a garntee, then
when the new lock comes, he'll give the money back to us.
All/right, Uncle Alec?' That could have been all of it, would
have been all probably, except for Pettigrew. Not that they
had forgotten him nor even assimilated him; they had simply
sealed----'healed' (so they thought)---him into their civic
crisis as the desperate and defenseless oyster immobilises
the atom of inevictable grit. He came forward now, among and
between them yet displacing none nor even brushing aside anyone, as though he had no substance; you would have said that he
had oozed to the front except for that quality durable as ada-
mant. ~~[struck through]~~ He spoke in a voice bland, reasonable and happy.

~~'Uncle Alec hasn't lost any lock.~~' That was
the ~~United~~ States government.

Somebody said, 'What?' He ~~stood~~ there, be-
ing looked at, ~~weightless and childsized~~, impregnable as diamond ~~manifest with perfect~~

mant; he spoke in a voice bland, reasonable and paternal, and then stood there being looked at: weightless and childsized, impregnable as diamond, manifest with portent and doom: who had brought into that log backwoods room a thousand miles in pathless wilderness the whole vast incalculable weight of federality, not representing the government nor even himself the government, but more: for that moment he was the United States.

'Uncle Alec hasn't lost any lock,' he said. 'That was the United States.'

After a moment someone said, 'What?'

'That's right,' Pettigrew said; now his voice became rapid and glib, dry, heatless, impersonal, uninterested: 'Whoever first put that lock of Holston's on that mail pouch either made a voluntary gift to the United States, or he or they done something else.'

'What else?' Ratcliffe said.

'Committed a violation of act of Congress as especially made and provided for the defacement of government property, penalty of five thousand dollars and not less than one year in a Federal jail. Not to mention whoever cut them two slits in the pouch to put the lock in, act of xxngraxxxsxesex Congress as especially made and provided for the xxxxx injury or destruction of government property, penalty of ten thousand dollars and not less than five years in a Federal jail. You can take your pick.' He spoke to old Alec: 'I reckon you're going to have supper here sooner or later or more or less, aint you?'

21.

'Wait,' Ratcliffe said. He turned to Compson. 'Is that true?'

'What the hell difference does it make whether it's true or not?' Compson said. 'What do you think he's going to do as soon as he gets to Nashville?' He said violently to Pettigrew: 'You were supposed to leave for Nashville this morning. What were you hanging around here for?

'Maybe I was helping,' Pettigrew said. 'You dont want any mail. You aint got any way to lock it// up.'

'So we aint,' Ratcliffe said. 'Let the United States hunt for its lock, then.' This time Pettigrew didn't look at anybody.

'Act of Congress as especially made and provided for the unauthorised removal and or use or felonious use or misuse or loss of government property, penalty the value of the article plus five hundred to ten thousand dollars and thirty days to ten years in a Federal jail. They may even make a new one when they find out you have charged a lost post office department lock to the bureau of Indian affairs.' He moved; now he was speaking to old Alec again: 'I'm going to set a while with my horse. When this caucus is over and you get around to cooking and eating again, you can send your nigger for me.'

He went out. They looked at one another. 'What do you reckon he hopes to get out of this?' Ratcliffe said. 'A reward?' But that was wrong; they knew it; it violated his whole character.

'He's already getting what he wants out of it,' Compson said, and cursed again. 'Confusion.' But that was not it either; Peabody saw it at once and said so:

'No, that's wrong too. A man that will ride six hundred miles through this country twice a month with nothing but a foxhorn, aint really interested in confusion anymore than he is in money.' So they didn't know what was in Pettigrew's mind. They didn't even know what he was going to do. But they knew him; they had known him for the three years now during which, fragile and inviolable and undeviable and preceeded for a mile or more by the strong sweet ringing of the horn, on his strong and tireless horse he would complete the bi-monthly trip from Nashville to the settlement; they knew that they dared not chance it, sitting for a while longer in the darkening room while old Alec still smoked, his back still squarely presented to them and their quandary too, then dispersing to their own cabins for the evening meal--- with what appetite they could bring to it, since presently they had drifted back through the summer darkness when by ordinary they would have been already in bed, to the back room of Ratcliffe's store now, to sit again until suddenly Peabody stirred and said, 'Wait a minute.'

'What?' somebody said. But he hadn't quite

23.

broke in on Compson's profane and savage recapitulation (and on ~~Ratli~~ Ratcliffe too; his attitude puzzled them a little too/: ~~kxxxx~~ a mixture of bewilderment and alarm, but with something of respect too; he was still unshakably convinced that Pettigrew's aim was a material one; it was as though Pettigrew had divined or invented some form of material recompense of which he, Ratcliffe, was incapable not only of gaining but even of imagining) to say sharply to no one: 'Wait.'

'What?' someone said. But Peabody didn't answer. He said to Ratcliffe:

'You'll know if anybody does. What's his ~~christian~~ name?'

'Whose name?' Ratcliffe said. 'Oh, Pettigrew's.' Ratcliffe told him. 'Why?' But Peabody wouldn't say. But there was something in his mind: hope: a straw perhaps, but at least a straw; so much more than they had had until now that they were even willing to know no more until Peabody was ready to tell them, even to the extent of letting Peabody and Compson walk away together toward Compson's cabin when they broke up.

'All right,' Compson said. 'What?'

'It may not work,' Peabody said. 'But you'll have to back me up. When I speak for the whole settlement, you'll have to make it stick. Will you?'

Compson cursed. 'Why the hell waste time asking? Just tell me something of what I'm going to have to guarantee.' So Peabody told him, a little of it, and the next morning entered the stall in the Holston House stable where Pettigrew was grooming his ugly hammerheaded ironbottomed horse.

24.

'We decided not to charge that lock to old Mo Ha Taha, after all,' Peabody said.

'That so?' Pettigrew said. 'Nobody in Washington would ever catch it, certainly not the ones that can read.'

'We're going to pay for it ourselves,' Peabody said. 'In fact we're going to do a little more than that, even. We've got to repair that jail wall, anyhow. So we're going to build a courthouse too.' Now Pettigrew stood up. He had been hissing between his teeth at each stroke of the brush, like an Irish groom; looking at Peabody, he made one last gentle half-hiss half-whistle.

'A courthouse?' he said.

'So we can have a town,' Peabody said. 'We've already got a church, and we're going to build a school too, so we can have a real town, and name her. It'll take a little time to raise the school, but the courthouse wont take long, since we've got to repair the jail anyhow. But we dont need to wait at all to name her. We've decided to do that today.'

They looked at one another. 'So?' Pettigrew said.

'Ratcliffe tells me your name's Jefferson,' Peabody said.

'That's right,' Pettigrew said. 'Thomas Jefferson Pettigrew. I'm from old Ferginny.'

'Any kin?' Peabody said.

'No,' Pettigrew said. 'My ma named me for

him, so I'd have some of his luck.'

'Luck?' Peabody said.

'That's right,' Pettigrew said. 'She didn't mean luck. She never had no schooling. She didn't know how to say what she meant.'

'Have you had it?' Peabody said. Pettigrew looked at him. 'I'm sorry,' Peabody said. 'Try to forget it.' He said, 'We decided to name her Jefferson.' Now Pettigrew didn't even seem to breathe. He just stood there, small, frail, less than boysize, childless and bachelor, incorrigibly tieless, looking at Peabody. Then he breathed and, raising the hand holding the brush, he turned back to the horse and for an instant Peabody though he was about to resume the grooming. But instead of making the xxxx stroke, he laid the hand and the brush against the horse's shoulder and stood for a moment, his head and face turned slightly away and lowered a little. Then he raised his head and turned it back to face Peabody.

'You could call that lock 'axel grease' on that Indian account,' he said.

'Fifty dollars worth of axel grease?' Peabody said.

'To grease the wagons for Oklahoma,' Pettigrew said.

'So we could,' Peabody said. 'Only her name's Jefferson now. We cant forget that anymore now.'

26-27

'So we could,' Peabody said. 'Only her name's Jefferson now. We cant ever forget that anymore now.' So they built the courthouse. They restored the jail wall and cut the logs and slit the shakes and raised the little floorless lean-to against it and moved the iron chest from the back room of Ratcliffe's store. It took only two days and cost nothing but the labor

~~from its communal slumber into a rush of Rotary and Lions~~

~~clubs and Chambers of Commerce and City Beautifuls~~, a furious

beating of hollow drums ~~toward nowhere but merely~~ to sound
              h
louder than the next little human clotting to its north or

south or east or west, dubbing itself ~~city as~~ Napoleon dubbed

himself emperor ~~and~~ defending the expedient by padding its

census ~~rolls---a fever, a delirium in which it would confuse~~

~~forever seething with motion, and motion with~~ progress) found

itself possessed of another ~~municipal~~ receptacle or edifice,

~~with nothing to put in it.~~

~~Because of the jailbreak, a gang--~~three or four---of Natchez

~~Trace bandits captured by an incidental band of civilian more-~~

~~or-less militia~~

tireless lift and rythm as if they had the same aim and hope,

which they did have as far as the Negro was capable, as even

Ratcliffe, son of a long pure line of Anglo-Saxon mountain people

and /destined/ father of an equally long and pure line of white

trash tenant farmers who never owned a slave and never would

since each had and would imbibe with his mother's milk a person-

al violent antipathy not at all to slavery but to black skins,

could have explained: the slave's simple child's mind had fired

at once with the thought that he

42.

REQUIEM FOR A NUN

ACT I

The courthouse is less old than the town, which began as a
Chickasaw Agency and trading-post. But even the simple dispossession of Indians begot a certain minimum of archives and records, which were presently moved, lock stock and barrel and,
including the sort of iron pirate's chest in which they were
kept, from the back room of the postoffice-tradingpost-store
to a small lean-to room like a wood- or tool-shed built against
one outside wall of the jail.

So even this first specific Yoknapatawpha County office or at
least storage-shed or anyway dumping-place of records was even
less old than the jail

north Mississippi and west Tennessee too as ~~The Academy.~~ The
Female Institute; old Alec Holston died and bequeathed back to
the town the fifteen dollars it had reimbursed him for the lock,
and Louis Grenier had died two years ago and his heirs had de-
livered to the town the fifteen hundred dollars his will had
devised them, and that summer there was a committee, Compson
and Peabody and Sartoris(and (in absentia) Sutpen ; nor did the
town ever know exactly how much of the additional sum Sartoris
and Sutpen contributed), and the next year the/unjointed marble [eight]
columns were disbarked from the Italian ship at New Orleans,
into a steamboat up the Mississippi to Vicksburg, and into a
smaller steamboat up the Yazoo and the Sunflower and the Talla-
hatchie, to Ikkemotubbe's old landing which Sutpen himself now
owned, and thence eight miles by oxen into Jefferson: the two
identical four-column porticoes, one on the north and one on
the south, each with its balcony of wrought-iron New Orleans
grillwork, ~~wherexinxtheirxMayxandxNovemberxfrom~~ one of which [on]
(the south one) in 1861 Sartoris stood in the first Confederate
uniform the town had ever seen, while ^on the ~~lawn~~ below a [Square]
Richmond mustering officer enrolled the regiment which ~~Sartos~~
Sartoris as its colonel would take to Virginia as a part of
Bee, to be Jackson's extreme left in front of the Henry house
at First Manassas, and from both of which each May and November
for a hundred years, bailiffs in their ~~in~~ orderly appointive
almost hereditary succession would cry/ 'Oyes oyes honorable [without inflection or punctuation!]
circuit court of yoknapatawpha county come all and ye shall
be heard' because when in 1863 a Union force burned the Square,

Gowan is four years older. He looks exactly like what he is: only child of a widow living in a New Orleans hotel apartment, who went three years to the University of Virginia without graduating due to the fact that he got married through what he believed was a sense of honor and chivalry, and has spent the subsequent six years living up to it,—a face almost typical in the south which during the first quarter of the century was full of it, but a face to which something—tragedy—something it had not counted on, had had no way to foreknow ~~and guard~~ nor equipment fend against, has happened, and which is now trying, really and sincerely trying, not at all/to look stronger than it is, but merely to be stronger. He and Stevens both wear topcoats, unbuttoned, and carry their hats. Stevens stops. Gowan drops his hat onto the sofa in passing and follows to where Temple, at the table, is stripping off one of her gloves. His attitude toward her is V
watchful, hovering, protective/. ~~for the moment almost completely selfless.~~

She kneels, facing the burning fire, her back to Stevens. He
watches her. Then he crosses toward her, taking the handkerchief
from his breat pocket, stops behind and over her and extends the
handkerchief. She turns her head, looks at the handkerchief,
then at him. Her face is quite calm.

                    TEMPLE
What's that for?

                    STEVENS
For tomorrow, then.

                    TEMPLE
~~The fourteenth of March, you mean. The day after~~
~~The fourteenth of March, maybe?~~ Oh, I see. For cinders.
On the train. We're going by air; hadn't Gowan told
you? We leave from the Memphis airport at midnight;
we're driving up after supper. Then California tomor-
                                            in the
row morning; maybe we'll even go on to Hawaii ~~later~~
spring. No; wrong season. Canada. Lake Louise, in May and
June ----

There is a sound from beyond the dining-room door as if Gowan
were about to return. Neither move, watching each other.

                    TEMPLE
So why the handkerchief? Not a threat, because you

TEMPLE (cont)
dont have anything to threaten me with. And not a
bribe, because I dont have anything you want. Do I?
         (they watch each other: quickly)
All right. Put it this way. I dont know what you want,
because I dont care. Because whatever it is, you wont
get it from me

                    TEMPLE (cont)
        She rises quickly, turns, and pauses, listening for an instant
                    toward the dining-room door.
                    TEMPLE (rapid, tense, voice down)
            Now he'll give you a drink, and then he'll ask you what
            you want, why you followed us home. I'm going to answer
            you. The answer's No. If what you came for is to see
            me weep, I doubt if you'll even get that. But you cer-
            tainly wont get anything else. Not from me. Do you
            understand that?

                    STEVENS
            I hear you.

                    TEMPLE
            Meaning, you dont believe it.

                    GOWAN

Right, dear.
                    (to Stevens)
You see? Not just a napkin: the right napkin. That's
how I'm trained.
                    (he stops suddenly, noticing Temple,
                    who has done nothing apparently: just
                    standing there holding the milk. But he
                    seems to know what is going on: to her)
What's this for?

                    TEMPLE
I dont know.

but
He moves; they kiss, not long and not a peck; definitely a kiss
between a man and a woman. Then, carrying the milk, Temple
crosses toward the hall door.

                    TEMPLE (to Stevens)
Goodbye until then until next June. Gee Gee will send
you and Maggie a postcard.
                    (she goes on to the door, pauses and
                    looks back at Stevens)
I may even be wrong about Temple Drake's odor too; if
you should happen to hear something you haven't heard
yet and it's true, I may even ratify it. ~~Perhaps~~ Maybe you
can even believe that.— if you can believe you are
going to hear anything that you haven't heard yet.

                    STEVENS
Do you?

67.

46 *Requiem for a Nun*, II, verso of preceding page

GOWAN (cont)

tend to---provided you can catch us before

we cross the Tennessee line tonight.

You see? Not just a clean set a bright napkin. That's

not lightabody. I know better. So maybe it's just my

own stinking after all that defying it tickles to

doubt. nothing apparently: just

Maps the Dubois

it) know what is going on: to her)

I'm not even going to take Gowan with me when

I say goodbye and go up stairs----and who knows? I may

even be wrong about Temple Drake's odor too; if she

should know to tell you anything between now and

the thirteenth of March, ratify it

He approaches. They kiss, maybe even briefly speak: definitely

a kiss between a man and a woman. Then carrying the milk, Tem-

Gowan enters toward the hall door tray with a glass of milk and

a napkin and salt shaker, comes on to the table.

TEMPLE (to Stevens)

Goodbye then until next June. Gee Gee will send you

what were you talking about now?

(she goes on to the door, pauses and

looks back)

Nothing. I was just telling Uncle Gavin that he had

something of Virginia or some kind of gentleman in him

too, he may have inherited from you through your grand-

father, and that I'm going upstairs and give Gee Bee

a bath and his supper.

(she touches the glass for heat, then

takes it up: to Gowan)

66.

TEMPLE (cont)
Thank you, dear.

GOWAN
Right. (to Stevens, not turning)
             just
You see? Not only a napkin, the right nap-
         That's
kin. how I am trained.
              (he stops suddenly, noticing Temple;
              she has done nothing apparently: just
              standing there holding the milk. But
              he seems to know what is going on;
              to Temple)
What's this for?

TEMPLE
I dont know.

He approaches; they kiss, not long but not a peck: definitely
a kiss. Carrying the milk, Temple crosses toward the hall door.

TEMPLE (to Stevens)
                until next June maybe
So goodbye then, and I'll send you a postcard. Or
Gee Gee will.

STEVENS
Do. Maybe even a letter. I mean Gee Gee by that time.
Who knows?

~~talking mostly, you know~~

She folds the paper back into its old creases, folds it still again. Stevens watches her.

STEVENS

Well? This is the eleventh. Is that the coincidence?

TEMPLE

No. This is.
>(she drops, tosses the folded paper onto the table, turns)

It was that afternoon---the sixth. We were on the beach, Gee Gee and I. I was reading, and he was---oh, talking mostly, you know---'Is California far from Jefferson, mamma?' and I say 'Yes, darling'---you know: still reading or trying to, and he says, 'How long will we stay in California, mamma?' and I say, 'Until we get tired of it' and he says, 'Will we stay here until they hang Nancy, mamma?' and it's already too late then; I should have seen it coming but it's too late now; I say, 'Yes, darling' and then he drops it right in my lap, right out of the mouths of---how is it?---babes and sucklings? 'Where will we go then, mamma?' And then we come back to the hotel, and there is you are too. Well?

STEVENS

Well what?

TEMPLE
Not enough. Try again.

STEVENS
You were there.

> (with her face averted, Temple reaches
> out, fumbles her hand until she finds
> the cigarette box, takes a cigarette
> and with the same hand fumbles until she
> finds the lighter, draws them both back
> to her lap). Stevens watches her)

At the trial. Every day, all day, from the time court opened----

TEMPLE (puts the cigarette into her
mouth, talking around it, the cigarette
bobbing)
The bereaved mother. Herself watching the accomplishment of her revenge. The tigress over the body of her dead cub----

STEVENS
----who should have been too immersed in grief to have thought of revenge----

TEMPLE (outwardly calm, her voice light
and casual, the cigarette bobbing)
Methinks she doth protest too much?

81.

STEVENS

Stevens doesn't answer, watching her as she snaps the lighter, lights the cigarette, puts the lighter back on the table. Leaning, Stevens pushes the ashtray along the table to where she can reach it.

TEMPLE

Thanks. It doesn't matter what I know, what you think I know, what might have happened, whether it ever happened or not. Because we wont need it. Now let grandmamma teach you how to suck an egg. All we need is an affidavit that she is crazy, has been for years.

STEVENS

I thought of that too. Only, it's too late. That should have been done about five months ago. The trial is over now. She has been convicted and sentenced. In the eyes of the law, she is already dead. In the eyes of the law, there is no such person as Nancy Mannigoe. Even if there wasn't a better reason than that. The best reason of all. We haven't got an affidavit.

Diversions: chronic: S.I.A.A. Basketball Tournament, Music Festival, Junior Auxiliary Follies, May Day Festival, State Tennis Tournament, Red Cross Water Pageant, State Fair, Junior Auxiliary Style Show, Horse Show Girl Scouts Horse Show, Feast of Carols.
Religion, Drama, Movies,
Diversions: acute: Churches, Theatres, Motion Pictures, Y.M.C.A., Baseball, Swimming, Tennis, Golf, Skeet, Riding.

After the beginning, Earth lurched, the ice fled infinitesimally
Equatorward, ~~intoxicatedxxxxxxxx~~ scouring out the valleys,
scoring the hills; a long long time ago, but not as long as God,
Who had the long view, decreeing down the long eras this
rounded knob, this gilded pustule, tilting Earth still further
to recede the sea: necklacerim on rim of crustacean-husks, recessional contour lines as trees aged ~~xxxxxxxxxxxxxxxxx~~
~~xxxxxxxxxxxxx~~ south and still south, baring their to
air the confluent continental swale, south and still south recessional the decrecent processional river towns: St Louis, Paducah, Memphis, Helena, Vicksburg, Baton Rouge, baring to air
the ~~primordial~~ primeval winterless unseasoned miasma not any of
earth or water or life but all of each, inextricable and indivisible; one seethe one mother-womb one furious tumescence, father mother one One vast ejaculation of itself incubent

52 *Requiem for a Nun*, II

Beyond the ice-cap, after the earth lynched, heaving darkward
the long continental flank, dragging beneath the polar cap that
furious equatorial womb, the shutter-lid of ice severing into the
black and heedless void one last sound, one cry, one puny fading
        incredulous
myriad ~~and tongueless~~ incrument, and then no more, the blind
                                              recordless
and tongueless earth splendid on, bearing the long noumbless
astral orbit, frozen, tideless xxxxxxxxxxx xxxxxxxxxxxxxxxxx il-
xxxxxxx continental swale, xxxxxxxxxxxxxxxxxxxxx the broad
blank mid-continental page for the first scratch of orderly xxxxxxxxx,xxx xxxxxxxxxxxxxxxxxx xxxxxxxxxx and temperate record-
ing---the laboratory-factory whose floor-plan covered twenty
states, established and ordained for the purpose of manufactur-
ing one: the ordered and unhurried whirl of seasons, of snow
and rain and ice and freeze and thaw and sun and drouth to
richen and aereate and loosen the dirt, the conflux of a hundred rivers into one vast father of rivers bearing the rich
dirt south and south, carving bluffs to bear the long march of
the river towns, spreading each vernal flood over the Mississippi lowlands, / spewning the rich dirt and the receeding,
raising   earth
~~building~~ inch by inch and foot and year and century the land
which one day would tremble for miles to the passing of a train
like when the cat crosses the suspension bridge

it anymore but a raccoon or a possum whose hide was worth at
the most two dollars, turning the earth into a howling waste
from which he would be the first to vanish, not
even on the heels but synchronous with the slightly darker wild
men whom he had dispossed, because, like them, only the wilderness could feed and nourish him. And so disappeared,
strutted his roering eupeptic hour, and was no more,
leaving his ghost, pariah and proscribed, scriptureless now and
armed only with the highwayman's, the murderer's, pistol,
haunting the fringes of the wilderness which he himself had
helped to destroy, because the river towns marched now recessional south by south along the professional bluffs: St Louis,
Paducah, Memphis, Helena, Vicksburg, Natchez, Baton Rouge, peopled by men in broadcloth and flowered waistcoats, who owned
with mouths full of law,
Negro slaves and   beds and buhl cabinets
imported Empire furniture and ormolu clocks, who strolled and smoked their cigars along the bluffs
and flatboat
beneath which in the shanty purlieus he rioted out the last
of his doomed evening, losing his worthless life again and again
to the fierce knives of his drunken and worthless kind;---
this in the intervals of being pursued and harried
in his vanishing avatars of Harpe and Hare and
Mason and Murrel, either shot on sight or hoicked, dragged out
secret
of what remained of his wilderness haunts along the overland Natchez Trace (one day someone brought a curious
seed into the land and inserted it into the earth, and now vast
fields of white not only covered the

with mouths

ACT II

THE GOLDEN DOME

(Beginning was)

JACKSON, Alt. 294 ft. Pop. (A.D.1950)---
Located by an expedition of three ~~appointed~~ Commissioners appointed and dispatched for that single purpose, on a high bluff above Pearl River at the approximate geographical center of the State, to be not a market town nor even ovum-foetus of the American industrial dream, nor even as a place for men to live, but to be a capital, the capital of a Commonwealth;

After the beginning, the earth lurched; the ice fled minuscule and infinitesimally equatorward, scouring out the valleys, scoring the hills;---a long long time ago but not as long as God already decreeing down the long arras out of the long irony pre-night this rounded knob, this golden pustule, tilting the earth still further to recede the sea by necklace-rim on -rim of crustacean-husks in recessional lines like the concentric whorls within the sewn stump telling the tree's age, baring south by recessional south to air the confluent continental swale, already decreeing a million years behind that steamy chairoscuro the processional river-towns: St Louis, ~~Cairo Girardeau Memphis~~ Paducah, ~~Memphis Natchez Vicksburg Baton Rouge~~

100.

ACT II

THE GOLDEN DOME

(Beginning Was)

JACKSON. Alt. 294 ft. Population.(A.D.1950)

Railroads: Illinois Central, Yazoo & Mississippi Valley, Alabama & Vicksburg, Gulf & Ship Island.

Bus: Tri-State Transit, Vanardo, Thomas, Greyhound, Dixie-Greyhound, Tech-Greyhound, Oliver.

Air: Delta, ~~Airlines~~ & Chicago & Southern.

Transport: Streets Busses, Taxis.

Accomodations: Hotels, Tourist Camps, Rooming Houses.

Radio: WJDX, WTJS.

~~Diversions~~, Moral: Churches.

~~Diversions, Mental: Theatres, Motion Pictures.~~

~~Diversions, Physical: Y.M.C.A., Baseball, Swimming, Tennis, Golf, Skeet, Riding, Basket Ball, Skating Rink~~

~~Diversions, Spiritual:~~ Music Festival, Follies, May Day, Style Show, Feast of Carols, ~~State Fair, Water~~ Carnival, ~~Horse Show.~~

After the ~~beginning, the~~ ~~first infinitesimally~~ Earth lurched; the ice fled infinitesimally Equatorward, into winterless miasma

e etarian amaze amid the heavy leather-flapped air, then the ice:
the earth lurched, heaving darkward the long continental flank,
dragging upward beneath the polar cap that furious equatorial
womb, the shutter-lid of cold severing off into blank and heedless void one last sound, one cry, one puny myriad incredulous
indictment already fading and then no more, the blind and
tongueless earth spinning on, looping the long recordless astral orbit, frozen, tideless; yet still was there, older than
the steam and more durable than the ice, this tiny gleam, this
spark, this gilded xxxxb buried crumb of man's eternal hope,
thisxroundedxknobxthisxgildedxpustulexdecreedxxxxinvinciblex
preordainedxandxinviolatexbidingxxxtxsleepxbutxstasis xxxxxx
this golden dome, this rounded knob, this gilded pustule decreed
and invincible, preordained and inviolate, biding, not sleep
but stasis; the earth lurched again sloughing; the ice fled
equatorward in minuscule and infinitesimal speed, scouring out
the valleys, scoring the hills, sloughing that iron pre-night,
tilting still further to recede the sea rim by necklace-rim of
crustacean husks in recessional contour-lines like the concentric whorls within the sawn stump telling the tree's age, baring south by recessional south to air and light the confluent
continental swale, carving bluffs to bear the long mutter of the
river-towns: St. Louis, Paducah, Memphis, Helena, Vicksburg,
Baton Rouge,

101.

ACT II
THE GOLDEN DOME
(Beginning Was)

JACKSON. Alt. 294 ft. Pop. (A.D. 1950) 201,092.

Located by an expedition of three Commissioners appointed and dispatched for that single purpose, on a high bluff above Pearl River at the approximate geographical center of the State, to be not a market town nor even ovum-foetus of the American industrial dream, nor even as a place for me to live, but to be a capital, the capital of a Commonwealth;

In the beginning was ~~already~~ ~~this gilded pustule, millions years beyond that~~ steamy ~~shit~~ chair-~~oscuro~~; that untimed unseasoned winterless ~~plasma~~ not any one of earth or water, or life but all of each, inextricable and indivisible; that one seethe one spawn one mother-womb, one ~~furious~~ tumescence, father-mother-one, ~~one what~~ incubant ejaculation ~~already fissionating in one boiling mass~~ of litter from the celestial work-bench, ~~that one spawling~~ crawl and creep printing with three-toed mastodonic tracks the steamy-green swaddling-cloths, grandfather of the coal and oil, above which soared the pea-brained reptilian ~~hands~~ heads in tentative veg-

100.

ACT II

THE GOLDEN DOME

(Beginning Was)

JACKSON. Alt. 294 ft. Pop. (A.D. 1950)

Located by an expedition of three appointed Commissioners, on high bluffs above Pearl River at the approximate geographical center of the State to be not a market town nor even ovum-foetus of the American industrial dream, but a capital, the capital of a commonwealth.

After the beginning, the earth lurched; the ice equatorward fled minuscule and infinitesimally, scouring out the valleys, scoring the hills;——a long long time ago but not as long as god already decreeing out down the long arras out of the long iron pre-night this rounded knob, this gilded pustule, tilting the earth still further to recede the sea: necklace-rim on rim of crustacean-husks, recessional contour-lines like the concentric whorls within the sawn severed stump telling the tree's age, baring south by recessional south to air the confluent continental swale, already decreeing a million years behind that steamy chairoscuro the processional river-towns: St Louis, Paducah, Cape Girardeau, Memphis, Helena, Vicksburg, Baton Rouge; baring to air the primordial primeval

100.

of earth or water or life but all of each, inextricable and
indivisible: one seethe, one mother-womb, one spawn one furious tumescence, father-mother-one, one vast troubant ejaculation already
fissionating in one furious moil of litter from that celestial experimental work-bench: one spawning crawl and creep
printing with three-toed mastodonic tracks the steamy-green
grandfathers of the coal and the oil,
tundra-dense swaddling cloths above which soared for a hundred
feet in tentative vegetarian amaze the pea-brained reptilian
necks, while the heavy air flapped with

"118.

tion;

And still the people and the railroads: the ~~Gulf Mobile~~ New Orleans and
Great Northern ~~Northern~~ down the Pearl River valley, ~~and the Gulf~~ the Gulf,
Mobile ~~and Northern~~ northeast, ~~in 1885~~ a line via Yazoo City
and the upper river towns to ~~xix~~ Chicago and the Great Lakes,
the Gulf and Ship Island which was the beginning of the south
Mississippi lumber boom, population doubled and trebled; ~~in
1895 the new Capitol~~ 1892 Millsaps College opened its doors to
~~become one of~~ the first in the State in higher learning, and in
~~1905~~

STEVENS (cont)

when the letters turned up, because she probably was.
Because she had forgotten about them, forgot she ever
wrote them probably. I mean, not surprised at ultimate
catastrophe. Not that she had been consciously ~~waiting~~
expecting ~~it~~, waiting for it constantly all the time,
all the ~~six~~ eight years. ~~Six~~ Eight years ago you moved say into
a new house, a strange house in the sense that this
one had a roof which could collapse on your head at
any moment. You didn't know it of course at the time,
or rather, didn't realise it at the time. You didn't
believe then that it wouldn't collapse about your ears,
not that it could not nor even that it might not, but
simply that it would not collapse on you for the simple
reason that the roofs of houses did not collapse on
the heads sheltering under them, else by this time people would have invented a substitute for houses or at
least roofs which would not ~~xxpx~~ collapse. You certainly didn't expect at first that this one would collapse
on you. Indeed, on the contrary, you not only didn't
expect it to collapse, ~~what if it did,--- ('so what?'~~
~~you would say if you were Temple Drake's age.) Cer-~~
~~tain experiences in your recent past had taught you~~
~~that the whole sky could rain on your head, doing---~~
~~in retrospect, when looking back---no harm at all---or at least~~
~~none that need concern anyone else, any outsider. And~~
this was just a roof, and (had you
expect it to collapse, what if it did/?--- ('so what?'
you would put it, in the ~~language~~ tongue suitable to eight

155.

F - L H of G   (cont)   3/21   135

                    CORNELIUS
            ~~There was a man — a roughneck — and the girl~~
            ~~while she believed you were a priest?~~

                    CARMODY
            No. At least, I ~~have~~ escaped that much censure
            ---is that it?

                    CORNELIUS
            You are ~~not being censured.~~ Your sin was not that.
            ~~I'm not even setting you a penance.~~ I don't have
            to. You did that for yourself

---had to hope. But at least she had nature, at least
for a little while, yet for almost three years in fact,
until the next child, xxxx The trauma of shock: you
are walking a tightrope, to cross an abyss; you,dont
have time to worry about the chasm beneath nor the
distance ahead; you are too busy thinking just the
next step ahead, setting that one foot planted and balanced;---in this case, the house: the progressing interminably and with no real xxxx advancement from one
cooking- or washing-gadget switch to the next, repo-
titive, endless, but enough, soporific and muff of anguish, as if deterrent were not a progressive diminishing chain, but a sprocket, a circle, in which she was
safe so long as it didn't break;---not to mention the
forgiveness and the being grateful for it: like the
juggler say, not with three durable and insentient
Indian clubs or replaceable plates or vases, but three
electric bulbs filled with nitroglycerin and not e-
nough hands for any single one: one hand to offer the
atonement with and another to receive the forgiveness
with and a third needed to offer the gratitude and

                    168.

141.

In my house.

R leads into the nursery where the child is asleep in its crib.
At rear, french windows open onto a terrace; this is a private
entrance into the house itself from outdoors. At L, a closet
door stands open. Garments are scattered on the floor about it,
indicating that it has been searched, not hurriedly so much as
savagely and ruthlessly. At R is a fireplace with a fire burning. A desk stands against the rear wall, showing the same savage and ruthless searching. A table center, beside the table are
two packed bags, obviously Temple's. A smaller one, obviously
for an infant, sits open and partly packed on the table. Temple's
hat, gloves, bag are on the table. The whole room indicates the
immediate departure of Temple, and that something has been
vainly, yet ruthlessly and perhaps frantically, searched for.

of the living-room, the scene is now:

Scene 2

Interior. Temple's private sitting- or dressing-room. 9:30 P.M.,
thirteenth
~~twelfth~~ September, ante.

A door L enters from the house proper. A door R leads into the
nursery where the child is asleep in its crib. At rear, french
windows open onto a terrace; this is a private entrance to the
house itself from outdoors. At L, a closet door stands open.
Garments are scattered about the floor near it, indicating that
the closet has been searched, not hurriedly so much as savagely
and ruthlessly and thoroughly. At R is a fireplace with a fire
burning. A desk against the rear wall is open, showing the same
savage and ruthless searching. A table center, beside the table
are two packed bags, obviously Temple's. A smaller one, obviously for an infant, sits open and partly packed on the table. Temple's hat, gloves and bag are on the table. The whole room indicates the immediate departure of Temple, and that something
has been vainly yet savagely and completely, ~~xxxxxxxxxxxx~~ perhaps even frantically, searched for.

When the lights go up, PETE is standing in the open closet door,
holding a final garment, a negligee, in his hands. He is between
25 and 30. He does not look like a criminal; that is, he is not
a standardised recognisable ~~gangster~~ type. He looks almost like
the general conception of a college man, or a successful young

173

F - L H of G 3/1   24.
L

peasants and goatherds, didn't matter because they were
not going anywhere, we were just a priest and a servant
travelling through the country. And even if we met a
caravan without having time to dodge, it would take the
same number of days for them to carry the word back to
Ch'ing that a priest had been seen, and the same number
of days again for Yang's gang to reach the place where
the priest had been seen. Because as soon as Yang
found out the next morning that Jim and I were missing,
and that the priest's robe was gone too, he would know
what had happened, he just didn't know where. An still
Jim never had told me why he decided to leave when we did.
I mean, about Yang's new idea for fun and games with that
whip, which after all could have been my business, since
it was my face Yang aimed to use, and like I told Jim, I'd
a heap rather take a whip across it than jump out of that
54 again onto a hundred miles of jagged mountain with
nothing on top of it but one thin cloud ——
what it was that happened so sudden that we had to pull out practically carrying
our own shoes in our hands.

CLOSE SHOT: CARMODY AND HANK ON THE MULES.
Carmody's beard is now gone and he is wearing the dead
priest's robe. Hank wears his usual clothes except for
a peasant jacket, to help with the idea that they are
a priest and a servant. Hank's voice continues over the
scene.

                    HANK'S VOICE
        And now we had already made three days.
        Only ten more to go and then we were
        safe as far as we were concerned, the
        whole country could rise up and holler
        to Ch'ing that they went that way when
        it happened.

They are nearing where the narrow mountain trail bends
around the shoulder of the hill. They are plodding steadily
along, they have been safe so long that they are a little
careless. When they ride around the corner it is too
late. About a hundred yards away is a caravan of laden
pack mules and five bearers, approaching up the trail.
Carmody and Hank rein up. Hank reacts violently.

                    HANK
        Back around the corner, quick.

                    CARMODY
                (Restrains him)
        It is too late now. Try to act like
        what you are supposed to be.

                    HANK
        What am I supposed to be right now except
        scared?

that the marble eyes under the marble palm stared not toward
the north and the enemy, but to the south, toward (if anything)
his own rear,---looking perhaps, the wits said, because the old
war was thirty-five years past now and you could even joke about
it,(except the women, the ladies, who even another thirty-five
years from now would still get up and stalk out of picture
houses showing Gone With The Wind), for reinforcements, or
perhaps not a combat soldier at all but a provost marshal's man
looking for deserters, or perhaps himself for a safe place to
run to. Because that old one was already dead: the sons of those
tottering irreconcilable old men in gray had already were died
in blue coats in Cuba, the new one already usurping the earth
before the blast of blank shotgun shells and the weightless
collapse of bunting unveiled it, already in a back yard on the
edge of town moving fast, faster: from the speed of two horses
on either side of a polished tongue, to that of thirty horses
then fifty horses and then a hundred horses under a tin hood,
which from almost the first explosion would have to be controlled
by law and police; already in a back yard on the edge of town
an ex-blacksmith's apprentice, a grease-covered man with the
eyes of a visionary monk, was building a gasoline buggy, casting
his own cylinders and rods, inventing his own coils and plugs
anx and valves as he found he needed them, which would run, and
did: crept popping and stinking out of the lane at the exact
moment when the banker Bayard Sartoris, the colonel's son,
passed in his carriage: as a result of which there is on the
books of Jefferson today a law prohibiting the operation of any

icebox on the back gallery for you, and the children in ~~rotating~~
rotational neighborhood gangs followed it, eating the fragments
of ice which the Negro driver chipped off for them; and that
year a specially built sprinkling cart began to make the rounds
of the streets every day: a new time, a new day, a new age; there
were screens in windows now; people could actually sleep in summer night air, finding it harmless, uninimical: as if there
waked suddenly in man (or anyway his womenfolks) a belief in his
inalienable civic right to be free of dust and bugs: a new age,
a new time; the old one had died, strutted its hour and vanished
from the stage; the town wrote its epilogue and epitaph: that
same year (1900) on Confederate Decoration Day, Mrs Virginia
Dupre, Colonel Sartoris's sister, pulled a cord and the spring-
restive bunting collapsed and flowed from the marble effigy---
the stone infantryman on his stone pedestal rising from the
exact spot where forty years ago the Richmond officer and the
local minister had mustered in Colonel Sartoris's regiment, and
the old men in ~~grayxuniforms~~ the gray and braided coats (all
officers now, none less in rank than captain) tottered into
the sunlight and fired shotguns at the bland sky and raised
their cracked ~~voicesxthexshri~~ quavering voices/the shrill
                                               e
hackle-lifting yelling which Lee_s_ and Jackson and Longstreet
and ~~the two Johnstones~~ (and Grant and Sherman and Hooker and _Pope_
and McClellan and Burnside _too_ for that matter!) had listened to
amid the smoke and the din; epilogue and epitaph, because neither
the U.D.C. ladies who instigated and bought the monument ~~nor~~
the architect and masons who erected it, apparently had noticed

49.

~~hixxxefxaxxxnhuxyxnaw~~ is no longer remembered by the vibration-
fading air; then the turn of a century, the long-ago iron dream
of a railroad ftom Memphis all the way to the Atlantic ocean
was now an intricate accomplishment covering the south and east
like the veins in an oak leaf and creating millionaires by the
trainload almost, and twenty-five years ago Colonel Sartoris
and General Compson and a third man (whose name was not even always remembered except by the older people who had been coeval
with the duel in which he had killed ~~Colonel~~ Sartoris; he---Red-
mond---had the money: a Northerner, a cotton and quartermaster
supplies speculator who had followed the Federal armies to Mem-
phi^s in '61 and thence down into Mississippi and Yoknapatawpha
County, bringing no family with him and leaving no kin behind)
had built one from Jefferson up into Tennessee to connect with
it, which in its turn was now part of a system, you could get
on a train in Jefferson now and ~~wkmx~~ wake up tomorrow in New
Orleans or Chicago; there were electric lights and running water
in almost every house in town except the Negro cabins, and now
the town ~~bought~~ and brought from a great distance a kind of gray
crushed ballast-stone which it called macadam and paved the whole
street leading from the depot to the Square and the hotel, so
that no more would the train-meeting hacks carrying the drummers
and the lawyers and court-witnesses need to lurch and heave
and strain through the winter mudholes; every morning a wagon
came to your very door with artificial ice and put it in your
~~icebox on the back gallery for you, and that year a specially~~
~~built sprinkling cart began to make the rounds~~

48.

ing, beacon and focus and lodestar, higher and taller than any other out of the rapid and fading wilderness, the wilderness not receeding from the rich and arable fields as tide recedes, but (as though) the fields themselves rich and inexhaustible to the plow rising sunward and airward out of swamp and morass, themselves thrusting back brake and thicket, bayou and bottom and forest along with/the wild men and the animals which its copeless denizens--- haunted them and (once) dreamed of, imagined, wanted, no other; drawing the people---the men and women and children, the maidens, the marriageable girls and the young men---flowing, pouring in with their tools and goods and cattle and slaves (gold, money, too) behind ox or mule teams, by steamboat up and down the rivers and thence across the country (soon there would be talk of even a railroad in the country, not a hundred miles away, running all the way from Memphis to Charleston on the Atlantic Ocean), and now there was another newcomer in Yoknapatawpha County, a man named John Sartoris, with slaves and gear and money too like Grenier and Sutpen, but who was an even better balance to Sutpen than old Louis had been because he, Sartoris, could have even coped/with Sutpen in the sense that a individually man with a sabre or rapier and heart enough for it could cope with one with an axe; now it was the seventh summer, Sutpen's Paris architect had long since gone back to wherever it was he came from and had made his one abortive midnight try to return, but his trickle, flow of bricks had never even faltered, his molds and kilns had built two brick churches and were now raising the wall and what would be known through all

45.

and presently Compson began to own the Indian accounts for tobacco and calico and jeans pants and cooking-pots on Ratcliffe's books (in time he would own Ratcliffe's books too) and one day Ikkemotubbe owned the race horse and Compson owned the land ~~itsel~~ itself, some o~~f~~ which the city fathers~~would~~ would have to buy from him at his price in order to establish a town; and Pettigrew with his tri-weekly mail, and then a ~~singe~~ monthly stage and the new faces coming in faster than old Alex Holston, arthritic and irascible, ^hunched^ ~~squatting~~ like an old surly bear over his smoldering hearth even in the heat of summer (he alone now of that original three, since old Grenier no longer came in to the settlement, and old Doctor Habersham was dead, and the old Doctor's son, in the opinion of the settlement, had already turned Indian and renegade even at the age of twelve or fourteen) ~~no~~ ^any^ longer made any effort, wanted, to associate names with; ~~until a day when not only Ikkemotubbe and his Chickasaws, but Habersham and Holston and Grenier too, were there on sufferance, anachronistic and forgotten~~ and now indeed the last moccasin print vanished from that dusty widening, the last towed-in heel-less light soft quick long-striding print pointing west for an instant, then trodden from the sight and memory of may by ~~the~~ a heavy leather heel engaged not in tne traffic of endurance and hardihood and survival, but in money,---taking with it (the print) not only the moccasins but the deer-hide leggins and jerkin too, because Ikkemotubbe's Chickasaws now wore ~~jeans and~~ eastern factory-made jeans and shoes sold them on credit out of

214.

overtaken, caught in the swamp not by Sutpen and Sutpen's wild
West Indian ~~headman~~ headman and Sutpen's bear hounds, nor by
Sutpen's destiny nor even by his (the architect's) own, but by
the destiny of Jefferson, the town; not his own fate nor even
just his luck, but the long arm of Progress reaching out into
~~that~~ midnight swamp, to pluck him out of ~~that bayed~~ circle of
dogs and half-naked Negroes and pine torches in order to stamp
the town with him: who (the architect) ~~maixaaly~~ in planning the
courthouse and the jail, planned the town too; who designed not
merely two buildings, but created a city, ~~xxx~~ then vanished, was
gone, none knew where nor—so rapid was change—had time to
wonder, not flung out of the town by Progress, once his work
was done, but as though, inattentive too, Progress had merely
relaxed its fingers, opened its hand; gone, leaving behind the
~~trickle and flow~~ of bricks which never even faltered, his molds
and kilns having built the two brick churches and by tomorrow
would have raised the walls of ~~the~~ that Female ~~Xaxxxxy~~ Academy a certificate
from which, to a young woman of North Mississippi or West Tenn-
essee, would have the same almost mystic value as an invitation
dated from Windsor castle signed by Queen Victoria would for a
young female from Long Island or ~~Pennsylvania~~ Philadelphia;
tomorrow, and the railroad ran unbroken from Memphis to Carolina, the light-wheeled bulb-stacked wood-burning engines
shrieked among the swamps and cane-brakes where bear and panther
still lurked, and across the open woods where the ~~deer~~ browsing still
drifted in pale herds like unwinded ~~smoke: they~~—the wild animals, the beasts—remained, they coped, they would endure; a

220.

by something capable of moving faster than thirty miles an hour
and now the last forest tree was gone from the court house yard
too, replaced by formal synthetic evergreen shrubs bred and
trained in Wisconsin greenhouses,(and now there squats on rubber
tires,on the other flank of the Confederate monument, a tank-
destroying weapon captured from a regiment of Germans in an
African desert by a regiment of American Japanese whose mothers
and fathers were in a California detention camp for enemy aliens) and from the fronts of the stores, the old brick made of
native clay in Sutpen's architect's old molds, replaced now by
sheets of glass taller than a man and longer than a wagon and
team, pressed intact in Pittsburg factories, beyond which,
bathed in the shadowless corpse-glare of fluorescence, farmers
and their wives and children, in clothes manufactured last year
in New York sweat-shops, bargain for clothes manufactured last
week in New York sweat-shops;

And now and at last, silence too from the American earth, the
one American air ululant with ceaseless radio because now and
at last there was only one American air; no longer anywhere,
one last irreconciliable foothold of fastness from which to enter the United States because at last even the last old sapless
indomitable unvanquished unvanquishable women had died and the
old deathless Lost Cause had become a faded(though still select)
social club or caste, or form of behavior when you remembered
it on the occasions when young men from Brooklyn, exchange students at Mason and Dixon universities, vended tiny confederate

240.

sinecure under the designation of United States marshal, an office held back in reconstruction times, when the state of Mississippi was a United States military district, by a Negro man still living in 1925firemaker, sweeper, janitor and furnaceattendant to five or six lawyers and doctors
and one of the banksand still known as "Mulberry" from the
avocation which he had followed before and during and after his
illicit
incumbency as marshal: peddling whiskey in pint and halfpint
bottles from a cache beneath the roots of a big mulberry tree
behind the drugstore of his pre1865 owner)put it) in both;
W.P.A. and NYZ indeed marked the town as war itself
had not: gone now was the last of the forest trees which had
                                                   continuous
followed the shape of the Square, shading the/secondstorey
wroughtironbalustraded balcony, onto which the lawyers' and
doctors' offices opened, which had shaded the fronts of the
stores and the walkway beneath; and now gone was even the balcony itself with its wroughtiron balustrade on which in the
long summer afternoons the lawyers would prop their feet to
talk; and the continuous chain looping from wooden post to
post along the circumference of the court house yard, for the
farmers to hitch their teams to: and the public water trough
                                                    wagon
where they could water them because gone was the last to
stand on the Square during a spring or summer or fall Saturday
or tradingday, the team reversed and tied to the back end of
it, munching corn or hay over the tailgate, because not only
the Square but the streets leading into it were paved now,
                            t   d   applicable
with fixed signs of indirection and direction violatable only

239.

247.

and merely harried and urgent and short of time now to get on
to Alabama, to see the condition of his farm or---for that mat-
ter---if he still had a farm; the frail and workless girl not
only not capable of milking a cow, but of whom it was not even
demanded to substitute for her father in drying the dishes,
mounting pillon behind on the mule before she and her husband
had had time to discover one another's food-preferences or re-
ligious convictions or middle names; riding, hurrying, to face
a future which was not even frontier: a primitive wilderness
touched only by the light hand of God/:but/ but/an old land instead was
ruined by the iron palm of man

moment
~~rxingxporkxfat;~~ the visitor would descry to be ~~a name and a~~
~~date~~; not at first of course, but after a moment, a second, because at first he would be a little puzzled, a little impatient because of his illness-at-ease from having been dragged here into the kitchen of a strange woman busy cooking a meal; he would /t think merely <u>what? So what?</u> until suddenly, even while he was still thinking it, something would happen: the faint ~~scratches~~ frail illegible meaningless even inferential-less scratchings in the ancient poor-quality glass would seem to move, to coalesce, ~~in~~ actually to enter into other senses than vision---a scent, a whisper filling that hot cramped room already fierce with the sound and smell of frying pork-fat, the two of them in conjunction---the old milky/glass and the obsolete scratches in it---the tender ownerless obsolete name and the old dead date---murmuring of a time as old as lavender, older ~~album or stereoptican: as old as daguerrotype itself,---the~~ voice itself of a girl young enough to have ~~xxxxxx~~ idle time enough to scratch her name with/ a diamond ring into a ~~shxxtxsfxwhxx~~ sheet of glass, saying to him across ~~xixtkyx~~ the ninety years since 1861: <u>Listen</u>, stranger; this was I, this was myself ~~xxxxxxxxxxxxxx;~~ sheet of glass,---the voice itself, not an echo ~~of it, saying to him across the ninety years since 1861: 'Listen, stranger; this was I, this was myself'~~

of installment-plan rugs; they had never had to go to the jail on the morning after Juneteenth or July Fourth or Thanksgiving or Christmas or New Years (or for that matter, on almost any Monday morning) and pay the fine of the ~~Negro servant~~ houseman or gardener ~~so that~~ or handyman so that he could come home and milk the cow and clean the furnace or mow the ~~yard~~ lawn;

Only the old citizens knew it: not old in years, but in the constancy of the town, or against it, ~~coeval~~ concordant with (not coeval of course, since this was a century and a quarter ago now, but in accord against that continuation) that this durable continuity born a hundred and twenty-five years ago out of a handful of bandits captured by a drunken militia squad, and a bitter ironical incorruptible wilderness mail-rider, and a monster wrought-iron padlock,---that steadfast and durable and unhurryable continuity upon which the glittering ephemerae of progress and alteration washed in substanceless repetitive evanescent waves, as with each dawn the wash and glare of the neon sign on what was still known as the Holston House, ~~faded from the diagonally across the street, faded from~~ the brick walls of the jail; only the old citizens (not old people: old citizens) still knew ~~it~~ it: the intractible and obsolescent, who still insisted on wood ranges and ~~handymen~~ cows and vegetable gardens and handymen who had to be taken out of hock on the mornings after holidays or merely after Saturday nights, or the Negroes who spent the Saturday- and holiday-nights there for ~~drinking~~ drunkenness or fighting or gambling---the servants,

247.

Mississippians but Yoknapatawphians:// by which time---who knows?---not merely the pane but the whole window, perhaps the entire wall even, may have been removed and embalmed into a museum by an historical, or perhaps even a mere culture club of ladies; why, by that time, they may not even know, or even need to know: only that it is that old, has lasted that long: one small rectangle of wavy, crudely-made, almost opaque glass, bearing a few light scratches, evocative yet significant-less, apparently no more durable than the thin dried slime left by a snail, yet which has lasted a hundred years) there are still one or two of them capable of leading you (with courteous neighborly apologies to the jailor's wife stirring or turning on the stove the peas and potatoes and side-meat--- purchased in bargain-lot quantities by shrewd and indefatiguable shopping---which she will serve to the prisoners for dinner or supper at so much a head payable by the County, which is no mean factor in the sinecure of hers and her husband's incumbency) to the window in what is now the jailor's kitchen, and so up to the cloudy pane bearing the faint scratches which after a moment he would think merely What? So what?

the housemen and gardeners and handymen, who would be taken out
the next morning by their white folks, and the others, ~~the New~~
~~Negroxxwho~~ what the town called the New Negro, independent of
that commodity, who would sleep there every night while they
worked out their fines on the street; and (known) to the County
too, since the County's cattle-thieves and ~~men~~ moonshiners and
bootleggers went to ~~jailxfrom~~ trial from there, and its murder-
ers---hanged once but electrocuted now (such, so fast, was
Progress)---went to eternity from there; and still, not a factor perhaps, but at least an integer, a cipher, in the county's
political establishment; at least still used by the Board of
Supervisors, ~~if not as a lever,~~ at least as something like
Punch's stuffed club, not intended to break bones, not aimed
to leave any permanent scars;

They---the old ones---still knew it; even in 1951, eighty-six
years afterward (and in 1965, a hundred years afterward, there
would probably be more, ~~six~~ dozens, because by that time the
children of that second outland invasion---that of the war years
between '40 and '50---would also have become not just Mississippians but ~~Yoknapatawphaians, by which time---who knows?---~~
not merely the pane but the whole window, perhaps the entire
wall, may have been removed and embalmed into a museum by an
historical, or perhaps even merely a cultural club, of Ladies:
why---by that time---they may not even know, or even need to
know; only that it is that old, has lasted that long: one small
rectangle of wavy, crudely-made, almost opaque glass, bearing
a few light scratches evocative yet significantless, apparently

248.

no more durable than the thin dried slime left by a snail, yet
which has lasted a hundred years) there are still one or two
capable of leading you (with courteous neighborly apologies to
the jailor's wife still stirring or turning on the stove the peas
and ~~milk~~ grits and side-meat---purchased in bargain-lot quantities by shrewd and indefatigueable shopping ---which she will
serve to the prisoners for dinner or supper at so much a head
payable by the County, which is no mean factor in the sinecure
of her husband's incumbency) to the window is what is now the
jailor's family kitchen, and so to the cloudy pane bearing the
faint scratches which, after a ~~moment~~ moment, the visitor would
descry to be a name and a date; not at first, of course, but
after a moment, a second, because at first he would be a little
puzzled, a little impatient because of his illness-at-ease
from having been dragged here into the kitchen of a strange woman
cooking a meal; he would think merely ~~xxx~~ What? So what? annoyed
and even a little outraged, until suddenly, even while he was
still thinking, something would happen; the faint frail illegible meaningless even inferential-less scratching on the ancient
poor-quality glass he was staring at, would seem to move, to coalesce, actually to enter into another sense or senses than
vision: a scent, a whisper, filling that hot cramped room already fierce with the sound and reek of frying pork-fat; the
two of them in conjunction---the old ~~milk~~ milky obsolete glass,
and the scratches on it---the tender ownerless obsolete name
and the old dead date---murmuring of a time old as lavender,
older than album or stereoptican: as old in fact as daguerrotype

249.

itself: Cecilia Farmer April 16th 1861;

And, being a stranger and a guest, the visitor would be courteous and polite to ask the questions expected of him; and, being a human being and curious, he would even want to know; and, being the host, the guide would try to tell him; perhaps the guide even knew: that little of it: since he had been moved to the trouble to bring the guest here, make the polite apologies to the woman/over the seething skillets and pots on the *sweating and seething too* wood-burning range: what little there was to be told out of the town's composite heritage of remembering that long back: the ~~The frail and war-fragile and workless~~ girl (they would not even remember the color of her hair in the window now, which has probably changed from blonde to brunette to blonde to brunette a hundred times since), the sudden rush and thunder of hooves, the dust, the crackle and splatter of pistols: and gone: and ~~still the girl in the window~~, not even waiting: musing; a year, which is nothing, since there is still the girl, not even waiting: meditant, not even unimpatient, but patienceless, in the sense that blindness ~~is colorless~~ or zenith are colorless; then out of the long north-eastern panorama of valor and defeat and dust and fading smoke, the mule ~~which was a better mule in 1865 than the blood mare had been in 1862 and '-3 and '-4, for the reason that this was 1865~~ and the man---the mule which was a better mule in 1865 than the blood mare had been a horse in 1862 and '-3 and '-4, for the reason that ~~~~ this was 1865; the man, the youth, still ~~gaunt~~ and undefeated the housemen and gardeners and handymen, who would be taken out ~~animix~~ the next morning by their ~~white~~ folks, and the others, the New Negro, who had no white folks and would sleep there every night while they worked out their fines on the street; and (known) to the County too, since the county's ~~ixi~~ cattle-thieves and moonshiners went to trial from there, and its murderers were hanged (electrocuted now) from there; and still, not a factor perhaps but at least an integer, a cipher, in the county's political ~~establishment~~; at least/used by the Board of Supervisors, if not as a lever, at least as something like Punch's stuffed club, not intended to break any bones, not aimed to leave any ~~xxxxx~~ permanent scars;

They---the old ones---still knew it; even in 1951, eighty-six years afterward (and ~~xxxx~~ in 1965, ~~xxxx~~ a hundred afterward, there would probably be more, dozens, because by that time the children of that second outland invasion---that of the war years between '40 and '50---would/also have become not just ~~Mississippians but Yoknapatawphians. There are one or two of them capable of~~ leading ~~you (with a courteous neighborly apologies to the jailer's wife stirring or burning on the stove the peas and potatoes and side-meat (purchased in bargain-lot quantities by whose shrewd and indefatigable shopping which she will serve them supper to the prisoners for dinner at supper at so much a plate payable by the county, which is~~

or New Orleans, the other the stranger, the outlander from the Atlantic seaboard or the Northern lakes or the Pacific slopes, passed through Jefferson by chance on his way to some- ~~whereelse~~ defeated land, across a whole disastrous year, more inescapable than lodestar;

That face not demanding more but simply requiring more, requir-
                                                          r
ing all: Lilith's face drawing the substance---the will and hope and aspiration and imagination---of all men into that one bright fragile net and snare,---indeed the imagination: these two also: the host and the guest in the small hot kitchen furious with frying ~~mmxt~~ fat---the one who in three generations had never been further from Yoknapatawpha County than Memphis or New Orleans, the other the stranger, the outlander from the Atlantic seaboard or the Northern lakes or the Pacific slopes, passed through Jefferson by simple chance on his way to somewhere else

touch, if there actually was a girl under the calico and the
shawls; there was no time for that yet; but simply to get her
up so they could start) onto the mule, to ride a hundred miles
to become the ~~mother of~~ farmless mother of farmers (she would
have a dozen, all boys, herself no older, still fragile, still
workless among the churns and stoves and brooms and stacks of
wood which even a woman could split into kindlings; unchanged),
bequeathing to them in their matronymic the heritage of that
invincible inviolable ineptitude;

Then suddenly, that was nowhere near enough, not for that face;
---bridehood, motherhood, grandmotherhood, ~~knowing whose~~ then
widowhood and then the grave,---the long peaceful connubial
progress toward matriarchy in a rocking chair nobody else was
ever allowed to sit in, then a headstone in a country church-
yard;---not for that passivity, that stasis, that invincible
captaincy of soul which didn't even need to wait but simply to
be, to breathe tranquilly, and take food,---infinite not only
in capacity but in scope too; that face, one maiden muse which
had drawn a man across the running pell mell of a cavalry battle; out of a retreat; a stand; around the long iron perimeter
of duty from Yoknapatawpha County, Mississippi, across Tennessee
into Virginia and up to the fringe of Pennsylvania before ~~xxxx~~
curving
~~running~~ back into that closing fade along the ~~headwaters~~ headwa-
ters of the Appomattox where, a safe distance ~~at last~~ from the
town, the Court House, the furled and mourning flags and the
stacked arms, a straggle, a handful of men leading spent horses,

256.

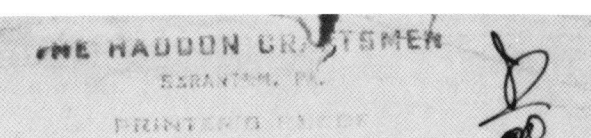

BANK L 7　　　　　SLIDE 62
2—Requiem for a Nun—1329
12 on 13 Bodoni Book (led. 2 pts.—x 22; 8 Bod. Bold

WILLIAM FAULKNER

REQUIEM
for a NUN

RANDOM HOUSE　　　　NEW YORK

86 *Requiem for a Nun*, II

BANK L 7   **SLIDE 63**
3—Requiem for a Nun—1329
12 on 13 Bodoni Book (led. 2 pts. x 22; 8 Bod. Bold

CONTENTS

The Courthouse (A Name for the City)   3

Act One   the Word   000

The Golden Dome (Beginning Was   )   00

Act Two   00

Prologue (?)   The Jail 5   000
                (Nor Even Yet Quite Relinquish)

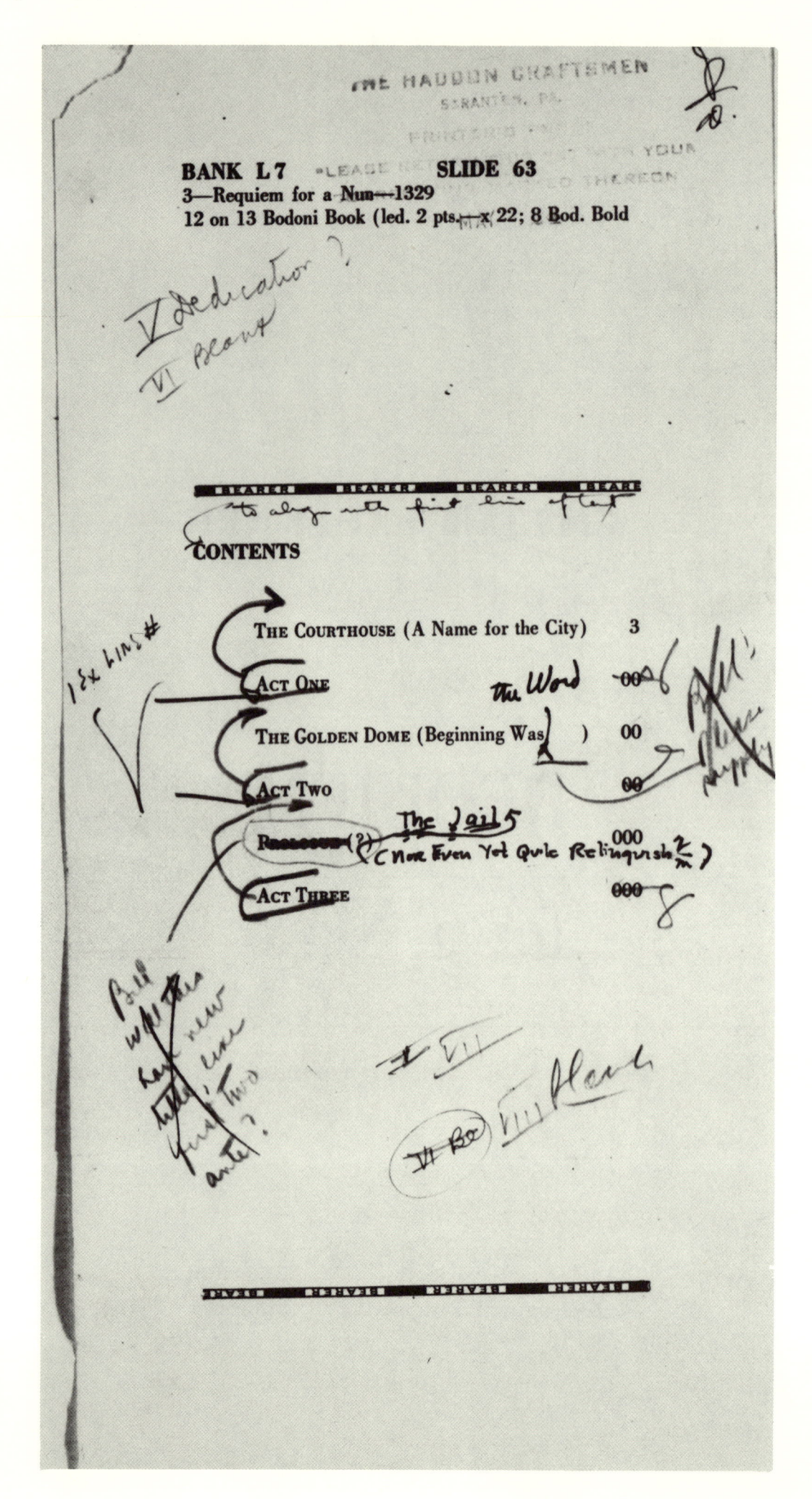

Act Three   000

BANK L 7   SLIDE 65
5—Requiem for a Nun—1329
12 on 13 Bodoni Book (led. 2 pts.—x 22; 8 Bod. Bold

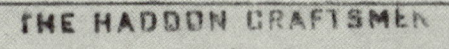

ACT ONE

THE COURTHOUSE (A Name for the City)

The courthouse is less old than the town, which began somewhere under the turn of the century as a Chickasaw Agency trading-post and so continued for almost thirty years before it discovered, not that it lacked a depository for its records and certainly not that it needed one, but that only by creating or anyway decreeing one, could it cope with a situation which otherwise was going to cost somebody money.

The settlement had the records; even the simple dispossession of Indians begot in time a minuscule of archive, let alone the normal litter of man's ramshackle confederation against environment—that time and that wilderness—in this case, a meagre, fading, dogeared, uncorrelated, at times illiterate sheaf of land-grants and patents and transfers and deeds, and tax- and militia-rolls, and bills of sale for slaves, and counting-house lists of spurious currency and exchange rates, and liens and mortgages, and listed rewards for escaped or stolen Negroes and other livestock, and diary-like annotations of births and marriages and deaths and public hangings and land-auctions, accumulating slowly for those three decades in a sort of iron pirate's chest in the back room of the postoffice-tradingpost-store, until that day thirty years later when, because of a jailbreak compounded by

3

BANK L 7   **SLIDE 66**
6—Requiem for a Nun—1329
12 on 13 Bodoni Book (led. 2 pts.) x 22; 8 Bod. Bold

tion with progress. But that was a hundred years away yet; now it was frontier, the men and women pioneers, tough, simple, and durable, seeking money or adventure or freedom or simple escape, and not too particular how they did it.) discovered itself faced not so much with a problem which had to be solved, as a Damocles sword of dilemma from which it had to save itself/

[no indent] [Even the jailbreak was fortuity: a gang—three or four—of Natchez Trace bandits (twenty-five years later legend would begin to affirm, and a hundred years later would still be at it, that two (if) the bandits were the Harpes themselves, Big Harpe anyway, since the circumstances, the method of the breakout left behind like a smell, an odor, a kind of gargantuan and bizarre playfulness at once humorous and terrifying, as if the settlement had fallen, blundered, into the notice or range of an idle and whimsical giant. Which—that they were the Harpes—was impossible, since the Harpes and even the last of Mason's ruffians were dead or scattered by this time, and the robbers would have had to belong to John Murrel's organization—if they needed to belong to any at all other than the simple fraternity of rapine.) captured by chance by an incidental band of civilian more-or-less militia and brought in to the Jefferson jail because it was the nearest one, the militia band being part of a general muster at Jefferson two days before for a Fourth-of-July barbecue, which by the second day had been refined by hardy elimination into one drunken brawling which rendered even the hardiest survivors vulnerable enough to be ejected from the settlement by the civilian residents, the band which was to make the capture having been carried, still comatose, in one of the evicting wagons to a swamp four miles from Jefferson known as Hurricane Bottoms, where they made camp to regain their strength or at least their legs, and where that night the four—or three—bandits, on the way across country to their hideout from their last exploit on the Trace, stumbled onto the campfire. And here report divided; some said that the sergeant in command of the militia recognised one of the bandits as a deserter from his corps, others said that one of the bandits recognised in the sergeant a former follower of his, the bandit's, trade. Anyway, on the fourth morning all of them, captors and

Galley 6A

prisoners, returned to Jefferson in a group, some said in confederation now seeking more drink, others said that the captors brought their prizes back to the settlement in revenge for having been evicted from it. Because these were frontier, pioneer times, when personal liberty and freedom were almost a physical condition like fire or flood, and no community was going to interfere with anyone's morals as long as the amoralist practised somewhere else, and so Jefferson, being neither on the Trace nor the River but lying about midway between, naturally wanted no part of the underworld of either/

But they had some of it now, taken as it were by surprise, unawares, without warning to prepare and fend off. They put the bandits into the log-and-mudchinking jail, which until now had had no lock at all since its clients so far had been amateurs—local brawlers and drunkards and runaway slaves—for whom a single heavy wooden beam in slots across the outside of the door like on a corncrib, had sufficed. But they had now what might be four—three—Dillingers or Jesse Jameses of the time, with rewards on their heads. So they locked the jail; they bored an auger hole through the door and another through the jamb and passed a length of heavy chain through the holes and sent a messenger on the run across to the postoffice-store to fetch the ancient Carolina lock from the last Nashville mail-pouch—the iron monster weighing almost fifteen pounds, with a key almost as long as a bayonet, not just the only lock in that part of the country, but the oldest lock in that cranny of the United States, brought there by one of the three men who were what was to be Yoknapatawpha County's coeval pioneers and settlers, leaving in it the three oldest names—Alexander Holston, who came as half groom and half bodyguard to Doctor Samuel Habersham, and half nurse and half tutor to the doctor's eight-year-old motherless son, the three of them riding horseback across Tennessee from the Cumberland Gap along with Louis Grenier, the Huguenot younger son who brought the first slaves into the country and was granted the first big land patent and so became the first cotton planter; while Doctor Habersham, with his worn black bag of pills and knives and his brawny taciturn bodyguard and his half orphan child, became the settlement itself (for a time, before it was named, the settlement was known as Doctor Habersham's, then Habersham's, then simply Habersham; a hundred years later, during a schism between two ladies' clubs over the naming of the streets in order to get free mail delivery, a movement was started; first, to change the name back to Habersham; then, failing that, to divide the town in two and call one half of it Habersham after the old pioneer doctor and founder)—friend of old Issetibbeha, the Chickasaw chief (the motherless Habersham boy, now a man of twenty-five, married one of Issetibbeha's grand-daughters and in the thirties emigrated to Oklahoma with his wife's dispossessed people), first unofficial, then official Chickasaw agent until he resigned in a letter of furious denunciation addressed to the President of the United States himself; and—his charge and pupil a man now—Alexander Holston became the settlement's first publican, establishing the tavern still known as the Holston House, the original log walls and puncheon floors and hand-morticed joints of which are still buried somewhere beneath the modern pressed glass and brick veneer and neon tubes. The lock was his

Fifteen pounds of useless iron lugged a thousand miles through a desert of precipice and swamp, of flood and drouth and wild beasts and wild Indians and wilder white men, displacing that fifteen pounds better given to food or seed to plant food or even powder to defend with, to become a fixture, a kind of landmark, in the bar of a wilderness ordinary, locking and securing nothing, because there was nothing behind the heavy bars and shutters needing further locking and securing; not even a paper weight because the only papers in the Holston House were the twisted spills in an old powder horn above the mantel for lighting tobacco; always a little in the way, since it had constantly to be moved: from bar to shelf to mantel then back to bar again until they finally thought about putting it on the bi-monthly mail-pouch; familiar, known, presently the oldest unchanged thing in the settlement, older than the people since Issetibbeha and Doctor Habersham were dead, and Alexander Holston was an old man crippled with arthritis, and Louis Grenier had a settlement of his own on his vast plantation, half of which was not even in Yoknapatawpha County, and the settlement rarely saw him; older than the town, since there were new names in it now even when the old blood ran in them—Sartoris and Stevens, Comp-

Galley 7A

son and McCaslin and Sutpen and Coldfield—and you no longer shot a bear or deer or wild turkey simply by standing for a while in your kitchen door, not to mention the pouch of mail—letters and even newspapers—which came from Nashville every two weeks by a special rider who did nothing else and was paid a salary for it by the Federal Government; and that was the second phase of the monster Carolina lock's transubstantiation into the Yoknapatawpha County courthouse/

The pouch didn't always reach the settlement every two weeks, nor even always every month. But sooner or later it did, and everybody knew it would, because it— the cowhide saddlebag not even large enough to hold a full change of clothing, containing three or four letters and half that many badly-printed one- and two-sheet newspapers already three or four months out of date and usually half and sometimes wholly misinformed or incorrect to begin with—was the United States, the power and the will to liberty, owning liegence to no man, bringing even into that still almost pathless wilderness the thin peremptory voice of the nation which had wrenched its freedom from one of the most powerful peoples on earth and then again within the same lifespan successfully defended it; so peremptory and audible that the man who carried the pouch on the galloping horse didn't even carry any arms except a tin horn, traversing month after month, blatantly, flagrantly, almost contemptuously, a region where for no more than the boots on his feet, men would murder a traveller and gut him like a bear or deer or fish and fill the cavity with rocks and sink the evidence in the nearest water; not even deigning to pass quietly where other men, even though armed and in parties, tried to move secretly or at least without uproar, but instead announcing his solitary advent as far ahead of himself as the ring of the horn would carry. So it was not long before Alexander Holston's lock had moved to the mail-pouch. Not that the pouch needed one, having come already the three hundred miles from Nashville without a lock. (It had been projected at first that the lock remain on the pouch constantly. That is, not just while the pouch was in the settlement, but while it was on the horse between Nashville and the settlement too. The rider refused, succinctly, in three words, one of which was printable. His reason was the lock's weight. They pointed out to him that this would not hold water,

BANK L7 **SLIDE 68**
8—Requiem for a Nun—1329
12 on 13 Bodoni Book (led. 2 pts.— x 22; 8 Bod. Bold

since not only—the rider was a frail irascible little man weighing less than a hundred pounds—would the fifteen pounds of lock even then fail to bring his weight up to that of a normal adult male, the added weight of the lock would merely match that of the pistols which his employer, the United States Government, believed he carried and even paid him for having done so, the rider's reply to this being succinct too though not so glib: that the lock weighed fifteen pounds either at the back door of the store in the settlement, or at that of the postoffice in Nashville. But since Nashville and the settlement were three hundred miles apart, by the time the horse had carried it from one to the other, the lock weighed fifteen pounds to the mile times three hundred miles, or forty-five hundred pounds. Which was manifest nonsense, a physical impossibility either in lock or horse. Yet indubitably fifteen pounds times three hundred miles was forty-five hundred something, either pounds or miles—especially as while they were still trying to unravel it, the rider repeated his first three succinct—two unprintable—words.) So less than ever would the pouch need a lock in the back room of the trading-post, surrounded and enclosed once more by civilization, where its very intactness, its presence to receive a lock, proved its lack of that need during the three hundred miles of rapine-haunted Trace; needing a lock as little as it was equipped to receive one, since it had been necessary to slit the leather with a knife just under each jaw of the opening and insert the lock's iron mandible through the two slits and clash it home, so that any other hand with a similar knife could have cut the whole lock from the pouch as easily as it had been clasped onto it. So the old lock was not even a symbol of security: it was a gesture of salutation, of free men to free men, of civilization to civilization across not just the three hundred miles of wilderness to Nashville, but the fifteen hundred to Washington: of respect without servility, allegiance without abasement to the government which they had helped to found and had accepted with pride but still as free men, still free to withdraw from it at any moment when the two of them found themselves no longer compatible, the old lock meeting the pouch each time on its arrival, to clasp it in iron and inviolable symbolism, while old Alec Holston, childless bachelor, grew a little older and grayer, a little more arthritic in flesh and temper too, a little stiffer and more rigid in bone and pride too, since the lock was still his, he had merely lent it, and so in a sense he was the grandfather in the settlement of the inviolability not just of government mail, but of a free government of free men too, so long as the government remembered to let men live free, not under it but beside it;

That was the lock; they put in on the jail. They did it quickly, not even waiting until a messenger could have got back from the Holston House with old Alec's permission to remove it from the mail-pouch or use it for the new purpose. Not that he would have objected on principle nor refused his permission except by simple instinct; that is, he would probably have been the first to suggest the lock if he had known in time or thought of it first, but he would have refused at once if he thought the thing was contemplated without consulting him. Which everybody in the settlement knew, though this was not at all why they didn't wait for the messenger. In fact, no messenger had ever been sent to old Alec; they didn't have time to send one, let alone wait until he got back; they didn't want the lock to keep the bandits in, since (as was later proved) the old lock would have been no more obstacle for the bandits to pass than the customary wooden bar; they didn't need the lock to protect the settlement from the bandits, but to protect the bandits from the settlement. Because the prisoners had barely reached the settlement when it developed that there was a faction bent on lynching them at once, out of hand, without preliminary—a small but determined gang which tried to wrest the prisoners from their captors while the militia was still trying to find someone to surrender them to, and would have succeeded except for a man named Compson, who had come to the settlement a few years ago with a race horse, which he swapped to Ikkemotubbe, Issetibbeha's successor in the chiefship, for a square mile of what was to be the most valuable land in the future town of Jefferson, who, legend said, drew a pistol and held the ravishers at bay until the bandits could be got into the jail and the auger holes bored and someone sent to fetch old Alec Holston's lock. Because there were indeed new names and faces too in the settlement now—faces so new as to have (to the older residents) no discernible antecedents other than mammalinity, nor past other than the simple years which had

BANK L 7   SLIDE 69
9—Requiem for a Nun—1329
12 on 13 Bodoni Book (led. 2 pts.—x 22; 8 Bod. Bold

scored them; and names so new as to have no discernible (nor discoverable either) antecedents or past at all, as though they had been invented yesterday, report dividing again: to the effect that there were more people in the settlement that day than the militia sergeant whom one or all of the bandits might recognise.

So Compson locked the jail, and a courier with the two best horses in the settlement—one to ride and one to lead—cut through the woods to the Trace to ride the hundred-odd miles to Natchez with news of the capture and authority to dicker for the reward; and that evening in the Holston House kitchen was held the settlement's first municipal meeting, prototype not only of the town council after the settlement would be a town, but of the Chamber of Commerce when it would begin to proclaim itself a city, with Compson presiding, not old Alec, who was quite old now, grim, taciturn, sitting even on a hot July night before a smoldering log in his vast chimney, his back even turned to the table (he was not interested in the deliberation; the prisoners were his already since his lock held them; whatever the conference decided would have to be submitted to him for ratification anyway before anyone could touch his lock to open it) around which the progenitors of the Jefferson city fathers sat in what was almost a council of war, not only discussing the collecting of the reward, but the keeping and defending it. Because there were two factions of opposition now: not only the lynching party, but the militia band too, who now claimed that as prizes the prisoners still belonged to their original captors; that they—the militia—had merely surrendered the prisoners' custody but had relinquished nothing of any reward: on the prospect of which, the militia band had got more whiskey from the trading-post store and had built a tremendous bonfire in front of the jail, around which they and the lynching party had now confederated in a wassail or conference of their own. Or so they thought. Because the truth was that Compson, in the name of a crisis in the public peace and welfare, had made a formal demand on the professional bag of Doctor Peabody, old Doctor Habersham's successor, and the three of them—Compson, Peabody, and the post trader (his name was Ratcliffe; a hundred years later it would still exist in the county, but by that

Galley 9A

time it had passed through two inheritors who had dispensed with the eye in the transmission of words, using only the ear, so that by the time the fourth one had been compelled by simple necessity to learn to write it again, it had lost the 'c' and the final 'fe' too) added the laudanum to the keg of whiskey and sent it as a gift from the settlement to the astonished militia sergeant, and returned to the Holston House kitchen to wait until the last of the uproar died; then the law-and-order party made a rapid sortie and gathered up all the comatose opposition, lynchers and captors too, and dumped them all into the jail with the prisoners and locked the door again and went home to bed—until the next morning, when the first arrivals were met by a scene resembling an outdoor stage setting: which was how the legend of the mad Harpes started: a thing not just fantastical but incomprehensible, not just whimsical but a little terrifying (though at least it was bloodless, which would have contented neither Harpe): not just the lock gone from the door nor even just the door gone from the jail, but the entire wall gone, the mud-chinked axe-morticed logs unjointed neatly and quietly in the darkness and stacked as neatly to one side, leaving the jail open to the world like a stage on which the late insurgents still lay sprawled and various in deathlike slumber, the whole settlement gathered now to watch Compson trying to kick at least one of them awake, until one of the Holston slaves—the cook's husband, the waiter-groom-hostler—ran into the crowd shouting, 'Whar de lock, whar de lock, ole Boss say whar de lock.'

It was gone (as were three horses belonging to three of the lynching faction). They couldn't even find the heavy door and the chain, and at first they were almost betrayed into believing that the bandits had had to take the door in order to steal the chain and lock, catching themselves back from the very brink of this wanton accusation of rationality. But the lock was gone; nor did it take the settlement long to realise that it was not the escaped bandits and the aborted reward, but the lock, and not a simple situation which faced them, but a problem which threatened, the slave departing back to the Holston House at a dead run and then reappearing at the dead run almost before the door, the walls, had had time to hide him, engulf and then eject him again, darting through the crowd and up to Compson himself now, saying, 'Ole Boss say fetch de lock'—not send the lock, but bring the lock. So Compson and his lieutenants (and this was where the mail rider began to appear, or rather, emerge—the fragile wisp of a man ageless, hairless and toothless, who looked too frail even to approach a horse, let alone ride one six hundred miles every two weeks, yet who did so, and not only that but had wind enough left not only to announce and precede but even follow his passing with the jeering musical triumph of the horn:—a contempt for possible—probable—despoilers matched only by that for the official dross of which he might be despoiled, and which agreed to remain in civilised bounds only so long as the despoilers had the taste to refrain)—repaired to the kitchen where old Alec still sat before his smoldering log, his back still to the room, and still not turning it this time either. And that was all. He ordered the immediate return of his lock. It was not even an ultimatum, it was a simple instruction, a decree, impersonal, the mail rider now well into the fringe of the group, saying nothing and missing nothing, like a weightless desiccated or fossil bird, not a vulture of course nor even quite a hawk, but say a pterodactyl chick arrested just out of the egg ten glaciers ago and so old in simple infancy as to be the worn and weary ancestor of all subsequent life. They pointed out to old Alec that the only reason the lock could be missing was that the bandits had not had time or been able to cut it out of the door, and that even three fleeing madmen on stolen horses would not carry a six-foot oak door very far, and that a party of Ikkemotubbe's young men were even now trailing the horses westward toward the River and that without doubt the lock would be found at any moment, probably under the first bush at the edge of the settlement: knowing better, knowing that there was no limit to the fantastic and the terrifying and the bizarre, of which the men were capable who already, just to escape from a log jail, had quietly removed one entire wall and stacked it in neat piecemeal at the roadside, and that they nor old Alec neither would ever see his lock again

Nor did they; the rest of that afternoon and all the next day too, while old Alec still smoked his pipe in front of his smoldering log, the settlement's sheepish and raging elders hunted for it, with (by now: the next afternoon) Ikkemotubbe's Chickasaws helping too, or anyway

Galley 11A

marvel (a little speculatively probably) at their own moderation, since they wanted nothing—least of all, to escape any just blame—but a fair and decent adjustment of the lock. They went back to where old Alec still sat with his pipe in front of his dim hearth. Only they had overestimated him; he didn't want any money at all, he wanted his lock. Whereupon what little remained of Compson's patience went too.

'Your lock's gone,' he told old Alec harshly. 'You'll take fifteen dollars for it,' he said, his voice already fading, because even that rage could recognise impasse when it saw it. Nevertheless, the rage, the impotence, the sweating, the *too much*—whatever it was—forced the voice on for one word more: 'Or—' before it stopped for good and allowed Peabody to fill the gap:

'Or else?' Peabody said, and not to old Alec, but to Compson. 'Or else what?' Then Ratcliffe saved that too.

'Wait,' he said. 'Uncle Alec's going to take fifty dollars for his lock. A guarantee of fifty dollars. He'll give us the name of the blacksmith back in Cal'lina that made it for him, and we'll send back there and have a new one made. Going and coming and all'll cost about fifty dollars. We'll give Uncle Alec the fifty dollars to hold as a guarantee. Then when the new lock comes, he'll give us back the money. All right, Uncle Alec?' And that could have been all of it. It probably would have been, except for Pettigrew. It was not that they had forgotten him, nor even assimilated him. They had simply sealed—healed him off (so they thought)—him into their civic crisis as the desperate and defenseless oyster immobilises its atom of inevictable grit. Nobody had seen him move yet he now stood in the center of them where Compson and Ratcliffe and Peabody faced old Alec in the chair. You might have said that he had oozed there, except for that adamantine quality which might (in emergency) become invisible but never insubstantial and never in this world fluid; he spoke in a voice bland, reasonable and impersonal, then stood there being looked at, frail and child-sized, impermeable as diamond and manifest with portent, bringing into that backwoods room a thousand miles deep in pathless wilderness, the whole vast incalculable weight of federality, not just representing the government nor even himself just the government; for that moment at least, he was the United States.

Galley 14A

on the second day they discovered what it was, because he was among them, busy too, sweating and cursing too, but rather like a single chip, infinitesimal, on an otherwise unbroken flood or tide, a single body or substance, alien and unreconciled, a single thin almost unheard voice crying thinly out of the roar of a mob: 'Wait, look here, listen—'

no indent [Because they were too busy raging and sweating among the dismantled logs and felling the new ones in the adjacent woods and trimming and notching and dragging them out and mixing the tenuous clay mud to chink them together with; it was not until the second day that they learned what was troubling Ratcliffe, because now they had time, the work going no slower, no lessening of sweat but on the contrary, if anything the work going even a little faster because now there was a lightness in the speed and all that was abated was the rage and the outrage, because somewhere between the dark and the dawn of the first and the second day, something had happened to them—the men who had spent that first long hot endless July day sweating and raging about the wrecked jail, flinging indiscriminately and savagely aside the dismantled logs and the log-like laudanum-smitten inmates in order to rebuild the one, cursing old Holston and the lock and the four—three—bandits and the eleven militiamen who had arrested them, and Compson and Pettigrew and Peabody and the United States of America —the same men met at the project before sunrise on the next day which was already promising to be hot and endless too, but with the rage and the fury absent now, quiet, not grave so much as sobered, a little amazed, diffident, blinking a little perhaps, looking a little aside from one another, a little unfamiliar even to one another in the new jonquil-colored light, looking about them at the meagre huddle of crude cabins set without order and every one a little awry to every other and all dwarfed to doll-houses by the vast loom of the woods which enclosed them—the tiny clearing clawed punily not even into the flank of pathless wilderness but into the loin, the groin, the secret parts, which was the irrevocable cast die of their lives, fates, pasts and futures—not even speaking for a while yet since each one probably believed (a little shamefaced too) that the thought was solitarily his, until at last one spoke for all and then it was all right since it had taken one conjoined breath to

BANK L 7   **SLIDE 76**
16—Requiem for a Nun—1329
12 on 13 Bodoni Book (led. 2 pts.—x 22; 8 Bod. Bold

or at least his strength of will. It was a matter of principle. It was he—they: the settlement (town now)—who had thought of charging the lock to the United States as a provable lock, a communal risk, a concrete ineradicable object, win lose or draw, let the chips fall where they may, on that dim day when some Federal inspector might, just barely might, audit the Chickasaw affairs; it was the United States itself which had voluntarily offered to show them how to transmute the inevictable lock into proofless and ephemeral axle grease—the little scrawny childsized man, solitary unarmed impregnable and unalarmed, not even defying them, not even advocate and representative of the United States, but *the* United States, as though the United States had said, 'Please accept a gift of fifteen dollars,' (the town had actually paid old Alec fifteen dollars for the lock; he would accept no more) and they had not even declined it but simply abolished it since, as soon as Pettigrew breathed it into sound, the United States had already forever lost it; as though Pettigrew had put the actual ponderable fifteen gold coins into—say, Compson's or Peabody's—hands and they had dropped them down a rathole or a well, doing no man any good, neither restoration to the ravaged nor emolument to the ravager, leaving in fact the whole race of man, as long as it endured, forever and irrevocably fifteen dollars deficit, fifteen dollars in the red.

That was Ratcliffe's trouble. But they didn't even listen. They heard him out of course, but they didn't even listen. Or perhaps they didn't even hear him either, sitting along the shade on Holston's gallery, looking, seeing, already a year away; it was barely the tenth of July; there was the long summer, the bright soft dry fall until the November rains, but they would require not two days this time but two years and maybe more, with a winter of planning and preparation before hand. They even had an instrument available and waiting, like providence almost: a man named Sutpen who had come into the settlement that same spring—a big gaunt friendless passion-worn untalkative man who walked in a fading aura of anonymity and violence like a man just entered a warm room or at least a shelter, out of a blizzard, bringing with him thirty-odd men slaves even wilder and more equivocal than the native wild men,

100 *Requiem for a Nun*, II

Galley 16A

the Chickasaws, to whom the settlement had become accustomed, who (the new Negroes) spoke no English but instead what Compson, who had visited New Orleans, said was the Carib-Spanish-French of the Sugar Islands, and who (Sutpen) had bought or proved on or anyway acquired a track of land in the opposite direction and was apparently bent on establishing a place on an even more ambitious and grandiose scale than Grenier's; he had even brought with him a tame Parisian architect—or captive rather, since it was said in Ratcliffe's back room that the man slept at night in a kind of pit at the site of the chateau he was planning, tied wrist to wrist with one of his captor's Carib slaves; indeed, the settlement had only to see him once to know that he was no docilier than his captor, any. more than the weasel or rattlesnake is no less untame than the wolf or bear before which it gives way until completely and hopelessly cornered:—a man no larger than Pettigrew, with humorous sardonic undefeated eyes which had seen everything and believed none of it, in the broad expensive hat and brocaded waistcoat and ruffled wrists of a half-artist half-boulevardier; and they—Compson perhaps, Peabody certainly—could imagine him in his mudstained brier-slashed brocade and lace standing in a trackless wilderness dreaming colonnades and porticoes and fountains and promenades in the style of David, with just behind each elbow an identical giant half-naked Negro not even watching him, only breathing, moving each time he took a step or shifted like his shadow repeated in two and blown to gigantic size.

So they even had an architect. He listened to them for perhaps a minute in Ratcliffe's back room. Then he made an indescribable gesture and said, 'Bah. You do not need advice. You are too poor. You have only your hands, and clay to make good brick. You dont have any money. You dont even have anything to copy: how can you go wrong?' But he taught them how to mold the brick; he designed and built the kiln to bake the brick in, plenty of them since they had probably known from that first yellow morning too that one edifice was not going to be enough. But although both were conceived in the same instant and planned simultaneously during the same winter and built in continuation during the next three years, the courthouse of course came first, and in March, with stakes and hanks of fishline, the archi-

BANK L 7   SLIDE 77
17—Requiem for a Nun—1329
12 on 13 Bodoni Book (led. 2 pts.) x 22; 8 Bod. Bold

tect laid out in a grove of oaks opposite the tavern and the store, the square and simple foundations, the irrevocable design not only of the courthouse but of the town too, telling them as much: 'In fifty years you will be trying to change it in the name of what you will call progress. But you will fail; but you will never be able to get away from it.' But they had already seen that, standing thigh-deep in wilderness also but with more than a vision to look at since they had at least the fishline and the stakes, perhaps less than fifty years, perhaps—who knew?—less than twenty-five even: a Square, the courthouse in its grove the center; quadrangular around it, the stores, two-storey, the offices of the lawyers and doctors and dentists, the lodge-rooms and auditoriums, above them; school and church and tavern and bank and jail each in its ordered place; the four broad diverging avenues straight as plumb-lines in the four directions, becoming the network of roads and by-roads until the whole county would be covered with it: the hands, the prehensile fingers clawing dragging lightward out of the disappearing wilderness year by year as up from the bottom of the receding sea, the broad rich fecund burgeoning fields, pushing thrusting each year further and further back the wilderness and its denizens —the wild bear and deer and turkey, and the wild men (or not so wild any more, familiar now, harmless now, just obsolete: anachronism out of an old dead time and a dead age; regrettable of course, even actually regretted by the old men, fiercely as old Doctor Habersham did, and with less fire but still as irreconcilable and stubborn as old Alec Holston and a few others were still doing, until in a few more years the last of them would have passed and vanished in their turn too, obsolescent too: because this was a white man's land; that was its fate, or not even fate but destiny, its high destiny in the roster of the earth)—the veins, arteries, life- and pulse-stream along which would flow the aggrandisement of harvest: the gold: the cotton and the grain/

[But above all, the courthouse: the center, the focus, the hub; sitting looming in the center of the county's circumference like a single cloud in its ring of horizon, laying its vast shadow to the uttermost rim of horizon; musing, brooding, symbolic and ponderable, tall as

to be hurried by man or men than the burgeoning of a crop, working (this paradox too to anyone except men like Grenier and Compson and Peabody who had grown from infancy among slaves, breathed the same air and even suckled the same breast with the sons of Ham: black and white, free and unfree, shoulder to shoulder in the same tireless lift and rhythm as if they had the same aim and hope, which they did have as far as the Negro was capable, as even Ratcliffe, son of a long pure line of Anglo-Saxon mountain people and—destined—father of an equally long and pure line of white trash tenant farmers who never owned a slave and never would since each had and would imbibe with his mother's milk a personal violent antipathy not at all to slavery but to black skins, could have explained: the slave's simple child's mind had fired at once with the thought that he was helping to build not only the biggest edifice in the country, but probably the biggest he had ever seen; this was all but this was enough) as one because it was theirs, bigger than any because it was the sum of all and, being the sum of all, it must raise all of their hopes and aspirations level with its own aspirant and soaring cupola, so that, sweating and tireless and unflagging, they would look about at one another a little shyly, a little amazed, with something like humility too, as if they were realising, or were for a moment at least capable of believing, that men, all men, including themselves, were a little better, purer maybe even, than they had thought, expected, or even needed to be. Though they were still having a little trouble with Ratcliffe: the money, the Holston lock-Chickasaw axle grease fifteen dollars; not trouble really because it had never been an obstruction even three years ago when it was new, and now after three years even the light impedeless chip was worn by familiarity and custom to less than a toothpick: merely present, merely visible, or that is, audible: and no trouble *with* Ratcliffe because he made one too contraposed the toothpick; more: he was its chief victim, sufferer, since where with the others was mostly inattention, a little humor, now and then a little fading annoyance and impatience, with him was shame, bafflement, a little of anguish and despair like a man struggling with a congenital vice, hopeless, indomitable, already defeated. It was not even

Galley 18A

the money any more now, the fifteen dollars. It was the fact that they had refused it and, refusing it, had maybe committed a fatal and irremediable error. He would try to explain it: 'It's like Old Moster and the rest of them up there that run the luck, would look down at us and say, Well well, looks like them durn peckerwoods down there dont want them fifteen dollars we was going to give them free-gratis-for-nothing. So maybe they dont want nothing from us. So maybe we better do like they seem to want, and let them sweat and swivet and scrabble through the best they can by themselves.'

Which they—the town—did, though even then the courthouse was not finished for another six years. Not but that they thought it was: complete: simple and square, floored and roofed and windowed, with a central hallway and the four offices—sheriff and tax assessor and circuit- and chancery-clerk (which—the chancery-clerk's office—would contain the ballot boxes and booths for voting)—below, and the courtroom and jury-room and the judge's chambers above—even to the pigeons and English sparrows, migrants too but not pioneers, inevictably urban in fact, come all the way from the Atlantic coast as soon as the town became a town with a name, taking possession of the gutters and eave-boxes almost before the final hammer was withdrawn, uxorious and interminable the one, garrulous and myriad the other. Then in the sixth year old Alec Holston died and bequeathed back to the town the fifteen dollars it had paid him for the lock; two years before, Louis Grenier had died and his heirs still held in trust on demand the fifteen hundred dollars his will had devised it, and now there was another newcomer in the county, a man named John Sartoris, with slaves and gear and money too like Grenier and Sutpen, but who was an even better stalemate to Sutpen than Grenier had been because it was apparent at once that he, Sartoris, was the sort of man who could even cope with Sutpen in the sense that a man with a sabre or even a small sword and heart enough for it could cope with one with an axe; and that summer (Sutpen's Paris architect had long since gone back to whatever place he came from and to which he had made his one abortive midnight try to return, but his trickle, flow of bricks had never even faltered: his molds and kilns had finished the jail and were now raising the walls of two churches and by the half-century would have comto the long weary increment since Genesis, had shattered the virgin pristine air with the first loud dingdong of time and doom.

SCENE I

Courtroom. 5:30 P.M. November thirteenth.

The curtain is down. As the lights begin to go up:

> **MAN'S VOICE**
> *(behind the curtain)*
> Let the prisoner stand.

The curtain rises, symbolising the rising of the prisoner in the dock, and revealing a section of the courtroom. It does not occupy the whole stage, but only the upper left half, leaving the other half and the bottom of the stage in darkness, so that the visible scene is not only spotlighted but elevated slightly too, a further symbolism which will be clearer when Act II opens—the symbolism of the elevated tribunal of justice of which this, a county court, is only the intermediate, not the highest, stage.

This is a section of the court—the bar, the judge, officers, the opposing lawyers, the jury. The defense lawyer is Gavin Stevens, about fifty. He looks more like a poet than a lawyer and actually is: a bachelor, descendant of one of the pioneer Yoknapatawpha County families, Harvard and Heidelberg educated, and returned to his native soil to be a sort of bucolic Cincinnatus, champion not so much of truth as of justice, or of justice as he sees it, constantly involving himself, often for no pay, in affairs of equity and passion and even crime too among his people, white and Negro both, sometimes directly contrary to his office of County Attorney which he has held for years, as is the present business.

The prisoner is standing. She is the only one standing in the room—a Negress, quite black, about thirty—that is, she could be almost anything between twenty and forty—with a calm impenetrable almost bemused face, the tallest, highest there with all eyes on her but she herself

Galley 21A

parents living in city apartment hotels, alumni of the best colleges, South or East, where they belonged to the right clubs; married now and raising families yet still alumni of their schools, performing acceptably jobs they themselves did not ask for, usually concerned with money: cotton futures, or stocks, or bonds. But this face is a little different, a little more than that. Something has happened to it—tragedy—something, against which it had had no warning, and to cope with which (as it discovered) no equipment, yet which it has accepted and is trying, really and sincerely and selflessly (perhaps for the first time in its life) to do its best with according to its code. He and Stevens wear their overcoats, carrying their hats. Stevens stops just inside the room. Gowan drops his hat onto the sofa in passing and goes on to where Temple stands at the table, stripping off one of her gloves.

TEMPLE
(takes cigarette from box on the table: mimics the prisoner; her voice, harsh, reveals for the first time repressed, controlled, hysteria)

Yes, God. Guilty, God. Thank you, God. If that's your attitude toward being hung, what else can you expect from a judge and jury except to accommodate you?

GOWAN
Stop it, Boots. Hush now. Soon as I light the fire, I'll buy a drink.
(to Stevens)
Or maybe Gavin will do the fire while I do the butler.

TEMPLE
(takes up lighter)

I'll do the fire. You get the drinks. Then Uncle Gavin wont have to stay. After all, all he wants to do is say Good-bye and send me a postcard. He can almost do that in two words, if he tries hard. Then he can go home.

Galley 23A
baby—

GOWAN

I said, stop it, Boots.

He carries a tray containing a pitcher of water, a bowl of ice, three empty tumblers and three whiskey glasses already filled. The bottle itself protrudes from his topcoat pocket. He approaches Temple and offers the tray.

GOWAN

That's right. I'm going to have one myself. For a change. After ~~six~~ years. Why not?

TEMPLE

Why not?
            (looks at the tray)
Not highballs?

GOWAN

Not this one.

She takes one of the filled glasses. He offers the tray to Stevens, who takes the second one. Then he sets the tray on the table and takes up the third glass.

GOWAN

Nary a drink in ~~~~ years; count 'em. So maybe this will be a good time to start again. At least, it wont be too soon.
            (to Stevens)
Drink up. A little water behind it?

As though not aware that he had done so, he sets his untasted glass back on the tray, splashes water from the pitcher into a tumbler and hands the tumbler to Stevens as Stevens empties his glass and lowers it, taking the tumbler. Temple has not touched hers either.

~~GOWAN~~

Now maybe Defense Attorney Stevens will tell us what he wants here.

STEVENS

Your wife has already told you. To say good-bye.

GOWAN

Then say it. One more for the road, and where's your hat, huh?

man's self-respect in the chastity of his wife and your child too, to pay for something your wife hadn't even lost, didn't even regret, didn't even miss? Is that why this poor lost doomed crazy Negro woman must die?

GOWAN
(tensely)

Get out of here. Go on.

STEVENS

In a minute.—Or else, blow your own brains out: stop having to remember, stop having to be forever unable to forget: nothing; to plunge into nothing and sink and drown forever and forever, never again to have to remember, never again to wake in the night writhing and sweating because you cannot, can never not, stop remembering? What else happened during that month, that time while that madman held her prisoner there in that Memphis house, that nobody but you and she know about, maybe not even you know about?

Still staring at Stevens, slowly and deliberately Gowan sets the glass of whiskey back on the tray and takes up the bottle and swings it bottom up back over his head. The stopper is out, and at once the whiskey begins to pour out of it, down his arm and sleeve and onto the floor. He does not seem to be aware of it even. His voice is tense, barely articulate.

GOWAN

So help me, Christ . . . So help me, Christ.

A moment, then Stevens moves, without haste, sets his own glass back on the tray and turns, taking his hat as he passes the sofa, and goes on to the door and exits. Gowan stands a moment longer with the poised bottle, now empty. Then he draws a long shuddering breath, seems to rouse, wake, sets the empty bottle back on the tray, notices his untasted whiskey glass, takes it up, a moment: then turns and throws the glass crashing into the fireplace, against the burning gas logs, and stands, his back to the audience, and draws another long shuddering breath and then draws both hands hard down his

Galley 29A

TEMPLE

Why not? Dont the philosophers and other gynecologists tell us that women will strike back with any weapon, even their children?

STEVENS

(watching the child)

Including the sleeping pill you told me you gave Gowan?

TEMPLE

All right.

(approaches table)

If I would just stop struggling: how much time we could save. I came all the way back from California, but I still cant seem to quit. Do you believe in coincidence?

STEVENS

(turns)

Not unless I have to.

TEMPLE

(at table, takes up a folded yellow telegraph form, opens it, reads) Dated Jefferson, March sixth. 'You have a week yet until the thirteenth. But where will you go then?' signed Gavin. She folds the paper back into its old creases, folds it still again. Stevens watches her.

STEVENS

Well? This is the eleventh. Is that the coincidence?

TEMPLE

No. This is.

(she drops, tosses the folded paper onto the table, turns)

It was that afternoon—the sixth. We were on the beach, C───── and I. I was reading, and he was—oh, talking mostly, you know—'Is California far from Jefferson, mamma?' and I say 'Yes, darling'—you know: still reading or try-

BANK L 7   SLIDE 90
30—Requiem for a Nun—1329
12 on 13 Bodoni Book (led. 2 pts.—x 22; 8 Bod. Bold

ing to, and he says, 'How long will we stay in California, mamma?' and I say, 'Until we get tired of it' and he says, 'Will we stay here until they hang Nancy, mamma?' and it's already too late then; I should have seen it coming but it's too late now; I say, 'Yes, darling' and then he drops it right in my lap, right out of the mouths of—how is it?—babes and sucklings? 'Where will we go then, mamma?' And then we come back to the hotel, and there you are too. Well?

STEVENS
Well what?

TEMPLE
All right. Let's for God's sake stop.
   (goes to a chair)
Now that I'm here, no matter whose fault it was, what do you want? A drink? Will you drink? At least, put your coat and hat down.

STEVENS
I dont even know yet. That's why you came back—

TEMPLE
   (interrupts)
I came back? It wasn't I who—

STEVENS
   (interrupts)
—who said, let's for God's sake stop.

They stared at each other: a moment.

TEMPLE
All right. Put down your coat and hat.

Stevens lays his hat and coat on a chair. Temple sits down. Stevens takes a chair opposite, so that the sleeping child on the sofa is between them in background.

TEMPLE
So Nancy must be saved. So you send for me, or you and ——— between you, or anyway here you are and here I am. Because apparently I know something I haven't told yet, or maybe you

TEMPLE

Or better still; wont it be obvious? a woman whose child was smothered in its crib, wanting vengeance, capable of anything to get the vengeance; then when she has it, realising she cant go through with it, cant sacrifice a human life for it, even a nigger whore's?

STEVENS

Stop it. One at a time. At least, let's talk about the same thing.

TEMPLE

What else are we talking about except saving a condemned whose trained lawyer has already admitted that he has failed?

STEVENS

Then you really dont want her to die. You did invent the coincidence.

TEMPLE

Didn't I just say so? At least, let's for God's sake stop that, cant we?

STEVENS

Done. So Temple Drake will have to save her.

TEMPLE

Mrs Gowan Stevens will.

STEVENS

Temple Drake.

She stares at him, smoking, deliberately now. Deliberately she removes the cigarette and, still watching him, reaches and snubs it out in the ashtray.

STEVENS

All right. Tell me again. Maybe I'll even understand this time, let alone listen. We produce—turn up with—a sworn affidavit that this murderess was crazy when she committed the crime.

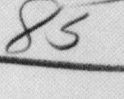

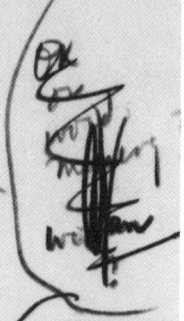

Galley 35A

against her face, her face calm, expressionless, cold, drops her hands, turns, picks up the crushed cigarette from beside the tray and puts it into the tray and takes up the tray and crosses to the fireplace, glancing down at the sleeping child as she passes the sofa, empties the tray into the fireplace and returns to the table and puts the tray on it and this time pauses at the sofa and stoops and tucks the blanket closer about the sleeping child and then goes on to the telephone and lifts the receiver.

TEMPLE
(into phone)

Maggie? Temple . . . Yes, suddenly . . . oh, I dont know; perhaps we got bored with sunshine . . . of course. I may drop in tomorrow. I wanted to leave a message for Gavin . . . I know; he just left here. Something I forgot . . . if you'll ask him to call me when he comes in . . . Yes . . . Wasn't it. Yes . . . If you will . . . Thank you.

She puts the receiver down and starts to turn back into the room when the telephone rings. She turns back, takes up the receiver.

Hello . . . Yes. Coincidence again; I had my hand on it; I had just called Maggie . . . Oh, the filling station. I didn't think you had had time. I can be ready in fifteen minutes. Your car, or ours? . . . All right. Listen . . . Yes, I'm here. Gavin . . . how much will I have to tell?
(hurriedly)
Oh, I know; you've already told me eight or ten times. But maybe I didn't hear it right. How much will I have to tell?
(she listens, quiet, frozen-faced, then slowly begins to lower the receiver toward the stand, quietly, without inflection)

Oh, God. Oh, God.

She puts the receiver down.

(Curtain)

see copy attached

add insert
Galley 35
as indicated

> (He turns, crosses again to the door without stopping nor
> looking back, exits, closes the door behind him. She is
> not watching him either now. For a moment after the door
> has closed, she doesn't move. Then she makes a gesture
> something like Gowan's in scene 2, except that she merely
> presses her palms for a moment hard against her face, her
> face calm, expressionless, cold, then drops her hands, turns,
> picks up the crushed cigarette from beside the tray and
> puts it into the tray and takes up the tray and crosses to
> the fireplace, glancing down at the sleeping child as she
> passes the sofa, empties the tray into the fireplace and
> returns to the table and puts the tray on it and this time
> pauses at the sofa and stoops and tucks the blanket closer
> about the sleeping child and then goes to the telephone
> and lifts the receiver.

TEMPLE
(into the phone)
Three two nine, please.

(While she stands waiting for the answer, there
is a slight movement in the darkness beyond the
open door at rear, just enough silent movement
to show that something or someone is there or
has moved there. Temple is unaware of it since
her back is turned. Then she speaks into the phone)

Maggie? Temple.... Yes, suddenly ... Oh, I dont know; perhaps we got
bored with sunshine .... Of course, I may drop in tomorrow. I wanted to
leave a message for Gavin... I know; he just left here. Something I forgot ... If you'll ask him to call me when he comes in .... Yes ....
Wasn't it. .... Yes .... If you will ... Thank you.

(She puts the receiver down and starts to turn
back into the room when the telephone rings. She
turns back, takes up the receiver, speaks into it)

Hello ... Yes. Coincidence again; I had my hand on it; I had just
called Maggie .... Oh, the filling station. I didn't think you had had
time I can be ready in thirty minutes. Your car, or ours? ... All
right. Listen. How much will I have to tell?
(hurriedly)

... Yes, I'm here Gavin ...

Oh, I know; you've already told me eight or ten times. But maybe I
didn't hear it right. How much will I have to tell?

(She listens a moment, quiet, frozen-faced, then
slowly begins to lower the receiver toward the
standard. speaks quietly, without inflection)

Oh, God. Oh, God.

TEMPLE (cont)
(She puts the receiver down, crosses to the sofa, snaps off the table lamp and takes up the child and crosses to the door to the hall, snaps off the remaining room lights as she goes out, so that the only light in the room now enters from the hall. As soon as she has disappeared from sight, Gowan enters from the door at rear, dressed except for his coat, vest and tie. He has obviously taken no sleeping pill. He goes to the phone and stands quietly beside it, facing the hall door and obviously listening until Temple is safely away. Now the hall light snaps off, and the stage is in complete darkness.

GOWAN'S VOICE (quietly)
Two three nine, please ... // Good evening, Aunt Maggie. Gowan ... / All right, thank you / ... / Sure, sometime tomorrow. As soon as Uncle Gavin comes in, will you have him call me? I'll be right here. Thank you.
(Sound of the receiver as he puts it back)

CURTAIN

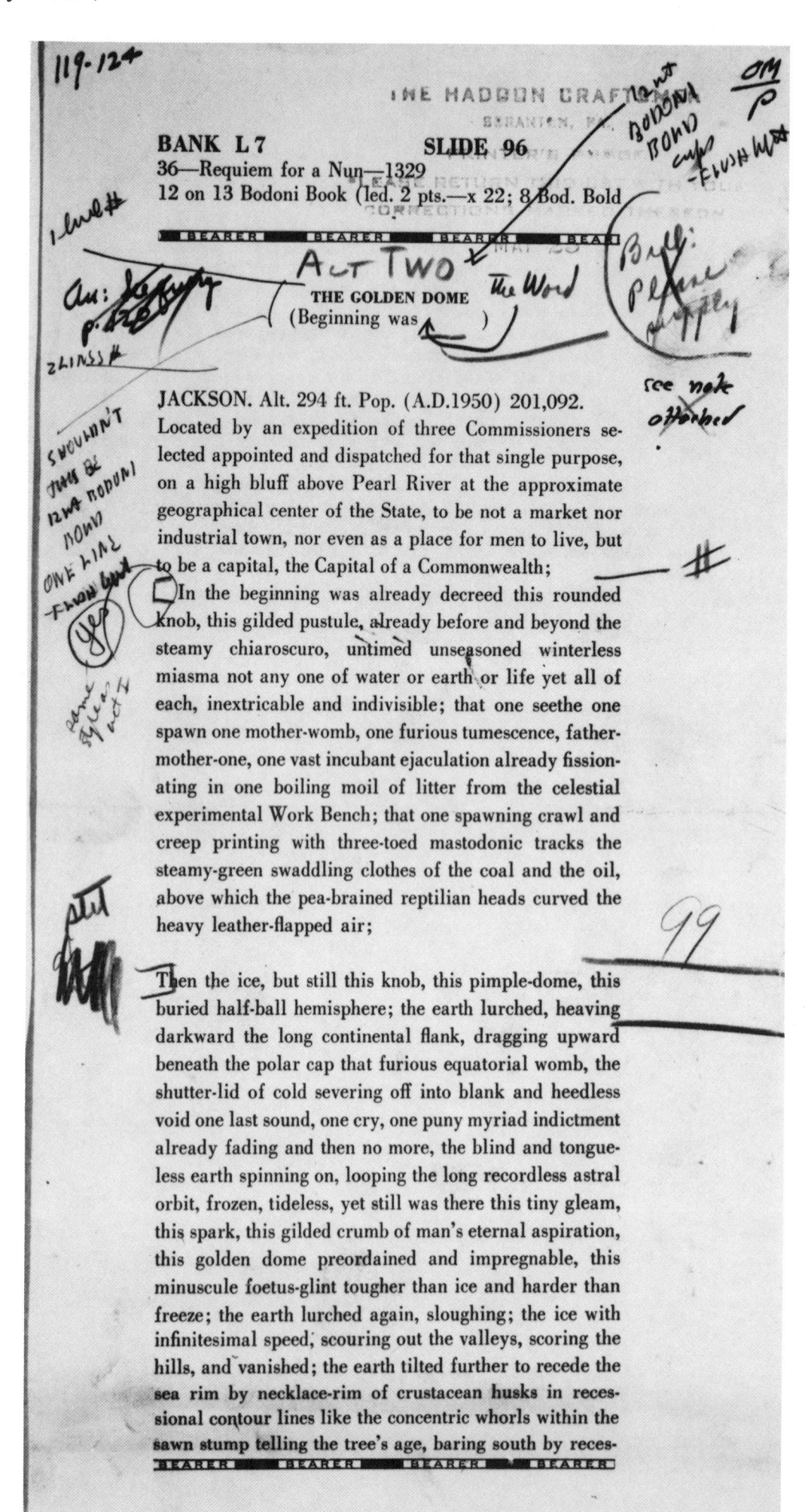

BANK L 7   SLIDE 96
36—Requiem for a Nun—1329
12 on 13 Bodoni Book (led. 2 pts.—x 22; 8 Bod. Bold

ACT TWO
THE GOLDEN DOME
(Beginning was the Word)

JACKSON. Alt. 294 ft. Pop. (A.D.1950) 201,092. Located by an expedition of three Commissioners selected appointed and dispatched for that single purpose, on a high bluff above Pearl River at the approximate geographical center of the State, to be not a market nor industrial town, nor even as a place for men to live, but to be a capital, the Capital of a Commonwealth; In the beginning was already decreed this rounded knob, this gilded pustule, already before and beyond the steamy chiaroscuro, untimed unseasoned winterless miasma not any one of water or earth or life yet all of each, inextricable and indivisible; that one seethe one spawn one mother-womb, one furious tumescence, father-mother-one, one vast incubant ejaculation already fissionating in one boiling moil of litter from the celestial experimental Work Bench; that one spawning crawl and creep printing with three-toed mastodonic tracks the steamy-green swaddling clothes of the coal and the oil, above which the pea-brained reptilian heads curved the heavy leather-flapped air;

Then the ice, but still this knob, this pimple-dome, this buried half-ball hemisphere; the earth lurched, heaving darkward the long continental flank, dragging upward beneath the polar cap that furious equatorial womb, the shutter-lid of cold severing off into blank and heedless void one last sound, one cry, one puny myriad indictment already fading and then no more, the blind and tongueless earth spinning on, looping the long recordless astral orbit, frozen, tideless, yet still was there this tiny gleam, this spark, this gilded crumb of man's eternal aspiration, this golden dome preordained and impregnable, this minuscule foetus-glint tougher than ice and harder than freeze; the earth lurched again, sloughing; the ice with infinitesimal speed, scouring out the valleys, scoring the hills, and vanished; the earth tilted further to recede the sea rim by necklace-rim of crustacean husks in recessional contour lines like the concentric whorls within the sawn stump telling the tree's age, baring south by reces-

ACT ~~TWO~~ One

SCENE I

Office of the Governor of the State. 2:00 A.M. March twelfth.

The whole bottom of the stage is in darkness, as in Scene I, Act One, so that the visible scene has the effect of being held in the beam of a spotlight. Suspended too, since it is upper left and even higher above the shadow of the stage proper than the same in Scene I, Act One, carrying still further the symbolism of the still higher, the last, the ultimate seat of judgment.

It is a corner or section of the office of the Governor of the Commonwealth, late at night, about two A.M.—a clock on the wall says two minutes past two—, a massive flat-topped desk bare except for an ashtray and a telephone, behind it a high-backed heavy chair like a throne; on the wall behind and above the chair, is the emblem, official badge, of the State, sovereignty (a mythical one, since this is rather the State of which Yoknapatawpha County is a unit)—an eagle, the blind scales of justice, a device in Latin perhaps, against a flag. There are two other chairs in front of the desk, turned slightly to face each other, the length of the desk between them.

The Governor stands in front of the high chair, between it and the desk, beneath the emblem on the wall. He is symbolic too: no known person, neither old nor young; he might be someone's idea not of God but of Gabriel perhaps, the Gabriel not before the Crucifixion but after it. He has obviously just been routed out of bed or at least out of his study or dressing-room; he wears a dressing gown, though there is a collar and tie beneath it, and his hair is neatly combed.

Temple and Stevens have just entered. Temple wears the same fur coat, hat, bag, gloves etc. as in Act One, Scene II, Stevens is dressed exactly as he was in Scene One, Act III, is carrying his hat. They are moving toward the two chairs at either end of the desk.

Gal. 40A

STEVENS

Good morning, Henry. Here we are.

GOVERNOR

Yes. Sit down.
              (as Temple sits down)
Does Mrs Stevens smoke?

STEVENS

Yes. Thank you.

He takes a pack of cigarettes from his topcoat pocket, as though he had come prepared for the need, emergency. He works one of them free and extends the pack to Temple. The Governor puts one hand into his dressing-gown pocket and withdraws it, holding something in his closed fist.

TEMPLE

              (takes the cigarette)
What, no blindfold?
              (The Governor extends his hand across the desk. It contains a lighter. Temple puts the cigarette into her mouth. The Governor snaps on the lighter)
But of course; Uncle Gavin and I have already agreed that Temple Drake is already dead. So all we need to do is, fire away—and hope that at least the volley rids us of the metaphor.

GOVERNOR

Metaphor?

TEMPLE

The blindfold. The firing squad. Or is metaphor wrong? Or maybe it's the joke. But dont apologise; a joke that has to be diagrammed is like trying to excuse an egg, isn't it? The only thing you can do is, bury them both, quick.
              (The Governor approaches the flame to Temple's cigarette. She leans and accepts the light, then sits back)
Thanks.

Gal. 40A

STEVENS

Good morning, Henry. Here we are.

GOVERNOR

Yes. Sit down.
        (as Temple sits down)
Does Mrs Stevens smoke?

STEVENS

Yes. Thank you.

He takes a pack of cigarettes from his topcoat pocket, as though he had come prepared for the need, emergency. He works one of them free and extends the pack to Temple. The Governor puts one hand into his dressing-gown pocket and withdraws it, holding something in his closed fist.

TEMPLE
        (takes the cigarette)

What, no blindfold?
        (The Governor extends his hand across the desk. It contains a lighter. Temple puts the cigarette into her mouth.

But of course, the only one waiting execution is back there in Jefferson. So all we need to do here is fire away, and hope that at least the volley rids us of the metaphor.

TEMPLE

The blindfold. The firing squad. Or is metaphor wrong? Or maybe it's the joke. But dont apologise; a joke that has to be diagrammed is like trying to excuse an egg, isn't it? The only thing you can do is, bury them both, quick.
        (The Governor approaches the flame to Temple's cigarette. She leans and accepts the light, then sits back)

Thanks.

BANK L 7   **SLIDE 101**
41—Requiem for a Nun 1329
12 on 13 Bodoni Book (led. 2 pts—x 22; 8 Bod. Bold

The Governor closes the lighter, sits down in the tall chair behind the desk, still holding the lighter in his hand, his hands resting on the desk before him. Stevens sits down in the other chair across from Temple, laying the pack of cigarettes on the desk beside him.

                 GOVERNOR

What has Mrs Gowan Stevens to tell me?

                 TEMPLE

Not Mrs Gowan Stevens: Temple Drake. You remember Temple Drake: the all-Mississippi debutante whose finishing school was the Memphis sporting house—about eight years ago, remember? not that anyone, certainly not the sovereign state of Mississippi's first paid servant, need be reminded of that, provided they could read newspapers five years ago or were kin to someone who could read five years ago or even had a friend who could or even just hear or even just remember or just believe the worst or even just hope for it.

                 GOVERNOR

I think I remember. What does Temple Drake have to tell me, then?

                 TEMPLE

Everything, of course. To save our murderess. But first, how much? How much that you dont already know? It's two oclock in the morning; you want to—maybe even need to—sleep some, even if you are our first paid servant; maybe because of that—

             (she stops: only a second;
             her tone is still brittle, emo-
             tionless)

You see? I'm already lying. What does it matter to me how much sleep the state's first paid servant loses, any more than it matters to the first paid servant, a part of whose job is being paid to lose sleep over the Nancy Mannigoes and Temple Drakes? How much do you already know about Temple Drake, so that I wont ...

             (she stops again, sits quite
             still erect and tense on the

Gal. 41A

        edge of the chair. They
        watch her)

And still lying. I cant understand why I should find either so difficult: the lying or not lying either. But I do. This is what I am trying to say—or maybe trying not to say. How much will I have to tell you, say, speak out loud so that anyone with ears can hear it, about Temple Drake that I never thought that anything on earth, certainly not the murder of my child, would ever make me say? That I came here to wake you up at two oclock in the morning for you to listen to, after five years of being safe or at least quiet? You know: how much will I have to tell, to make it good and painful of course, but quick too, so that you can commute the sentence or whatever you do to it—provided you are going to do it—and we can all go back home to sleep or at least to bed. Because I seem to have been wrong about the blindfold. Temple Drake doesn't seem to be quite dead, after all. This is going to be a little . . . painful, to put it euphoniously—at least 'euphoniously' is right, isn't it?—no matter who bragged.

GOVERNOR

Death is. A shameful one, even more so—which is not too euphonious, even at best.

TEMPLE

At least, you escape the shame.

GOVERNOR

How?

TEMPLE

By dying. Or am I the dense one?

GOVERNOR

Whose death and whose shame? This—woman—

STEVENS

Mannigoe. Nancy Mannigoe.

TEMPLE

All right. Touché. Nancy Mannigoe has no shame. All she has to do is, die. But touché for me too;

haven't I come here and waked you up at two oclock in the morning to tell you about Temple Drake's shame?

STEVENS

Tell him, then.

GOVERNOR
(to Stevens)
Hush, Gavin.
(to Temple)
Tell me. Give her the blindfold.

TEMPLE

You haven't answered my question yet. How much will I have to tell?

GOVERNOR

I know who Temple Drake was: the young woman student at the University five years ago who left on the special train of students to attend a baseball game at State College and disappeared from the train and was not seen again until she was produced six weeks later as a witness in a murder trial in Jefferson, by the Memphis lawyer acting for a notorious psychopathic criminal who had kidnapped her at the scene of the murder, who—the psychopath—himself was hanged the following year in Alabama for another crime.

TEMPLE

Which is not enough. Not near enough, nothing at all in fact, to save a murderess with—if you really intend to save her, which, incidentally, you've never said yet, either yes or no:—which, yes or no, if either of us, Temple Drake or Mrs Gowan Stevens either, had any sense, would be the first thing we would demand of you.

GOVERNOR

Do you want to bargain with me first, then?

TEMPLE

No.

Gal. 42A

GOVERNOR

Why not?

TEMPLE

You know why not. You might say no.

GOVERNOR

(watches her: after a moment)

Whether yes or whether no, you've got to tell me. And as long as you dont hear no, you will?

TEMPLE

A little stiffer than that. I've got to say it, or I wouldn't be here. But unless I can believe you might say yes, I dont see how I can. Which is another touché for somebody: God, maybe; certainly He, if anybody, knows you cant tell about Temple Drake's shame without telling about Nancy Mannigoe.

GOVERNOR

Then start with Nancy—Nancy—

STEVENS

Mannigoe.

GOVERNOR

Mannigoe? Oh yes: Manigault, the old Charleston name.

STEVENS

Further back than that. Maingault. Nancy's heritage—or anyway her name—runs Norman blood.

TEMPLE

Yes.

(she puffs rapidly at the cigarette, removes it from her mouth, leans and crushes it out in the ashtray and sits erect again, unrelaxed. She speaks in a hard rapid brittle emotionless voice)

whore, dopefiend; hopeless, already damned before she was ever born, whose only reason for living was to get the chance to die a

TEMPLE

Not tell you: ask you. No, that's wrong. I could have asked you to revoke or commute or whatever you do to a sentence to hang when we——Uncle Gavin telephoned you last night.
(to STEVENS)
Go on. Tell him. Aren't you the mouthpiece?——isn't that how you say it? Don't lawyers always tell their patients——I mean clients—— never to say anything at all: to let them do all the talking?

GOVERNOR

That's only before the client enters the witness stand.

TEMPLE

So this is the witness stand.

GOVERNOR

You have come all the way here from Jefferson at two o'clock in the morning. What would you call it?

TEMPLE

All right. Touché then. But not Mrs. Gowan Stevens: Temple Drake. You remember Temple: the all-Mississippi debutante whose finishing school was the Memphis sporting house? About eight years ago, remember? Not that anyone, certainly not the sovereign state of Mississippi's first paid servant, need be reminded of that, provided

2 - 1 - 4

TEMPLE (cont'd.)
they could read newspapers eight years ago or were kin to somebody
who could read eight years ago or even had a friend who could or
even just hear or even just remember or just believe the worst or
even just hope for it.

GOVERNOR
I think I remember. What has Temple Drake to tell me then?

TEMPLE
That's not first. The first thing is, how much will I have to tell?
I mean, how much of it that you don't already know, so that I won't
be wasting all of our times telling it over? It's two o'clock in the
morning; you want to——maybe even need to——sleep some, even if you
are our first paid servant; maybe even because of that—— You see?
I'm already lying. What does it matter to me how much sleep the
state's first paid servant loses, anymore than it matters to the
first paid servant, a part of whose job is being paid to lose sleep
over Nancy Mannigoes and Temple Drakes?

[margin: The]

STEVENS
Not lying.

TEMPLE
All right. Stalling, then. So maybe if his excellency or his
honor or whatever they call him, will answer the question, we can
get on.

STEVENS
Why not let the question go, and just get on?

GOVERNOR
(to TEMPLE)
Ask me your question. How much of what do I already know?

TEMPLE
(after a moment; she doesn't answer at
first, staring at the GOVERNOR; then:)
Uncle Gavin's right. Maybe you are the one to ask the questions.
Only, make it as painless as possible. Because it's going to
be a little §... painful, to put it euphoniously——at least
'euphonious' is right, isn't it?——no matter who bragged about
blindfolds.

GOVERNOR
Tell me about Nancy——Mannihoe, Mannikoe——how does she spell it?

[margin: 2nd gal. 4]

TEMPLE
She doesn't. She can't. She can't read or write either. You
are hanging her under Mannigoe, which may be wrong too, though after
tomorrow morning it won't matter.

2 - 1 - 5

GOVERNOR

Oh yes, Manigault. The old Charleston name.

STEVENS

Older than that. Maingault. Nancy's heritage——or anyway her patronym——runs Norman blood.

GOVERNOR

Why not start by telling me about her?

TEMPLE

You are so wise. She was a dopefiend whore that my husband and I took out of the gutter to nurse our children. She murdered one of them and is to be hung tomorrow morning. We——her lawyer and I——have come to ask you to save her.

GOVERNOR

Yes. I know all that. Why?

TEMPLE

Why am I, the mother whose child she murdered, asking you to save her? Because I have forgiven her.
  (the GOVERNOR watches her, he and STEVENS
  both do, waiting. She stares back at the
  GOVERNOR, steadily, not defiant: just alert)
Because she was crazy.
  (the GOVERNOR watches her: she stares back,
  puffing rapidly at the cigarette)
All right. You don't mean why I am asking you to save her, but why I——we hired a whore and a tramp and a dopefiend to nurse our children.
  (she puffs rapidly, talking through the smoke)
To give her another chance——a human being too, even a nigger dope-fiend whore——

STEVENS

Nor that, either.

TEMPLE

  (rapidly, with a sort of despair)
Oh yes, not even stalling now. Why can't you stop lying? You know: just stop for a while or a time like you can stop playing tennis or running or dancing or drinking or eating sweets during Lent. You know: not to reform: just to quit for a while, clear your system, rest up for a new tune or set or lie? All right. It was to have someone to talk to. And now you see? I'll have to tell the rest of it in order to tell you why I had to have a dopefiend whore to talk to, why Temple Drake, the white woman, the all-Mississippi debutante, descendant of long lines of statesmen and soldiers high and proud in the high proud annals of our sovereign state, couldn't find anybody except a nigger dopefiend whore that could speak her language——

BANK L 7   **SLIDE 103**

43—Requiem for a Nun 1329

> murderess on the gallows.—Who not only entered the home of the socialite Gowan Stevenses out of the gutter, but made her debut into the public life of her native city while lying in the gutter with a white man trying to kick her teeth or at least her voice back down her throat.—You remember, Gavin: what was his name? it was before my time in Jefferson, but you remember: the cashier in the bank, the pillar of the church or anyway in the name of his childless wife; and this Monday morning and still drunk, Nancy comes up while he is unlocking the front door of the bank and fifty people standing at his back to get in, and Nancy comes into the crowd and right up to him and says, 'Where's my two dollars, white man?' and he turned and struck her, knocked her across the pavement into the gutter and then ran after her, stomping and kicking at her face or anyway her voice which was still saying 'Where's my two dollars, white man?' until the crowd caught and held him still kicking at the face lying in the gutter, spitting blood and teeth and still saying, 'It was two dollars more than two weeks ago and you done been back twice since'—

She stops speaking, presses both hands to her face for an instant, then removes them.

TEMPLE

No, no handkerchief; Lawyer Stevens and I made a dry run on handkerchiefs before we left home tonight. Where was I?

GOVERNOR

(quotes her)

'It was already two dollars'—

TEMPLE

That was Nancy Mannigoe. Temple Drake was in more than just a two-dollar Saturday night house. You see? We've already reached Temple Drake. But then, I said touché, didn't I?

She leans forward and starts to take up the crushed cigarette from the ashtray. Stevens picks up the pack

murderess on the gallows.—Who not only entered the home of the socialite Gowan Stevenses out of the gutter, but made her debut into the public life of her native city while lying in the gutter with a white man trying to kick her teeth or at least her voice back down her throat.—You remember, Gavin: what was his name? it was before my time in Jefferson, but you remember: the cashier in the bank, the pillar of the church or anyway in the name of his childless wife; and this Monday morning and still drunk, Nancy comes up while he is unlocking the front door of the bank and fifty people standing at his back to get in, and Nancy comes into the crowd and right up to him and says, 'Where's my two dollars, white man?' and he turned and struck her, knocked her across the pavement into the gutter and then ran after her, stomping and kicking at her face or anyway her voice which was still saying 'Where's my two dollars, white man?' until the crowd caught and held him still kicking at the face lying in the gutter, spitting blood and teeth and still saying, 'It was two dollars more than two weeks ago and you done been back twice since'—

She stops speaking, presses both hands to her face for an instant, then removes them.

TEMPLE

No, no handkerchief; Lawyer Stevens and I made a dry run on handkerchiefs before we left home tonight. Where was I?

GOVERNOR

(quotes her)
'It was already two dollars'—

TEMPLE

So now I've got to tell all of it. Because that was just Nancy Mannigoe. Temple Drake was in more than just a two-dollar Saturday night house. But then, I said touché, didn't I?

She leans forward and starts to take up the crushed cigarette from the ashtray. Stevens picks up the pack

Gal. 43A

from the desk and prepares to offer it to her. She withdraws her hand from the crushed cigarette and sits back.

TEMPLE
(to the proffered cigarette in Stevens' hand)
No, thanks; I wont need it, after all. From here out, it's merely anticlimax. *Coup de grace.* The victim never feels that, does he?—Where was I?
(quickly)
Never mind. I said that before too, didn't I?
(she sits for a moment, her hands gripped in her lap, motionless)
There seems to be some of this, quite a lot of this, which even our first paid servant is not up on; maybe because he has been our first paid servant for less than two years yet. Though that's wrong too; he could read ~~five~~ *eight* years ago, couldn't he? In fact, he couldn't have been elected Governor of even Mississippi if he hadn't been able to read at least three years in advance, could he?

STEVENS
Temple.

GOVERNOR
(watching Temple)
Hush, Gavin.
(to Temple)
Coup de grace not only means mercy, but is. Deliver it. Give her the cigarette, Gavin.

TEMPLE
(sits forward again)
No, thanks. Really.
(after a second)
Sorry.
(quickly)
You'll notice, I always remember to say that, always remember my manners,—'raising' as we put it. Showing that I really sprang from gentlefolks, not Norman knights like Nancy did, but at least people who dont insult the host in his own house, especially at two oclock in the morning. Only, I just sprang too far, where Nancy merely

[margin note: TEMPLE (to Stevens) why not? It's just talking, isn't it?]

147-150

OM/P

BANK L 7   SLIDE 104

stumbled modestly: a lady, again, you see.
>   (after a moment)
> There again. I'm not even ~~lying~~ now: I'm faulting
> —what do they call it? burking. You know: here
> we are at the fence again; we've got to jump it
> this time, or crash. You know: slack the snaffle,
> let her mouth it a little, take hold, a light hold,
> just enough to have something to jump against;
> then touch her. So here goes. Temple Drake, the
> foolish virgin, that is, as far as anyone at least
> disproved, a virgin, but a fool certainly; seven-
> teen and more of a fool than simply being a vir-
> gin or even being seventeen could have excused
> or accounted for; indeed, being capable of that
> height of folly which even seven or three, let
> alone virginity, could hardly have matched; get-
> ting off the train as soon as she could persuade
> someone to stop it, to make the rest of the trip in
> an automobile; not to get anywhere any sooner;
> just to ride in the automobile: and that mainly
> because all the other girls were either not brave
> enough to be that foolish or not virgin enough
> to—

stalling

124

STEVENS
—or too lucky to have a boy-friend who owned
or at least could borrow his mother's car. That
was her husband.

GOVERNOR
What?

TEMPLE
Shut up, Gavin.

STEVENS
           (to Governor)
The one who met her with the automobile when
she got off the train. My nephew. They were
married the next year.

TEMPLE
           (sharply)
Gavin.
           (to Governor)
Listen to me—

125

insert

Gal. 44A

STEVENS

The Virginia gentleman. That is, trained at the University of Virginia not only in drinking but in gentility too, only he pulled off the course before he had run it completely out. Or rather, ran out of both the drink and the gentility simultaneously back in Mississippi that morning five years ago; wrecked the car hunting for another drink and left them both stranded at the moonshiner's in time for her to be present at the murder—and then permitted the murderer to kidnap her and carry her to Memphis and hide her in the brothel against the day when he would need her in his alibi.

TEMPLE

But had a relapse into one of them at least. Because a year afterward, he married her. Why dont you add that?

STEVENS

Into both of them. He hasn't had a drink since, either. That's correct, isn't it?

TEMPLE

Correct. And much better. For a moment it looked like Temple Drake was going to have to make this confession not only from behind Mrs Gowan Stevens's skirts but from behind her husband's virtue too. Because how could his honor or his excellency or whatever he is have accepted Temple Drake as reason enough to save Nancy Mannigoe, if Temple Drake was revealed to be simply another victim of evil associations too? Or is that wrong, and our Uncle Gavin threw his nephew to the wolves not to help save anybody but just to make it a little harder for Temple Drake to bare her soul, because saving Nancy Mannigoe is not what we came here for at all—

STEVENS

Temple.

GOVERNOR

Hush, Gavin.

2-1-7

TEMPLE (cont'd.)
No, thanks; I won't need it, after all. From here out, it's merely
anticlimax. <u>Coupe de grace</u>. The victim never feels that, does
he? — Where was I?
   (Quickly)
Never mind. I said that before too, didn't I?

   (SHE sits for a moment, her hands
   gripped in her lap, motionless)

There seems to be some of this, quite a lot of this, which even our
first paid servant is not up on; maybe because he has been our first
paid servant for less than two years yet. Though that's wrong too;
he could read eight years ago, couldn't he? In fact, he couldn't
have been elected Governor of even Mississippi if he hadn't been
able to read at least three years in advance, could he?

STEVENS
Temple.

TEMPLE (to STEVENS)
Why not? It's just stalling, isn't it?

GOVERNOR
   (Watching TEMPLE)
Hush, Gavin.
   (To TEMPLE)
<u>Coupe de grace</u> not only means mercy, but is. Deliver it. Give
her the cigarette, Gavin.

TEMPLE
   (Sits forward again)
No, thanks. Really.
   (After a second)
Sorry.
   (Quickly)
You'll notice, I always remember to say that, always remember my
manners, — 'raising' as we put it. Showing that I really spring
from gentlefolks, not Norman knights like Nancy did, but at least
people who don't insult the host in his own house, especially at
two o'clock in the morning. Only, I just sprang too far, where
Nancy merely stumbled modestly: a lady again, you see. There again
I'm not even stalling now; I'm faulting — what do they call it? —
burking. You know: here we are at the fence again; we've got to
jump it this time, or crash. You know, slack the snaffle, let
her mouth it a little, take a hold, a light hold, just enough to have
something to jump against, then touch her — So here we are, right
back where we started, and so we can start over. So how much will
I have to tell, say, speak out loud so that anybody with ears can
hear it, about Temple Drake that I never thought that anything on
earth, least of all the murder of my child and the execution of a
nigger dopefiend where, would ever make me tell? That I came here

Pick up insert for Galley 44 here

2 - 1 - 8

TEMPLE (cont'd.)
at two o'clock in the morning to wake you up to listen to, after eight years of being safe or at least quiet? You know: how much will I have to tell, to make it good and painful of course, but quick too, so that you can revoke or commute the sentence or whatever you do to it, and we can all go back home to sleep or at least to bed? Painful of course, but just painful enough—— I think you said 'euphoniously' was right, didn't you?

GOVERNOR
Death is painful. A shameful one, even more so——which is not too euphonious, even at best.

Start

TEMPLE
Oh, death. We're not talking about death now. We're talking about shame. Nancy Mannigoe has no shame; all she has is, to die. But touché for me too; haven't I brought Temple Drake all the way here at two o'clock in the morning for the reason that all Nancy Mannigoe has, is to die?

STEVENS
Tell him, then.

TEMPLE
He hasn't answered my question yet.
            (to GOVERNOR)
Try to answer it. How much will I have to tell? Don't just say 'everything'. I've already heard that.

GOVERNOR
I know who Temple Drake was: the young woman student at the University eight years ago who left the school one morning on a special train of students to attend a baseball game at another college, and disappeared from the train somewhere during its run, and vanished, nobody knew where, until she reappeared six weeks later as a witness in a murder trial in Jefferson, produced by the lawyer of the man who, it was then learned, had abducted her and held her prisoner——

TEMPLE
——in the Memphis sporting house: don't forget that.

GOVERNOR
——in order to produce her to prove his alibi in the murder——

TEMPLE
——that Temple Drake knew had done the murder for the very good reason that——

2 - 1 - 9

STEVENS

Wait. Let me play too. She got off the train at the instigation of a young man who met the train at an intermediate stop with an automobile, the plan being to drive on to the ball game in the car, except that the young man was drunk at the time and got drunker, and wrecked the car and stranded both of them at the moonshiner's house where the murder happened, and from which the murderer kidnapped her and carried her to Memphis, to hold her until he would need his alibi. Afterward he——the young man with the automobile, her escort and protector at the moment of the abduction——married her. He is her husband now. He is my nephew.

TEMPLE
(to STEVENS, bitterly)
You too. So wise too. Why can't you believe in truth? At least that I'm trying to tell it. At least trying now to tell it.
(to GOVERNOR)
Where was I?

GOVERNOR (quotes)
That Temple Drake knew had done the murder for the very good reason that——

TEMPLE

Oh yes. —— for the very good reason that she saw him do it, or at least his shadow; and so produced by his lawyer in the Jefferson courtroom so that she could swear away the life of the man who was accused of it. Oh yes, that's the one. And now I've already told you something you nor nobody else but the Memphis lawyer knew, and I haven't even started. You see? I can't even bargain with you. You haven't even said yes or no yet, whether you can save her or not, whether you want to save her or not, will consider saving her or not; which, if either of us, Temple Drake or Mrs. Gowan Stevens either, had any sense, would have demanded first of you.

GOVERNOR
Do you want to ask me that first?

TEMPLE
I can't. I don't dare. You might say no.

GOVERNOR
Then you wouldn't have to tell me about Temple Drake.

TEMPLE
I've got to do that. I've got to say it all, or I wouldn't be here. But unless I can still believe that you might say yes, I don't see how I can. Which is another touché for somebody: God, maybe——if there is one. You see? That's what's so terrible.

2 - 1 - 10

TEMPLE (cont'd.)
We don't even need Him. Simple evil is enough. Even after eight years, it's still enough. It was eight years ago that Uncle Gavin said——oh yes, he was there too; didn't you just hear him? He could have told you all of this or anyway most of it over the telephone and you could be in bed asleep right this minute——said how there is a corruption even in just looking at evil, even by accident; that you can't haggle, traffic, with putrefaction——you can't, you don't dare——
   (she stops, tense, motionless)

GOVERNOR
Take the cigarette now.
   (to STEVENS)
Gavin——
   (STEVENS takes up the pack and prepares
   to offer the cigarette)

TEMPLE
No, thanks. It's too late now. Because here we go. If we can't jump the fence, we can at least break through it——

STEVENS (interrupts)
Which means that anyway one of us will get over standing up.
   (as TEMPLE reacts)
Oh yes, I'm still playing; I'm going to ride this one too. Go ahead.
   (prompting)
Temple Drake——

TEMPLE
——Temple Drake, the foolish virgin; that is, a virgin as far as anybody went on record to disprove, but a fool certainly by anybody's standards and computation; seventeen, and more of a fool than simply being a virgin or even being seventeen could excuse or account for; indeed, showing herself capable of a height of folly which even seven or three, let alone mere virginity, could scarcely have matched——

STEVENS
Give the brute a chance. Try at least to ride him at the fence and not just through it.

TEMPLE
You mean the Virginia gentleman.
   (to GOVERNOR)
That's my husband. He went to the University of Virginia, trained, Uncle Gavin would say, at Virginia not only in drinking but in gentility too——

STEVENS
——and ran out of both at the same instant that day eight years ago when he took her off the train and wrecked the car at the moonshiner's house.

                    TEMPLE
But relapsed into one of them at least because at least he married
me as soon as he could.
          (to STEVENS)
You don't mind my telling his excellency that, do you?

                    STEVENS
A relapse into both of them. He hasn't had a drink since that day
either. His excellency might bear that in mind too.

                    GOVERNOR
I will. I have.
          (he makes just enough of a pause to cause
          them both to stop and look at him)
I almost wish——
          (they are both watching him; this is the
          first intimation we have that something
          is going on here, an undercurrent: that
          the GOVERNOR and STEVENS know something
          which TEMPLE doesn't: to TEMPLE)
He didn't come with you.

                    STEVENS (mildly yet quickly)
Won't there be time for that later, Henry?

                    TEMPLE (quick, defiant, suspicious, hard)
Who didn't?

                    GOVERNOR
Your husband.

                    TEMPLE (quick and hard)
Why?

                    GOVERNOR
You have come here to plead for the life of the murderess of your
child. Your husband was its parent too.

                    TEMPLE
You're wrong. We didn't come here at two o'clock in the morning to
save Nancy Mannigoe. Nancy Mannigoe is not even concerned in this
because Nancy Mannigoe's lawyer told me before we ever left Jefferson
that you were not going to save Nancy Mannigoe. What we came here
and waked you up at two o'clock in the morning for is just to give
Temple Drake a good fair honest chance to suffer — you know: just
anguish for the sake of anguish, like that Russian or somebody who
wrote a whole book about suffering, not suffering for or about
anything, just suffering, like somebody unconscious not really
breathing for anything but just breathing. Or maybe that's wrong
too and nobody really cares, suffers, anymore about suffering than
they do about truth or justice or Temple Drake's shame or Nancy
Mannigoe's worthless nigger life —

BANK L7　　　　　　　SLIDE 105
45—Requiem for a Nun 1329
12 on 13 Bodoni Book (led. 2 pts—x 22; 8 Bod. Bold

TEMPLE

—because in fact according to something Nancy Mannigoe's lawyer said before we left home tonight, his honor or his excellency is not going to save Nancy Mannigoe anyway; that we came here just to give Temple Drake a good fair honest chance to suffer;—you know: just anguish for the sake of anguish, like that Russian or somebody who wrote a whole book about suffering, not suffering for or about anything, just suffering, like somebody unconscious not really breathing for anything but just breathing. Or maybe that's wrong too and nobody really cares, suffers, anymore about suffering than they do about truth or justice or Temple Drake's shame or Nancy Mannigoe's worthless nigger life.

STEVENS

Temple.

She stops speaking, sitting quite still, erect in the chair, her face raised slightly, not looking at either of them while they watch her.

GOVERNOR

Give her the handkerchief now.

Stevens takes a fresh handkerchief from his pocket, shakes it out and extends it toward Temple. She does not move, her hands still clasped in her lap. Stevens rises, crosses, drops the handkerchief into her lap, returns to his chair.

TEMPLE

Thanks really. But it doesn't matter now; we're too near the end; you could almost go on down to the car and start it and have the engine warming up while I finish.

(to Governor)

You see? All you'll have to do now is just be still and listen. Or not even listen if you dont want to: but just be still, just wait. And not long either now, and then we can all go to bed and turn off the light. And then, night: dark: sleep even maybe, when with the same arm you turn off the light and pull the covers up with, you can put

Gal. 45A

aw— forever Temple Drake and whatever it is you have done about her, and Nancy Mannigoe and whatever it is you have done about her, if you're going to do anything, if it even matters anyhow whether you do anything or not, and none of it will ever have to bother us anymore. I'll have the cigarette now, please.

Stevens takes up the pack, rising and working the end of a cigarette free, and extends the pack. She takes the cigarette, already speaking again while Stevens puts the pack on the desk and takes up the lighter which the Governor, watching Temple, shoves across the desk where Stevens can reach it. Stevens snaps the lighter on and holds it out. Temple makes no effort to light the cigarette, holding the cigarette in her hand and talking. Then she lays the cigarette unlighted on the ashtray and Stevens closes the lighter and sits down again, putting the lighter down beside the pack of cigarettes.

TEMPLE

Oh yes, already bad and lost before she ever started for the ball game. Because she only went to the ball game because she would have to make a train trip to get there, so that she could slip off the train the first time it stopped so she could get into the automobile to make the rest of the hundred-mile trip with a young man who could be depended on to be wrong about how much he could drink. You know: an optimist. I dont mean the young man, he was just doing the best he knew, could. He didn't want to make the trip anyway, the automobile was Temple's idea. She was the optimist, eternally hopeful; not that she had foreseen, planned ahead either; she simply had every trust and confidence in her parents' acquaintance with evil, and was simply doing the best thing she could invent or think of that she knew her father and brothers would have forbidden her to do. And they were right and so of course she was right, though still having to fight a little for her rights and destiny even then, even driving the car for a while after we began to realise that the young man had been mistaken about the drink, driving and insisting on the wrong turn which finally got u—them lost—

Because Uncle Gavin was only partly right. It's not that you must never even look on evil and corruption; sometimes you can't help that, you are not always warned. It's not even that you must resist it always. Because you've got to start much sooner than that. You've got to be already prepared to resist it, say no to it, long before you see it; you must have already said no to it long before you even know what it is. ~~I'll have the cigarette now, please.~~

you're going to do anything, if it even matters anyhow whether you do anything or not, and none of it will ever have to bother us anymore. I'll have the cigarette now, please.

Stevens takes up the pack, rising and working the end of a cigarette free, and extends the pack. She takes the cigarette, already speaking again while Stevens puts the pack on the desk and takes up the lighter which the Governor, watching Temple, shoves across the desk where Stevens can reach it. Stevens snaps the lighter on and holds it out. Temple makes no effort to light the cigarette, holding the cigarette in her hand and talking. Then she lays the cigarette unlighted on the ashtray and Stevens closes the lighter and sits down again, putting the lighter down beside the pack of cigarettes.

TEMPLE

Oh yes, already bad and lost before she ever started for the ball game. Because she only went to the ball game because she would have to make a train trip to get there, so that she could slip off the train the first time it stopped so she could get into the automobile to make the rest of the hundred-mile trip with a young man who could be depended on to be wrong about how much he could drink. You know: an optimist. I dont mean the young man, he was just doing the best he knew, could. He didn't want to make the trip anyway, the automobile was Temple's idea. She was the optimist, eternally hopeful; not that she had foreseen, planned ahead either; she simply had every trust and confidence in her parents' acquaintance with evil, and was simply doing the best thing she could invent or think of that she knew her father and brothers would have forbidden her to do. And they were right and so of course she was right, though still having to fight a little for her rights and destiny even then, even driving the car for a while after we began to realise that the young man had been mistaken about the drink, driving and insisting on the wrong turn which finally got u—them lost—

153-156

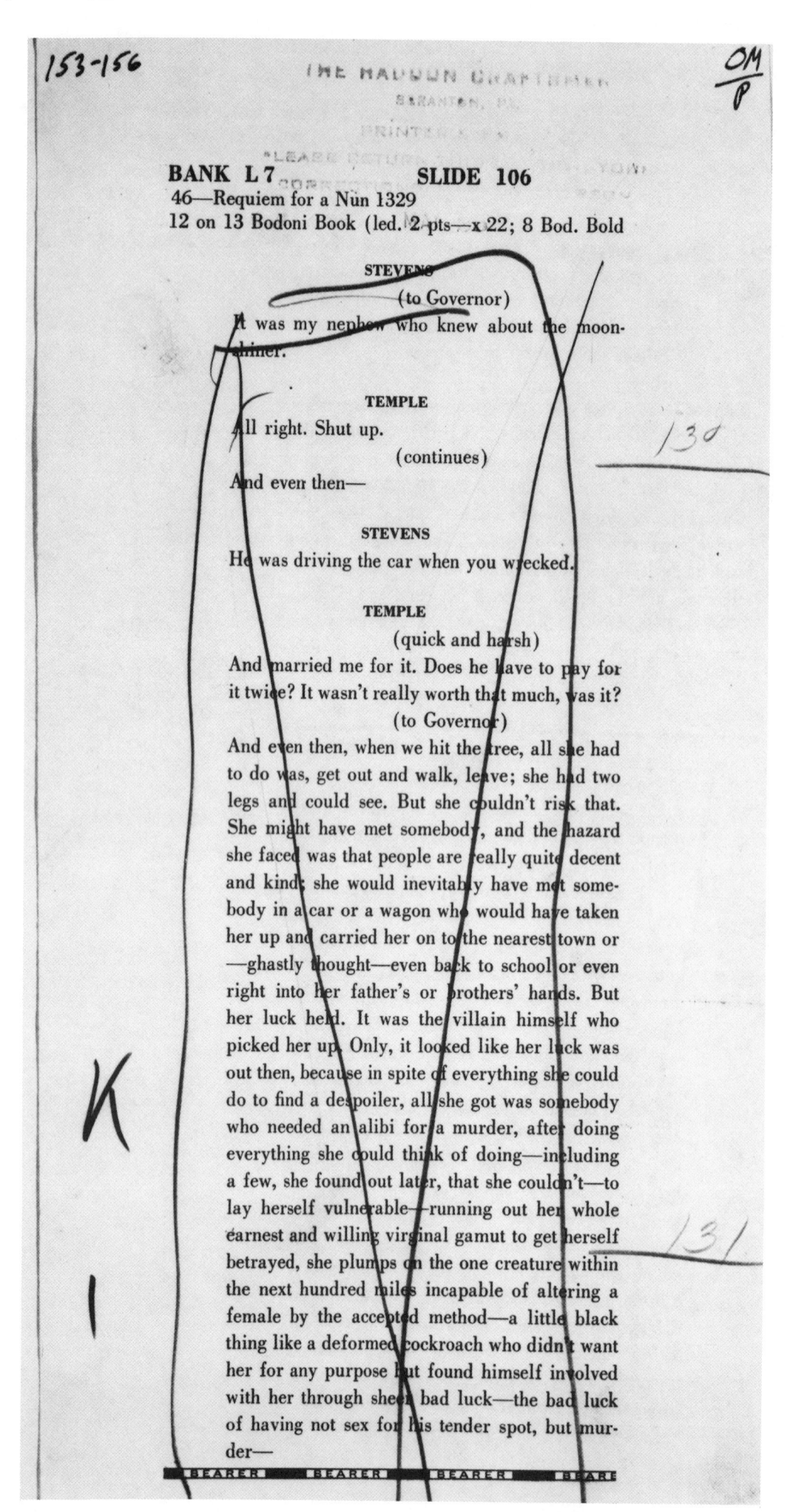

BANK L 7   SLIDE 106
46—Requiem for a Nun 1329
12 on 13 Bodoni Book (led. 2 pts—x 22; 8 Bod. Bold

STEVENS
(to Governor)
It was my nephew who knew about the moonshiner.

TEMPLE
All right. Shut up.
(continues)
And even then—

STEVENS
He was driving the car when you wrecked.

TEMPLE
(quick and harsh)
And married me for it. Does he have to pay for it twice? It wasn't really worth that much, was it?
(to Governor)
And even then, when we hit the tree, all she had to do was, get out and walk, leave; she had two legs and could see. But she couldn't risk that. She might have met somebody, and the hazard she faced was that people are really quite decent and kind; she would inevitably have met somebody in a car or a wagon who would have taken her up and carried her on to the nearest town or —ghastly thought—even back to school or even right into her father's or brothers' hands. But her luck held. It was the villain himself who picked her up. Only, it looked like her luck was out then, because in spite of everything she could do to find a despoiler, all she got was somebody who needed an alibi for a murder, after doing everything she could think of doing—including a few, she found out later, that she couldn't—to lay herself vulnerable—running out her whole earnest and willing virginal gamut to get herself betrayed, she plumps on the one creature within the next hundred miles incapable of altering a female by the accepted method—a little black thing like a deformed cockroach who didn't want her for any purpose but found himself involved with her through sheer bad luck—the bad luck of having not sex for his tender spot, but murder—

Gal. 46A

(she stops, sitting motionless, erect, her hands
clenched into fists on her lap,
looking at neither of them;
she speaks again in a tone of
quiet and despairing amaze-
ment)

You see? I'm lying again. The harder I try to
tell the truth, the more trouble I seem to have
with it. I'm like trying to drive a hen into a barrel. Maybe if you could just make the hen—tell
the hen— If everybody just acted like they were
trying to keep her out of the barrel—

STEVENS

It's not a barrel. It's a culvert. A thoroughfare.
The other end is open too. Go through it. Not a
seducer—

TEMPLE

(rapidly, once more glib and
apparently composed)

—worse. Worse than a father or uncle. Worse
than a father confessor with an acolyte. It was
almost horticultural, like the orchid-grower with
his one prize stalk: carried her to Memphis—
and she still had the legs and the eyes; she could
have climbed down the rainspout anytime, the
only difference being that she didn't—and shut
her up in the sporting house as pure and insulated as any Spanish bride, with the madam herself to watch her more eagle-eyed than any mama
because why not since here was the one industry
in America where maidenhead was a marketable
commodity. So there she was, a prisoner, watched
night and day by the madam and a faithful Negro
maid; a prisoner of course but gilded, with every
wish granted before she even thought of it—perfume by the quart, a fur coat, with nowhere to
wear it because he wouldn't let her out, and in
May too, too warm to wear a fur coat even if he
had let her out—and a nasty mind would say he
had waited until May to buy the fur coat, but
they would have been wrong; nothing was too
good for her really—snazzy underwear, negligees, of course he did all the shopping, select-

(STEVENS takes up the pack, raising
and working the end of a cigarette free,
and extends the pack. SHE takes the
cigarette, already speaking again while
STEVENS puts the pack on the desk and takes up
the lighter which the GOVERNOR, watching TEMPLE,
shoves across the desk where STEVENS can reach
it. STEVENS snaps the lighter on and holds it
out. TEMPLE makes no effort to light the
cigarette, holding the cigarette in her hand
and talking. Then SHE lays the cigarette
unlighted on the ashtray and STEVENS closes
the lighter and sits down again, putting the
lighter down beside the pack of cigarettes)

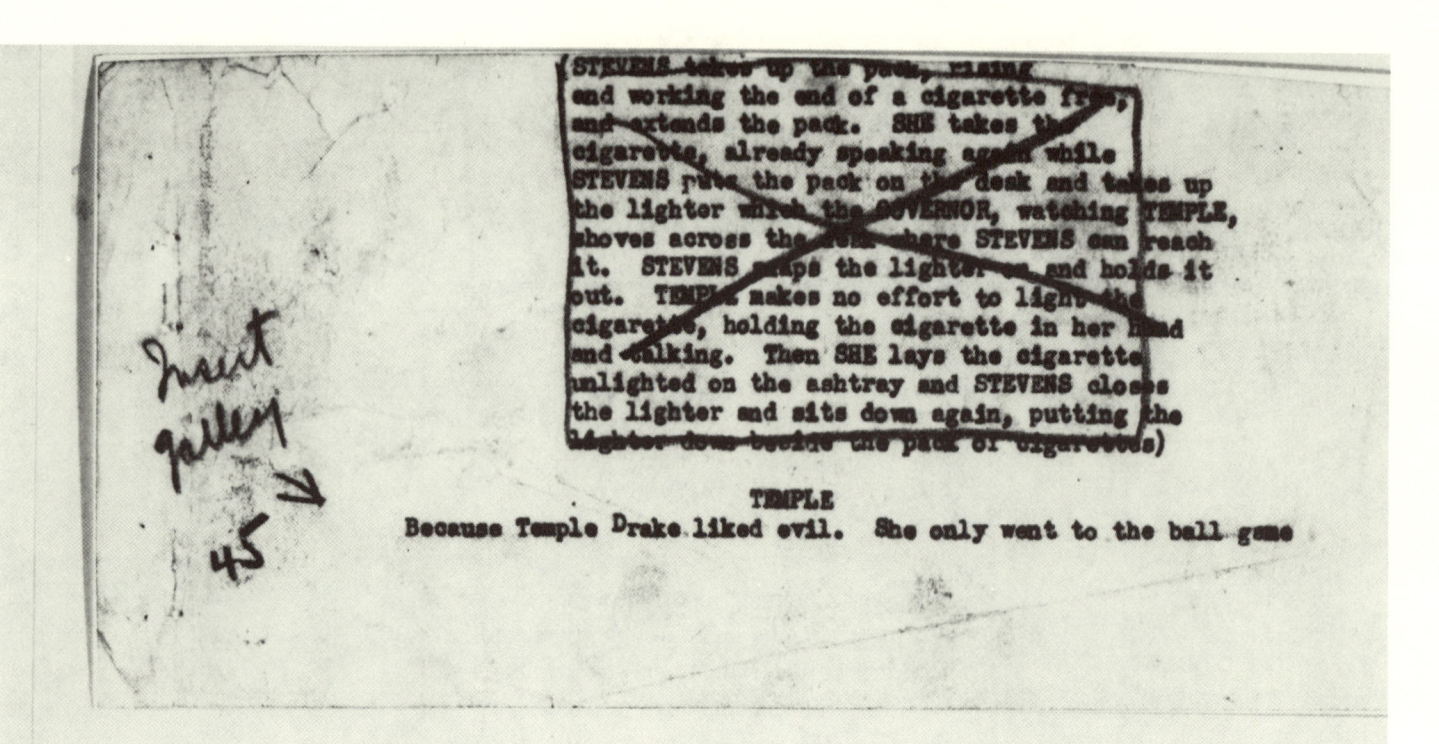

TEMPLE
Because Temple Drake liked evil. She only went to the ball game

Insert galley 45 →

2 - 1.- 13

TEMPLE (Con'd)
because she would have to get on a train to do it, so that she
could slip off the train the first time it stopped, and get into
the car to drive a hundred miles with a man——

STEVENS
——who couldn't hold his drink.

TEMPLE (to STEVENS)
All right. Aren't I just saying that?
(to GOVERNOR)
An optimist. Not the young man; he was just doing the best he knew,
could. It wasn't him that suggested the trip: it was Temple——

STEVENS
It was his car though. Or his mother's.

TEMPLE (to STEVENS)
All right. All right.
(to GOVERNOR)
No, Temple was the optimist: not that she had foreseen, planned
ahead either: she just had unbounded faith that her father and
brothers would know evil when they saw it, so all she had to do was,
do the one thing which she knew they would forbid her to do if they
had the chance. And they were right about the evil, and so of course
she was right too, though even then it was not easy: she even had to
drive the car for a while after we began to realize that the young
man was wrong, had graduated too soon in the drinking part of his
Virginia training——

STEVENS
It was Gowan who knew the moonshiner and insisted on going there.

TEMPLE
—— and even then——

STEVENS
He was driving when you wrecked.

TEMPLE (to STEVENS: quick and harsh)
And married me for it. Does he have to pay for it twice? It wasn't
really worth paying for once, was it?
(to GOVERNOR)
And even then——

GOVERNOR
How much was it worth?

TEMPLE
Was what worth?

GOVERNOR
His marrying you.

2-1-14

TEMPLE

You mean to him, of course. Less than he paid for it.

GOVERNOR

Is that what he thinks too?
            (They stare at one another, TEMPLE
            alert, quite watchful, though rather
            impatient than anything else)
You're going to tell me something that he doesn't know, else you would have brought him with you. Is that right?

TEMPLE

Yes.

GOVERNOR

Would you tell it if he were here?
            (TEMPLE is staring at the GOVERNOR.
            Unnoticed by her, STEVENS makes a
            faint movement. The GOVERNOR stops
            him with a slight motion of one
            hand which also TEMPLE does not
            notice)
Now that you have come this far, now that, as you said, you have got to tell it, say it aloud, not to save Nan——this woman, but because you decided before you left home tonight that there is nothing else to do but tell it.

TEMPLE

How do I know whether I would or not?

GOVERNOR

Suppose he was here —— sitting in that chair where Gav —— your uncle is ——

TEMPLE

——or behind the door or in one of your desk drawers, maybe? He's not. He's at home. I gave him a sleeping pill.

GOVERNOR

But suppose he was, now that you have got to say it. Would you still say it?

TEMPLE

All right. Yes. Now will you please shut up too and let me tell it? How can I, if you and Gavin won't hush and let me? I can't even remember where I was. —— Oh yes. So I saw the murder, or anyway the shadow of it, and the man took me to Memphis, and I know that too, I had two legs and I could see, and I could have simply screamed up the main street of any of the little towns we passed, just as I could have walked away from the car after Gow —— we ran it into the tree, and stopped a wagon or a car which would have carried me to the nearest town or railroad station or even back to school or for that matter, right on back home into my father's or brothers' hands. But not me, not Temple. I choose the murderer——

2 - 1 - 15

              STEVENS (to GOVERNOR)
He was a psychopath, though that didn't come out in the trial, and
when it did come out, or could have come out, it was too late. I
was there; I saw that too: a little black thing with an Italian name,
like a neat and only slightly deformed cockroach: a hybrid, sexually
incapable. But then, she will tell you that too.

              TEMPLE (with bitter sarcasm)
Dear Uncle Gavin.
       (to GOVERNOR)
Oh yes, that too, her bad luck too: to plump for a thing which didn't
even have sex for his weakness, but just murder——
       (She stops, sitting motionless,
        erect, her hands clenched on her
       lap, her eyes closed)
If you both would just hush, just let me. I seem to be like trying
to drive a hen into a barrel. Maybe if you would just try to act
like you wanted to keep her out of it, from going into it——

              GOVERNOR
Don't call it a barrel. Call it a tunnel. That's a thoroughfare,
because the other end is open too. Go through it. There was no ——
sex.

              TEMPLE
Not from him. He was worse than a father or uncle. It was worse
than being the wealthy ward of the most indulgent trust or insurance
company: carried to Memphis and shut up in that Manuel Street
sporting house like a ten-year-old bride in a Spanish convent, with
the madam herself more eagle-eyed than any mamma——and the Negro maid
to guard the door while the madam would be out, to wherever she would
go, wherever the madams of cat houses go on their afternoons out, to
pay police court fines or protection or to the bank or maybe just
visiting, which would not be so bad because the maid would unlock the
door and come inside and we could ——
       (She falters, pauses for less than
       a second; then quickly)
Yes, that's why —— talk. A prisoner of course, and maybe not in a
very gilded cage, but at least the prisoner was. I had perfume by
the quart; some salesgirl chose it of course, and it was the wrong
kind, but at least I had it, and he bought me a fur coat——with
nowhere to wear it of course because he wouldn't let me out, but I
had the coat——and snazzy underwear and negligees, selected also by
salesgirls but at least the best or anyway the most expensive——the
taste at least of the big end of an underworld big shot's wallet.
Because he wanted me to be contented, you see; and not only contented,
he didn't even mind if I was happy too: just so I was there when or in
case the police finally connected him with that Mississippi murder;
not only didn't mind if I was happy; he even made the effort himself
to see that I was. And so at last we have come to it, because now I
have got to tell you this too to give you a valid reason why I waked
—— up at two in the morning to ask you to save a murderess.

~~ing himself; but at least his taste was based on the big end of an underworld caesar's pocketbook, like the perfume which at least came in quarts. Because he wanted her to be contented; he wouldn't really mind if she was even happy too probably, since all he wanted was to have her in hand when the meddling police finally connected him with the murder back in Mississippi at the moonshiner's house.~~

She stops speaking, reaches and takes the unlighted cigarette from the tray, then realises it is unlit. Stevens takes up the lighter from the desk and starts to get up. Still watching Temple, the Governor makes to Stevens a slight arresting signal with his hand. Stevens pauses, then pushes the lighter along the desk to where Temple can reach it, and sits back down. Temple takes the lighter, snaps it on, lights the cigarette, closes the lighter and puts it back on the desk. But after only one puff at the cigarette, she lays it back on the tray and sits again as before, speaking again.

TEMPLE

But still a prisoner, not even allowed to meet or even see the other girls, the co-laborers in that vineyard, not even allowed to sit with them after hours and talk shop while they counted the chips or compared blisters or whatever they would do sitting on one another's beds and hashing over the exigencies—that's surely the right word, isn't it?—of their merry trade. But not her, not Temple: shut up in one room twenty-four hours a day with nothing to do but hold solitary fashion shows in front of a two-foot mirror in the fur coat and the flash pants and negligees, hanging bone-dry and safe in the middle of sin and pleasure like being suspended twenty fathoms deep in an ocean diving bell. But not Temple, not always, not even very long, because Temple's luck was Temple; driven to any extreme of course, but then, Temple was capable of any extreme. And so she fell in love.

GOVERNOR

Ah.

Gal. 47A

STEVENS

He—Popeye—brought the man there himself,—Red he was called, Arkansas Red. Not a criminal himself: just a thug, probably cursed more by eupepsia than anything else, including amorality. He was a houseman—bouncer, they call them—in a nightclub which Popeye owned a piece of. He died shortly afterward in a back street alley of a bullet bearing a marked resemblance to the one responsible for the Mississippi murder, though Popeye got himself hung in Alabama for one he didn't commit, before the pistol was ever found and connected with him.

GOVERNOR

Ah. This—Popeye . . .

STEVENS

Say it. 'Sold her to the man called Red and then reneged his bargain with a pistol.' Because what else can you believe, being a Southerner and gently bred? Only, how can you say that in the presence of the victim who is not only a Southerner and gently bred too, but far worse: a female Southerner and gently bred?

TEMPLE
(sharply)

Gavin!

STEVENS
(still to the Governor)

Sorry. You underrate this *precieux*, this flower, this jewel. Vitalli. What a name for him. A hybrid, impotent. He was hanged the next year to be sure. But even that was wrong: his very effacement debasing, flouting, even what dignity man has been able to lend to necessary human abolishment. He should have been crushed somehow under a vast and mindless boot, like a spider. He didn't sell her; you violate and outrage his very memory with that crass and material impugnment. He was a purist, an amateur always: he did not even murder for base profit. It was not even for simple lust. He was a gourmet, a sybarite, centuries, perhaps hemispheres before his time; in spirit and glands he was of that age

2 - 1 - 16

                      TEMPLE (Cont'd)
(SHE stops speaking, reaches and takes the unlighted cigarette from the tray, then realizes it is unlit. STEVENS takes up the lighter from the desk and starts to get up. Still watching TEMPLE, the GOVERNOR makes to STEVENS a slight arresting signal with his hand. STEVENS pauses, then pushes the lighter along the desk to where TEMPLE can reach it, and sits back down. TEMPLE takes the lighter, snaps it on, lights the cigarette, closes the lighter and puts it back on the desk. But after only one puff at the cigarette, SHE lays it back on the tray and sits again as before, speaking again) [crossed out]

Insert galley 47 →

Because I still had the two arms and legs and eyes; I could have climbed down the rainspout at any time, the only difference being that I didn't. I would never leave the room except late at night, when he would come in a closed car the size of an undertaker's wagon, and he and the chauffeur on the front seat, and me and the madam in the back, rushing at forty and fifty and sixty miles an hour up and down the back alleys of the redlight district. Which—— the back alleys——was all I ever saw of them too. I was not even permitted to meet or visit with or even see the other girls in my own house, not even to sit with them after work and listen to the shop talk while they counted their chips or blisters or whatever they would do, sitting on one another's beds in the elected dormitory....
            (SHE pauses again, continues in a
            sort of surprise, amazement)
Yes, it was like the dormitory at school: the smell: of women, young women all busy thinking not about men but just man: only a little stronger, a little calmer, less excited, —— sitting on the temporarily idle beds discussing the exigencies——that's surely the right one, isn't it?——of their trade. But not me, not Temple: shut up in that room twenty-four hours a day, with nothing to do but hold fashion shows in the fur coat and the flash pants and negligees, with nothing to see it but a two-foot mirror and a Negro maid; hanging bone dry and safe in the middle of sin and pleasure like being suspended twenty fathoms deep in an ocean diving bell. Because he wanted her to be contented, you see. He even made the last effort himself. But Temple didn't want to be just contented. So she had to do what us sporting girls call fall in love.

                      GOVERNOR
Ah.

                      STEVENS
That's right.

                TEMPLE (quickly: to STEVENS)
Hush.

STEVENS (to TEMPLE)

Hush yourself.
 (to GOVERNOR)
He----Vitelli----they called him Popeye----brought the man there himself.
He----the young man----.

TEMPLE

Gavin! No, I tell you!

STEVENS (to TEMPLE)

You are drowning in an orgasm of abjectness and moderation when all you need is truth.
 (to GOVERNOR)
----was known in his own circles as Red, Alabama Red; not to the police, or not officially, since he was not a criminal, or anyway not yet, but just a thug, probably cursed more by simple eupepsia than by anything else. He was a houseman----the bouncer----at the nightclub, joint, on the outskirts of town, which Popeye owned and which was Popeye's headquarters. He died shortly afterward in the alley behind Temple's prison, of a bullet from the same pistol which had done the Mississippi murder, though Popeye too was dead, hanged in Alabama for a murder he did not commit, before the pistol was ever found and connected with him.

GOVERNOR

I see. This -- Popeye----

STEVENS

----discovered himself betrayed by one of his own servants, and took a princely vengeance on his honor's smircher? You will be wrong. You underrate this *precieux*, this flower, this jewel. Vitelli. What a name for him. A hybrid, impotent. He was hanged the next year, to be sure. But even that was wrong; his very effacement debasing, flouting, even what dignity man has been able to lend to necessary human abolishment. He should have been crushed somehow under a vast and mindless boot, like a spider. He didn't sell her; you violate and outrage his very memory with that crass and material impugnment. He was a purist, an amateur always: he did not even murder for base profit. It was not even for simple lust. He was a gourmet, a sybarite, centuries, perhaps hemispheres before his time; in spirit and glands he was of that age of princely despots to whom the ability even to read was vulgar and plebeian and, reclining on silk amid silken airs and scents, had eunuch slaves for that office, commanding death to the slave at the end of each reading, each evening, that none else alive, even a eunuch slave, shall have shared in, partaken of, remembered, the poem's evocation.

GOVERNOR

I don't think I understand.

STEVENS

Try to. Uncheck your capacity for rage and revulsion -- the sort of rage and revulsion it takes to step on a worm. If Vitelli cannot evoke that in you, his life will have been indeed a desert.

of princely despots to whom the ability even to read was vulgar and plebeian and, reclining on silk amid silken airs and scents, had eunuch slaves for that office, commanding death to the slave at the end of each reading, each evening, that none else alive, even a eunuch slave, shall have shared in, partaken of, remembered, the poem's evocation.

GOVERNOR

I dont think I understand.

STEVENS

Try to. Uncheck your capacity for rage and revulsion—the sort of rage and revulsion it takes to step on a worm. If Vitelli cannot evoke that in you, his life will have been indeed a desert.

~~**TEMPLE**

(quickly, harshly)~~

~~Or dont try. You're a lawyer—or were, weren't you?—dont lawyers not only have the right to not be interested in anything but facts, they dont even need to have to be interested in anything else? Dont even want to be?~~

STEVENS

~~Which is not only good English, but good advice too. So sustain an objection then, and delete everything else from the record and leave only the facts. Beginning right here with the ones that her husband doesn't know.~~

GOVERNOR

~~Doesn't know what? About the man, or about the love?~~

STEVENS

~~About both of course, though only the man is important. The other would be just one more outrageous and indefensible thing for my nephew to have to refuse. The man is enough. And why should her husband have to know about either, who was already equipped and even doomed to believe the worst? What would another name or two or face or two matter?~~

Gal. 48A

TEMPLE

Or body or two in the bed? Or three or four? Dear Uncle Gavin.

(to the Governor: fiercely)

Your honor—excellency—whatever they call you. I'm trying to tell it: cant you see? But cant you make him let me alone? Make him for God's sake let me?

GOVERNOR

(to Stevens: watching Temple)

No more, Gavin.

(to Temple)

So he brought the man there, and you fell in love with him.

TEMPLE

Thank you for that. I mean, the 'love'. And how right. *I. I* fell in love. You see? How quickly we have got through Temple and right to Mrs Gowan Stevens? Because it was there all the time: the bad, the lost: who could have climbed down the gutter or lightning rod any time and got away, or even simpler, a better story than the lightning rod: disguised herself as the nigger maid, with a stack of towels and a bottle opener and change for ten dollars and walked right out the front door. But not . . . .

She pauses, stops; she and the Governor look at one another.

GOVERNOR

That's right. Let's abolish Temple once and for all, and stick to *I* and *me*. Shall we?

TEMPLE

Yes.

(they look at one another a moment)

So I wrote the letters. I would write one each time . . . afterward, after they—he left, and sometimes I would write two or three when it would be two or three days between, when they—he wouldn't—

BANK L 7   **SLIDE 109**
49—Requiem for a Nun 1329
12 on 13 Bodoni Book (led. 2 pts+ x 22; 8 Bod. Bold

GOVERNOR
What? What's that?

TEMPLE
—you know: something to do, be doing, filling the time, better than the fashion parades in front of the two-foot glass with nobody to be disturbed even by the . . . pants, or even no pants. Good letters—

GOVERNOR
Wait. What did you say?

TEMPLE
I said they were good letters, even for—

GOVERNOR
You said, after *they* left.
> (they look at one another. Temple doesn't answer: to Stevens, though still watching Temple)

Am I being told that this . . . Vitalli would be there in the room too?

STEVENS
Yes. That was why he brought him. You can see now what I meant by connoisseur and gourmet.

GOVERNOR
And what you meant by the boot too. You can assure me he's dead?

STEVENS
Oh yes. And I said 'purist' too. To the last: hanged the next summer in Alabama for a murder he didn't even commit and which nobody involved in the matter really believed he had committed, only not even his lawyer could persuade him to admit that he couldn't have done it if he had wanted to, or wouldn't have done it if the notion had struck him. Oh yes, he's dead too; we haven't come here for vengeance.

GOVERNOR
(to Temple)

Gal. 49A

Yes. Go on. The letters

TEMPLE

Yes. The letters. They were good leters. I mean . . . good ones. Better than you would expect from a seventeen-year-old amateur. I mean, you would have wondered how anybody just seventeen and not even through sophomore in college could have learned the . . . words. But then . . . Temple was a fast learner and even just one lesson . . . not to mention after three or four or a . . . dozen—

(rapidly)

But the old bad, the old lost, was already there, just waiting; all she would have needed would be some old dictionary back in Shakespeare's time when, so they say, people hadn't yet learned how to blush at just words. So I wrote them, I dont know how many, does it matter? enough, more than enough; and then it was all over: he was dead, shot from a car while he was walking along the street coming to me—the one time, the first time, the only time when we thought we had dodged, escaped him, to be together alone, just the two of us, at last after all the . . . other—if love can be, mean anything except the newness, the learning, the peace, the privacy, no shame and if you haven't had that you have had nothing—

(rapidly)

But all over now, and then the courtroom in Jefferson and there were my father and brothers come for me and then the year in Europe, Paris, and then it was as if it had never happened, never been. You know: somebody—Hemingway, wasn't it?—wrote a book about how it had never actually happened to a g—woman, if she just refused to accept it, no matter who remembered, bragged. And besides, the ones who could . . . remember were both dead. Then Gowan came to Paris that winter and we were married—at the Embassy, with a reception afterward at the Crillon, and if that couldn't fumigate an American past, what else this side of heaven could you hope for to remove stink? not to mention a new automobile

TEMPLE
Or don't try to. Just let it go. Just for God's sake let it go. I met the man, how doesn't matter, and I fell what I called in love with him and what it was or what I called it doesn't matter either because all that matters is that I wrote the letters——

GOVERNOR
I see. This is the part that her husband didn't know.

TEMPLE (to GOVERNOR)
And what does that matter either? Whether he knows or not? What can another face or two or name or two matter, since he knows that I lived for six weeks in a Manuel Street brothel? Or another body or two in the bed? Or three or four? I'm trying to tell it, enough of it. Can't you see that? But can't you make him let me alone so I can. Make him, for God's sake, let me alone.

GOVERNOR (to STEVENS; watching TEMPLE)
No more, Gavin.
    (to TEMPLE)
So you fell in love.

TEMPLE
Thank you for that. I mean, the 'love.' Except that I didn't even fall, I was already there: the bad, the lost; who could have climbed down the gutter or lightning rod any time and got away, or even simpler than that: disguised myself as the nigger maid with a stack of towels and a bottle opener and change for ten dollars, and walked right out the front door. So I wrote the letters. I would write one each time...afterward, after they — he left, and sometimes I would write two or three when it would be two or three days between, when they — he wouldn't —

GOVERNOR
What? What's that?

TEMPLE
— you know: something to do, be doing, filling the time, better than the fashion parades in front of the two-foot glass with nobody to be disturbed even by the...pants, or even no pants. Good letters —

GOVERNOR
Wait. What did you say?

TEMPLE
I said they were good letters, even for —

GOVERNOR
You said, after they left.
    (They look at one another. TEMPLE
    doesn't answer; to STEVENS, though

2 - 1 - 19

GOVERNOR (Cont'd)
(still watching TEMPLE)
Am I being told that this...Vitelli would be there in the room too?

STEVENS
Yes. That was why he brought him. You can see now what I meant by connoisseur and gourmet.

GOVERNOR
And what you meant by the boot too. But he's dead. You know that.

STEVENS
Oh yes. He's dead. And I said 'purist' too. To the last: hanged the next summer in Alabama for a murder he didn't even commit and which nobody involved in the matter really believed he had committed, only not even his lawyer could persuade him to admit that he couldn't have done it if he had wanted to, or wouldn't have done it if the notion had struck him. Oh yes, he's dead too; we haven't come here for vengeance.

GOVERNOR
(to TEMPLE)
Yes. Go on. The letters.

TEMPLE
The letters. They were good letters. I mean —— good ones.
(staring steadily at the GOVERNOR)
What I'm trying to say is, they were the kind of letters that if you had written them to a man, even eight years ago, you wouldn't —— would —— rather your husband didn't see them, no matter what he thought about your —— past.
(still staring at the GOVERNOR as she makes her painful confession)
Better than you would expect from a seventeen-year-old amateur. I mean, you would have wondered how anybody just seventeen and not even through freshman in college, could have learned the —— right words. Though all you would have needed probably would be an old dictionary from back in Shakespeare's time when, so they say, people hadn't learned how to blush at words. That is, anybody except Temple Drake, who didn't need a dictionary, who was a fast learner and so even just one lesson would have been enough for her, let alone three or four or a dozen or two or three dozen.
(staring at the GOVERNOR)
No, not even one lesson because the bad was already there waiting, who hadn't even heard yet that you must be already resisting the corruption not only before you look at it but before you even know what it is, what you are resisting. So I wrote the letters, I don't know how many, enough, more than enough because just one would have been enough. And that's all.

GOVERNOR
All?

                    TEMPLE
Yes. You've certainly heard of blackmail. The letters turned up
again of course. And of course, being Temple Drake, the first way to
buy them back that Temple Drake thought of, was to produce the material
for another set of them.

                    STEVENS (to TEMPLE)
Yes, that's all. But you've got to tell him why it's all.

                    TEMPLE
I thought I had. I wrote some letters that you would have thought
that even Temple Drake might have been ashamed to put on paper, and
then the man I wrote them to died, and I married another man and
reformed, or thought I had, and bore two children and hired another
reformed whore so that I would have somebody to talk to, and I even
thought I had forgotten about the letters until they turned up again
and then I found out that I not only hadn't forgot about the letters,
I hadn't even reformed——

                    STEVENS
All right. Do you want me to tell it, then?

                    TEMPLE
And you were the one preaching moderation.

                    STEVENS
I was preaching against orgasms of it.

                    TEMPLE (bitterly)
Oh, I know. Just suffering. Not for anything: just suffering.
Just because it's good for you, like calomel or ipecac.
          (to GOVERNOR)
All right. What?

                    GOVERNOR
The young man died——

                    TEMPLE
Oh yes. —— Died, shot from a car while he was slipping up the alley
behind the house, to climb up the same drainpipe I could have climbed
down at any time and got away, to see me——the one time, the first
time, the only time when we thought we had dodged, fooled him, could
be alone together, just the two of us, after all the ... other ones.
—— If love can be, mean anything, except the newness, the learning,
the peace, the privacy: no shame: not even conscious that you are
naked because you are just using the nakedness because that's a part
of it; then he was dead, killed, shot down right in the middle of
thinking about me, when in just one more minute maybe he would have
been in the room with me, when all of him except just his body was
already in the room with me and the door locked at last for just the
two of us alone; and then it was all over and as though it had never
been, happened; it had to be as though it had never happened, except

TEMPLE (Cont'd)
that that was even worse——
    (rapidly)
Then the courtroom in Jefferson and I didn't care, not about anything any more, and my father and brothers waiting and then the year in Europe, Paris, and I still didn't care, and then after a while it really did get easier. You know. People are lucky. They are wonderful. At first you think that you can bear only so much and then you will be free. Then you find out that you can bear anything, you really can and then it won't even matter. Because suddenly it could be as if it had never been, never happened. You know; somebody — Hemingway, wasn't it?——wrote a book about how it had never actually happened to a gir——woman, if she just refused to accept it, no matter who remembered, bragged. And besides, the ones who could——remember were both dead. Then Gowan came to Paris that winter and we were married — at the Embassy, with a reception afterward at the Crillon, and if that couldn't fumigate an American past, what else this side of heaven could you hope for to remove stink? Not to mention a new   and a honeymoon in a rented hideaway built for his European mistress by a Mohammedan prince at Cap Ferrat. Only——
    (She pauses, falters, for just an
    instant, then goes on)
—— we — I thought we — I didn't want to efface the stink really —
    (rapidly now, tense, erect, her hands
    gripped again into her fists on her
    lap)
You know; just the marriage would be enough: not the Embassy and the Crillon and Cap Ferrat but just to kneel down, the two of us, and say 'We have sinned, forgive us.' And then maybe there would be the love this time — the peace, the quiet, the no shame that I... didn't — missed that other time —
    (falters again, then rapidly
    again, glib and succinct)
Love, but more than love too: not depending on just love to hold two people together, make them better than either one would have been alone, but tragedy, suffering, having suffered and caused grief; having something to have to live with even when, because, you knew both of you could never forget it. And then I began to believe something even more than that: that there was something even better, stronger, than tragedy to hold two people together: forgiveness. Only, that seemed to be wrong. Only maybe it wasn't the forgiveness that was wrong, but the gratitude; and maybe the only thing worse than having to give gratitude constantly all the time, is having to accept it —

        STEVENS
Which is exactly backward. What was wrong wasn't —

        GOVERNOR
Gavin.

Gal. 50A

band's conscience. Is was his vanity: the Virginia-trained aristocrat caught with his gentility around his knees like the guest in the trick Hollywood bathroom. So the forgiving wasn't enough for him, or perhaps he hadn't read Hemingway's book. Because after about a year, his restiveness under the onus of accepting the gratitude began to take the form of doubting the paternity of their child.

TEMPLE

Oh God. Oh God.

GOVERNOR

Gavin.
(Stevens stops.)
No more, I said. Call that an order.
(to Temple)
Yes. Tell me.

TEMPLE

I'm trying to.
I expected our main obstacle in this would be the bereaved plaintiff. Apparently though it's the defendant's lawyer. I mean, I'm trying to tell you about one Temple Drake, and our Uncle Gavin is showing you another one. So already you've got two different people begging for the same clemency; if everybody concerned keeps on splitting up into two people, you wont even know who to pardon, will you? And now that I mention it, here we are, already back to Nancy Mannigoe, and now surely it shouldn't take long. Let's see, we'd got back to Jefferson too, hadn't we? Anyway, we are now. I mean, back in Jefferson, back home. You know: face it: the disgrace: the shame, face it down, good and down forever, never to haunt us more; together, a common front to stink because we love each other and have forgiven all, strong in our love and mutual forgiveness. Besides having everything else: The Gowan Stevenses, young, popular: a new bungalow on the right street to start the Saturday night hangovers in, a country club with a country-club younger set of rallying friends to make it a Saturday night hangover worthy the name of Sat-

BANK L 7   SLIDE 111
51—Requiem for a Nun 1329
12 on 13 Bodoni Book (led. 2 pts—x 22; 8 Bod. Bold

urday-night country-club hangover, a pew in the right church to recover from it in, provided of course they were not too hungover even to get to church. Then the son and heir came; and now we have Nancy: nurse: guide: mentor, not old cradle-rockin black mammy, because the Gowan Stevenses are young and modern, and besides, Al Jolson used that up, sang right through that and out the other side, consuming everything but the turban, so that it's really Al Jolson you see immortal in a headrag on the box of prefabricated battercake flour, but more, much more: the— what do you call it?—catalyst, glue, holding the whole lot of them together—

   (quickly she takes up the burning cigarette from the tray and puffs rapidly at it, talking between the puffs)

—not just a gravitational pull for the infantile orbit of heir apparent and the other princes and princesses too in their orderly appearance, but for the two big hunks too of mass or matter or dirt or whatever it is shaped in the image of God, in a semblance at least of order and respectability and security and peace—

   (puffs rapidly at the cigarette)

Wait. Just wait—

STEVENS
   (to Governor)
And while we are. She finally had somebody she could talk to.

TEMPLE
   (puts the cigarette on tray)
Oh yes, I'm going to tell that too. Just give me time. Yes, a confidante. You know: The big-time ball player, the worshipped, the idol on the pedestal; and the worshipper, the acolyte, the one that never had and never would, no matter how willing or how hard she tried, get out of the sandlots, the bush league. You know: the long afternoons, with the last electric button pressed on the last cooking or washing or sweeping gadget and

158 *Requiem for a Nun*, II

                                    2-1-22

                      STEVENS
Shut up yourself, Henry. What was wrong wasn't Temple's
It wasn't even her husband's conscience. It was his vanity: the
Virginia-trained aristocrat caught with his gentility around his
knees like the guest in the trick Hollywood bathroom. So the forgiving wasn't enough for him, or perhaps he hadn't read Hemingway's
book. Because after about a year, his restiveness under the onus of
accepting the gratitude began to take the form of doubting the
paternity of their child.

                      TEMPLE
Oh God. Oh God.

                      GOVERNOR
Gavin.
          (STEVENS stops)
No more, I said. Call that an order.
          (to TEMPLE)
Yes. Tell me.

                      TEMPLE
I'm trying to.

I expected our main obstacle in this would be the bereaved plaintiff.
Apparently though it's the defendant's lawyer. I mean, I'm trying
to tell you about one Temple Drake, and our Uncle Gavin is showing
you another one. So already you've got two different people begging
for the same clemency; if everybody concerned keeps on splitting up
into two people, you won't even know who to pardon, will you? And
now that I mention it, here we are, already back to Nancy Mannigoe,
and now surely it shouldn't take long. Let's see, we'd got back
to Jefferson too, hadn't we? Anyway, we are now. I mean, back in
Jefferson, back home. You know: face it: the disgrace, the shame,
face it down, good and down forever, never to haunt us more; together,
a common front to stink because we love each other and have forgiven
all, strong in our love and mutual forgiveness. Besides having everything else: the Gowan Stevenses, young, popular; a new bungalow on the
right street to start the Saturday night hangovers in, a country club
with a country-club younger set of rallying friends to make it a
Saturday night hangover worthy the name of Saturday-night country-
club hangover, a pew in the right church to recover from it in, provided
of course they were not too hungover even to get to church. Even the
son and heir came; and now we have Nancy: nurse: guide: mentor, catalyst,
glue, whatever you want to call it, holding the whole lot of them
together——not just a magnetic center for the heir apparent and the
other little princes or princesses in their orderly succession, to
circle around, but for the two bigger hunks too of mass or matter or
dirt or whatever it is shaped in the image of God, in a semblance at
least of order and respectability and peace; not one cradle-rocking
black mammy at all, because the Gowan Stevenses are young and

TEMPLE (Cont'd)
modern, so young and modern that all the other young Country Club
set applauded when they took an ex-dope fiend nigger whore out of
the gutter to nurse their children, because the rest of the young
Country-Club set didn't know that it wasn't the Gowan Stevenses
but Temple Drake who had chosen the ex-dope fiend nigger whore
for the reason that an ex-dope fiend nigger whore was the only
animal in Jefferson that spoke Temple Drake's language——
    (quickly takes up the burning cigarette
    from the tray and puffs at it, talking
    through the puffs)
Oh yes, I'm going to tell this too. A confidante. You know: the
big-time ball player, the idol on the pedestal, the worshipped;
and the worshipper, the acolyte, ~~the one that never had and never would,
no matter how willing or how hard she~~ tried, get out of the sandlots,
the bush league. You know: the long afternoons, with the last electric button pressed on the last cooking or washing or sweeping gadget
and the baby safely asleep for a while, and the two sisters in sin
swapping trade or anyway avocational secrets over Coca Colas in the
quiet kitchen. Somebody to talk to, as we all seem to need, want,
have to have, not to converse with you nor even agree with you, but
just keep quiet and listen. Which is all that people really want,
really need; I mean, to behave themselves, keep out of one another's
hair; the maladjustments which they tell us breed the arsonists and
rapists and murderers and thieves and the rest of the anti-social
enemies, are not really maladjustments but simply because the
embryonic murderers and thieves didn't have anybody to listen to
them: which is an idea the Catholic Church discovered two thousand
years ago only it just didn't carry it far enough or maybe it was
too busy being the Church to have time to bother with man, or maybe
it wasn't the Church's fault at all but simply because it had to
deal with human beings and maybe if the world was just populated with
a kind of creature half of which were dumb, couldn't do anything but
listen, couldn't even escape from having to listen to the other half,
there wouldn't even be any war. Which was what Temple had: somebody
paid by the week just to listen, which you would have thought would
have been enough; and then the other baby came, the infant, the
doomed sacrifice (though of course we don't know that yet) and you
would have thought this was surely enough, that now even Temple Drake
would consider herself safe, could be depended on, having two —— what
do sailors call them? Oh yes, sheet-anchors —— now. Only it wasn't
enough. Because Hemingway was right. I mean, the g——woman in his
book. All you have got to do is, refuse to accept ~~it. And you have
got to... refuse~~

STEVENS
Now, the letters——

GOVERNOR (watching TEMPLE)
Be quiet, Gavin.

Gal. 51A

the baby safely asleep for a while, and the two sisters in sin swapping trade or anyway avocational secrets over Coca-Colas in the quiet kitchen. Somebody to talk to, as we all seem to need, want, have to have, not to converse with you nor even agree with you, but just keep quiet and listen. Which is all that people really want, really need; I mean, to behave themselves, keep out of one another's hair; the maladjustments which they tell us breed the arsonists and rapists and murderers and thieves and the rest of the anti-social enemies, are not really maladjustments but simply because the embryonic murderers and thieves didn't have anybody to listen to them: which is an idea the Catholic Church discovered two thousand years ago only it just didn't carry it far enough or maybe it was too busy being the Church to have time to bother with man, or maybe it wasn't the Church's fault at all but simply because it had to deal with human beings and maybe if the world was just populated with a kind of creature half of which were dumb, couldn't do anything but listen, couldn't even escape from having to listen to the other half, there wouldn't even be any war. Which was what Temple had: somebody paid by the week just to listen, which you would have thought would have been enough; and then the other baby came, the infant, the doomed sacrifice (though of course we dont know that yet) and you would have thought this, was surely enough, that now even Temple Drake would consider herself safe, could be depended on, having two—what do sailors call them? oh yes, sheet-anchors—now. Only it wasn't enough. Because Hemingway was right. I mean, the woman in his book. All you have got to do is, refuse to accept. Only, you have got to . . . refuse—

STEVENS

Now, the letters

GOVERNOR (watching Temple)

Be quiet, Gavin.

BANK L 7 SLIDE 112
52—Requiem for a Nun 1329
12 on 13 Bodoni Book (led. 2 pts—x 22; 8 Bod. Bold

STEVENS

Yes, I'm going to talk some now. We'll even stick to the sports metaphor: a relay race this time, with our Stevens team far enough out in front for even the middleaged bat-boy (if I may mix it) to carry the . . . baton, grip, twig, switch, sapling, tree, stick—whatever you want to call the symbolical wood, up what trivial remains of the symbolical hill.

> (the lights flicker, grow slightly dimmer, then build back up and steady once more, as though in a signal, a warning)

The letters. The blackmail. The letters she wrote to the man, Red, whom Vitalli would bring to her room in the Memphis . . . house. The blackmailer was Red's younger brother—a criminal of course, but at least a man—

TEMPLE

Wont you for Christ's sake stop?

STEVENS

No. I'm going to carry your stick a while. It only goes up a hill, not a precipice. Besides, it's only a stick.

> (Temple puts both hands to her face, sits motionless and erect again. Stevens continues)

She was probably not even surprised. Shocked, of course, but not surprised. I dont mean not surprised when the letters turned up, because she probably was. Because she had forgotten about them, forgot she ever wrote them probably. I mean not surprised at ultimate catastrophe. Not that she had been consciously expecting catastrophe, waiting for it constantly all the time, not of course during all the eight years since that May day when, by slipping out of that baseball special train, she put her hand to a promissory note for trouble, nor even since the one six years ago in Paris when, by accepting matrimony and the prospect of motherhood, she relinquished all

162 *Requiem for a Nun*, II

Gal. 52A

immunity from her past. Six years ago you moved say into a new house, a strange house in the sense that this particular one had a roof which could collapse on your head at any moment. You didn't know it of course at the time, or rather, didn't realise it at the time. You didn't believe then that it wouldn't collapse about your ears, not that it could not nor even that it might not, but simply that it would not collapse on you for the simple reason that roofs of houses do not collapse on the heads sheltering beneath them, else by this time people would have invented a substitute for houses or anyway roofs which would not collapse. You certainly didn't expect at first that this one would collapse on you. Indeed, the contrary: you not only didn't expect it to collapse, what if it did?—('so what?' you would put it in the tongue suitable to two years past seventeen). Because certain experiences in your recent past had taught you that the whole sky could fall on your head, doing you—in retrospect—no permanent harm at all—or at least none that need concern anyone else, any outsider; and this was just a roof, and when you have just proved immune to the whole collapsing sky, you dont even have to think twice about a mere roof; indeed, if you thought about the roof at all, you probably thought that, granting any modicum of truth anywhere in the morality of society to which, by entering this particular house, you had affirmed your intention of subscribing for the rest of your life, this particular roof, frail though it be and was, would be capable of shielding your head from anything out of your past or future either of which might assail it. Not that you had deliberately entered the house for that reason, to be shielded from your past. Being nineteen and therefore invulnerable in your own right, let alone less than two years ago having had your invulnerability indubitably proved to you, you did not believe that you, *you* could need protection from anything. In fact, if you could have been persuaded of the precariousness of that roof, you might have moved into the house then for that very reason, even if you had not intended,

BANK **SLIDE 113**
53—Requiem for a Nun 1329
12 on 13 Bodoni Book (led. 2 pts—x 22; 8 Bod. Bold

planned to, before, out of sheer bravado, being nineteen and hence invulnerable;—not to mention being, marriage and threat of pregnancy and all to the contrary, alone, solitary, integrated, private, impregnable, neither giving nor accepting, wanting, anything from anyone—your own woman, no matter what priest or magistrate mumbled what shibboleth in the presence of what witnesses—and therefore able, competent, to leave it, quit it at any time, any moment—which, naturally, being sensible, you would. Besides, you hadn't been in the house very long, hardly long enough to realise that it had a roof, let alone one that might collapse, before you discovered that the potentialities of the roof were no threat to you; that your past nor future neither were going to descend on your head through that roof in one splendid crash, for the reason that they—it—the future and the past—were already inside the house with you something like a dripping water-tap; that you were going to have little if any time to spend watching a roof because you were going to have to spend a good part of your days (and nights too) being forgiven for that past; in being not only constantly reminded— well, maybe not reminded but say made—kept— aware—of your past so that you could be forgiven for it and be grateful for the forgiveness, but having to employ steadily and unflaggingly more and more of what tact you had (and the patience which you probably didn't know you had) to make your gratitude—in which you probably had as little experience and skill as in the patience—meet, match, the high standards of your forgiver. Well, you could cope with that too—then, or so you thought. You hadn't intended to have to cope with being constantly forgiven; you had heard of gratitude before, but then so had you heard of Buddhism too. You didn't know how you were going to cope with it, but you who had been invulnerable to the whole collapsing sky, could certainly resist a dripping water-tap, even when a little more time had passed and the dripping tap was rather more the

Gal. 53A

smell of escaping gas or even a dead rat in the wall. So you still stood it, coped, not only accepting, absorbing the forgiveness and supplying the gratitude on constant demand and doing what you could to make the gratitude palatable, swallowable; still coping even when you realised that the more gratitude you gave, the more you would have to give, and the more unpalatable to the swallower it would be. Because you could always, always, leave. You had not asked to enter the house; least and last of all had you ever eased for the privilege, an invitation, to enter it: you had not cared either way, and had never pretended any different. Do you accept that?

GOVERNOR
Go on.

STEVENS
Then you found out that you were wrong. You already knew that the whole sky could fall on you, because you had tried it, or rather, it had tried you, and failed. So obviously any roof could fall on anybody; it wasn't that you didn't believe the roof could fall, you just didn't need to bother about whether it could or not would or not or might or not, because you were invulnerable. But now something happened to you which not only showed you that you were not invulnerable, but showed it to you too late. Because it taught you that the thing which had made you invulnerable was not invulnerability at all but instead was the very thing which this new factor in your life had deprived you forever of: the solitariness, the inactness, the one-womanism, the ability and the right, privilege, to get up and leave, evacuate the roof whenever you liked. This new factor was a child. You hadn't expected that. It was not that you hadn't expected children. You hadn't expected to be sterile; you just hadn't thought one way or the other about the matter, possibility, not enough to take precautions one way or the other, because then, at first, you didn't believe that a child would, could, make any difference. That is, even if you had known about, been warned in advance, believed in the danger of this

178-181

BANK L 7   SLIDE 114
54—Requiem for a Nun 1329
12 on 13 Bodoni Book (led. 2 pts—x 22; 8 Bod. Bold

particular roof, even with a child you would still have been *you*, still invulnerable; you were probably not even conscious of having assumed that, being your child, it would automatically have inherited its own sufficient share of invulnerability; that is, the child would either be invulnerable in its own right, or you would have amply enough for two; or even better, even with the child to complicate and (in that sense) diffuse you, you would still be integrated, still be one and indivisible, or at worst one-and-a-fraction, and you could still quit the danger at any time you liked. But you were wrong. You found that you were not only not one, you were not even one-and-a-fraction; that you were the fraction to the child's *one*, and that the child, that barely sentient moiety unable to speak or walk or even raise itself up, capable only of hunger and satiety and sleep, was not *one* but *three*: not only itself and its progenitors, but the house, the roof too, and that what you had bequeathed it was no invulnerability to the roof, but the very roof itself which would destroy it. So for the first time in your invulnerable own-woman life probably you knew fear and terror and perhaps despair too: you could not only never flee, escape the house and the roof now, but on the contrary, by bringing that child into the world you had not merely forever forfeited that 'out' as you would say in school, your temerity in bringing the child into the world had very probably drawn upon you both disaster's eye which until now may have missed you. Despair too; frantic now for any straw, you probably told yourself that at least the child's innocence would save it, that God—if there was one—would save the child because it was innocent—knowing better, since all your observation showed you that God either would not or could not—anyway, did not—save innocence just because it was innocent; that when He said 'Suffer little children to come unto Me' He indeed meant suffer: that the adults, the fathers, the old in and capable of sin, must be ready and willing, nay, eager, to suffer at any time, that the little children shall come unto Him unanguished, unterrified, undefiled. So not God, but only she, and not to save the child nor even shield it, since at the last, all she could do would be to fling her body between the innocence and the disaster: whereupon its own futile and spurious corollary followed: if all she could do was to fling her willing and crushable body between them, then she could save the child at once and forever and always by destroying and effacing her body now, at once, without waiting for the roof: which would not be saving the child, because she would simply be escaping, fleeing, shirking the disaster which she had already realised that she had waited too late, forfeited forever her chance to escape. No, no hope to save the child at all: only the duty—no, the privilege, inexorable, inescapable—to endure, willing and abnegant and without hope of anguish's end; to try, to attempt— where the tough durable web of bone and meat, though capable of bearing all sin and all repentance too, would crumble at the first shatter of plaster—with no more than the willingness and the abnegation, to prop the whole falling sky. So ... she—

GOVERNOR

Yes, she. You've been saying it for almost a minute now. Go on.

STEVENS

—had no hope. But at least she had nature, at least for a little while, for almost three years in fact, until the next child. The trauma of shock: you are walking a tightrope, to cross an abyss; you dont have time to worry about the chasm beneath nor the distance ahead; you are too busy thinking just the next step ahead, getting that one foot planted and balanced—in this case, the house: the progressing interminably and with no real advancement from one cooking- or washing-gadget switch to the next, repetitive, endless, but enough, soporific and null of anguish, as if deferment were not a progressive diminishing chain, but a sprocket, a circle, in which she was safe so long as it didn't break—not to mention

BANK L 7   SLIDE 115
55—Requiem for a Nun 1329
12 on 13 Bodoni Book (led. 2 pts.) x 22; 8 Bod. Bold

the forgiveness and the being grateful for it: like the juggler say, not with three durable and insentient Indian clubs or replaceable plates or vases, but three electric bulbs filled with nitroglycerin and not enough hands for any single one: one hand to offer the atonement with and another to receive the forgiveness with and a third needed to offer the gratitude and still one more needed, a fourth one, more and more imperative as time passed to sprinkle steadily and constantly a little more and a little more sugar and seasoning on the gratitude to keep it palatable to the swallower. So when the circle broke at last—which it must, and did, and which she knew must and would break—there was perhaps something even of relief. What broke it was a child too. And she had indeed not expected this. She may really have expected to be sterile this time, not that she had done anything perhaps to deserve sterility, escape, this time, not out of justice to herself in return for having accepted the gambit of the other life she had created, but say out of the simple necessary balance between debit and credit, lacking which the whole ramshackle edifice of circumstance in which man lives would collapse about him and leave him naked, or even more than that perhaps: a balance in cosmos, universe: that God perhaps—if there was one—would at least play fair, be a gentleman, and since she had accepted the gambit which she had brought on her head with the first child and had declined the one 'out' of which she might have availed herself—in a word, accepted her mistake and fate without whining about it—would at least keep hands off, side not against her at least. Not that she put the onus on God; anything but that. It was her own doing, of course, hers alone. Because this time she had tried to prevent the child, done—or thought she had—everything possible to forefend it. But she had failed: carelessness perhaps; or—more than perhaps—maybe she had builded more than she realised on the fact that there even was, must be, something like taste, a dignity, an abhorrence of dull redundancy, in misfortune; that

Gal. 55 A

in fact even sin and evil, like poverty, took, would always take, care of their own; that perhaps even evil did not dare too great a triumph over virtue and innocence. But evil did dare; there was another child, another innocence, and now she knew that this was indeed the end, that God (if there is one) might have condoned, passed, putting it down to simple instinctive desperation, her apparent attempt to hide from her fate behind one innocence, one damp diaper, but never the involving of two of them in her doom. So now it was only a question of time; when the blackmailer finally appeared with the old letters, she was not surprised: she probably only wondered why it had taken him so long—not him so long nor them so long, but it: the disaster. Because she had never even known that Red had a brother, and she had forgot about the letters. She probably remembered now having written them of course, perhaps she had never really forgotten having written them. But now, and for six years now, they no longer had any existence, as dead and transposed back into anonymous unrecognisable original matter as was, and even along with, the man himself: the living flesh she had touched, felt, the hard masculine hands she had known or her flesh, the strength of the muscles, the physical pain, the voice, the words he spoke —taught her too until she could write them back to him in the letters—of which they (the letters) were a part, and as fragile and as mortal before the same bullet.

The lights flicker and dim further, then steady at that point.

STEVENS

And relief too. Because at last it was over; the roof had fallen, avalanche had roared; even the helplessness and the impotence were finished now, because now even the old fragility of bone and meat was no longer a factor—and, who knows? because of that fragility, a kind of pride, triumph: you have waited for destruction: you endured; it was inevitable, inescapable, you had no hope. Nevertheless, you did not merely cringe,

[Insert galley 5✓]

STEVENS

No, I'm going to talk a while now. We'll even stick to the sports metaphor and call it a relay race, with the senior member of the team carrying the... baton, twig, switch, sapling, tree——whatever you want to call the symbolical wood, up what remains of the symbolical hill.

> (the lights flicker, grow slightly
> dimmer, then flare back up and
> steady again, as though in a signal,
> a warning)

The letters. The blackmail. The blackmailer was Red's younger brother——a criminal of course, but at least a man——

[Gal 55]

TEMPLE

No! No!

STEVENS (to TEMPLE)

Be quiet too. It only goes up a hill, not over a precipice. Besides, it's only a stick. The letters were not first. The first thing was the gratitude. And now we have even come to the husband, my nephew. And when I say 'past,' I mean that part of it which the husband knows so far, which apparently was enough in his estimation. Because it was not long before she discovered, realized, that she was going to spend a good part of the rest of her days (nights too) being forgiven for it; in being not only constantly reminded - well, maybe not specifically reminded, but say made - kept - aware of it in order to be forgiven for it so that she might be grateful to the forgiver, but in having to employ more and more of what tact she had - and the patience which she probably didn't know she had, since until now she had never occasion to need patience - to make the gratitude - in which she had probably had as little experience as she had had with patience - acceptable to meet with, match, the high standards of the forgiver. But she was not too concerned. Her husband - my nephew - had made what he probably considered the supreme sacrifice to expiate his part in her past; she had no doubts of her capacity to continue to supply whatever increasing degree of gratitude the increasing appetite - or capacity - of its addict would demand, in return for the sacrifice which, so she believed, she had accepted for the same reason of gratitude. Besides, she still had the legs and the eyes; she could walk away, escape, from it at any moment she wished, even though her past might have shown her that she probably would not use the ability to locomote to escape from threat and danger. Do you accept that?

[Start]

GOVERNOR

All right. Go on.

STEVENS

Then she discovered that the child - the first one - was on the way. For that first instant, she must have known something almost like frenzy. Now she couldn't escape; she had waited too long. But it was worse than that. It was as though she realised for the first time

2 - 1 - 25

STEVENS (Cont'd)

that you - everyone - must, or anyway may have to, pay for your past; that past is something like a promissory note with a trick clause in it which, as long as nothing goes wrong, can be manumitted in an orderly manner, but which fate or luck or chance, can foreclose on you without warning. That is, she had known, accepted, this all the time and dismissed it because she knew that she could cope, was invulnerable through simple integration, own-womanness. But now there would be a child, tender and defenseless. But you never really give up hope, you know, not even after you finally realise that people not only can bear anything, but probably will have to, so probably even before the frenzy had had time to fade, she found a hope: which was the child's own tender and defenseless innocence: that God - if there was one - would protect the child - not her: she asked no quarter and wanted none; she could cope, either cope or bear it, but the child from the sight draft of her past—because it was innocent, even though she knew better, all her observation having shown her that God either would not or could not - anyway, did not - save innocence just because it was innocent; that when He said 'Suffer little children to come unto Me' He meant exactly that: He meant suffer; that the adults, the fathers, the old in and capable of sin, must be ready and willing - nay, eager - to suffer at any time, that the little children shall come unto Him unanguished, unterrified, undefiled. Do you accept that?

GOVERNOR

Go on.

STEVENS

So at least she had ease. Not hope: ease. It was precarious of course, a balance, but she could walk a tightrope too. It was as though she had struck, not a bargain, but an armistice with God - if there was one. She had not tried to cheat; she had not tried to evade the promissory note of her past by intervening the blank check of a child's innocence - it was born now, a little boy, a son, her husband's son and heir - between. She had not tried to prevent the child; she had simply never thought about pregnancy in this connection, since it took the physical fact of the pregnancy to reveal to her the existence of that promissory note bearing her post-dated signature. And since God - if there was one - must be aware of that, then she too would bear her side of the bargain by not demanding on Him a second time since He - if there was one - would at least play fair, would be at least a gentleman. And that?

GOVERNOR

Go on.

STEVENS

So you can take your choice about the second child. Perhaps she was too busy between the three of them to be careful enough; between the three of them: the doom, the fate, the past; the bargain

STEVENS (Cont'd)

with God; the forgiveness and the gratitude. Like the juggler says, not with three insentient replaceable Indian clubs or balls, but three glass bulbs filled with nitroglycerin and not enough hands for one even: one hand to offer the atonement with and another to receive the forgiveness with and a third needed to offer the gratitude, and still a fourth hand more and more imperative as time passed to sprinkle in steadily and constantly increasing doses a little more and a little more of the sugar and seasoning on the gratitude to keep it palatable to its swallower——that perhaps: she just didn't have time to be careful enough, or perhaps it was desperation, or perhaps this was when her husband first refuted or implied or anyway impugned – whichever it was – his son's paternity. Anyway, she was pregnant again; she had broken her word, destroyed her talisman, and she probably knew fifteen months before the letters that this was the end, and when the man appeared with the old letters she probably was not even surprised: she had merely been wondering for fifteen months what ~~form the destruction would take. And accept this too——~~

Set this line

~~(the lights dimmer and dim further)~~

then steady at that point)

And relief too. Because at last it was over; the roof had fallen, avalanche had roared; even the helplessness and the impotence were finished now, because now even the old fragility of bone and meat was no longer a factor — and, who knows? Because of that fragility, a kind of pride, triumph; you have waited for destruction: you endured; it was inevitable, inescapable, you had no hope. Nevertheless, you did not merely cringe, crouching, your head, vision, buried in your arms; you were not watching that poised arrestment all the time, true enough, but that was not because you feared it but because you were too busy putting one foot before the other, never for one instant really flagging, faltering, even though you knew it was in vain — triumph in the very fragility which no longer need concern you now, for the reason that the air, the very worst, which catastrophe can do to you, is crush and obliterate the fragility, you were the better man, you outfaced even catastrophe, outlasted it, compelled it to move first; you did not even defy it, not even contemptuous: with no other tool or implement but that worthless fragility, you held disaster off as with one hand you might support the weightless silken canopy of a bed, for six long years while it, with all its weight and power, could not possibly prolong the obliteration of your fragility over five or six seconds; and even during that five or six seconds you would still be the better man, since all that it — the catastrophe — could deprive you of, you yourself had already written off six years ago as being, inherently of and because of its own fragile self, worthless.

GOVERNOR

And now, the man.

STEVENS

I thought you would see it too. Even the first one struck out like

184-187

BANK L7   SLIDE 116
56—Requiem for a Nun 1329
12 on 13 Bodoni Book (led. 2 pts. x 22; 8 Bod. Bold

crouching, your head, vision, buried in your arms; you were not watching that poised arrestment all the time, true enough, but that was not because you feared it but because you were too busy putting one foot before the other, never for one instant really flagging, faltering, even though you knew it was in vain—triumph in the very fragility which no longer need concern you now, for the reason that the ~~all~~, the very worst, which catastrophe can do to you, is crush and obliterate the fragility; you were the better man, you outfaced even catastrophe, outlasted it, compelled it to move first; you did not even defy it, not even contemptuous: with no other tool or implement but that worthless fragility, you held disaster off as with one hand you might support the weightless silken canopy of a bed, for six long years while it, with all its weight and power, could not possibly prolong the obliteration of your fragility over five or six seconds; and even during that five or six seconds you would still be the better man, since all that it—the catastrophe —could deprive you of, you yourself had already written off six years ago as being, inherently of and because of its own fragile self, worthless. ~~But that was just triumph and relief. There was one more thing~~

GOVERNOR

And now, the man

STEVENS

I thought you would see it too, even the first one struck out like a sore thumb. Yes, he—
(he continues)
—relinquishment, release. The old bad, the old evil. She hadn't escaped that. She hadn't tried to, certainly not to shirk or evade it. She admitted it, accepted it; she had done her best, to cope with it when and if that was possible, but at least to live with it, in the same house with it, or that is with its aftermath; she continued to do her best even after she no longer really hoped her best would be good enough or in fact any good at all. So it was not even the ultimate catastrophe which was her doom and fate, but the old bad

Insert attached

Gal 56A

which sold her the railroad ticket for the baseball trip and then pulled the emergency signal cord which stopped the train so she could get out of it and into the car with the drunken driver, and then jammed the door handle so she couldn't get out of the car and run, somewhere, anywhere, when the driver wrecked it, and jammed or locked the Memphis window so she couldn't or anyway didn't climb through it and down the rainspout. So who's to chide her if, having done her best for two and three and five and six years to no avail, when the avalanche did roar, she elected to repudiate the vain clawing and scrabbling and instead to go with it, for those last five or six seconds anyway to ride it at least face-forward into abyss—not to mention the burden of forgiveness and the gratitude—not the burden of accepting the forgiveness nor even of giving the gratitude, but of keeping the gratitude fresh and acceptable—

GOVERNOR

Ah.

> (Stevens pauses. He and the
> Governor look at each other.
> Temple does not move)

So this time I am right.

STEVENS

Maybe. We'll see.

It was the man. At first, all he thought of, planned on, was interested in, intended, was the money —to collect for the letters, and beat it, get the hell out. Of course, even at the end, all he was really after was still the money, not only after he found out that he would have to take her and the child too to get it, but even when it looked like all he was going to get, at least for a while, was just a runaway wife and a six-months-old infant. In fact, Nancy's error, her really fatal action on that fatal and tragic night, was in not giving the money and the jewels both to him when she found where Temple had hidden them, and getting the letters and getting rid of him forever, instead of hiding the money and jewels from

174 *Requiem for a Nun*, II

2 - 1 - 27

Insert galley 56

GOVERNOR

The first what?

STEVENS (pauses, looks at the GOVERNOR)
The first man; Red. Don't you know anything at all about women? I never saw Red or this next one, his brother, either, but all three of them, the other two and her husband, probably all look enough alike or act enough alike - maybe by simply making enough impossible unfulfillable demands on her or by being drawn to her enough to accept, risk, almost incredible conditions - to be at least first cousins. Where have you been all your life?

GOVERNOR

All right. The man.

STEVENS

At first, all he thought of, planned on, was interested in, intended, was the money — to collect for the letters, and beat it, get the hell out. Of course, even at the end, all he was really after was still the money, not only after he found out that he would have to take her and the child too to get it, but even when it looked like all he was going to get, at least for a while, was just a runaway wife and a six-months-old infant. In fact, Nancy's error, her really fatal action on that fatal and tragic night, was in not giving the money and the jewels both to him when she found where Temple had hidden them, and getting the letters and getting rid of him forever, instead of hiding the money and jewels from Temple in her turn — which was what Temple herself thought too apparently, since she — Temple — told him a lie about how much the money was, telling him it was only two hundred dollars when it was actually almost two thousand. So you would have said that he wanted the money indeed, and just how much, how badly, to have been willing to pay that price for it. Or maybe he was being wise — "smart," he would have called it — beyond his years and time, and without having actually planned it that way, was really inventing a new and safe method of kidnapping: that is, pick an adult victim capable of signing her own checks - also with an infant in arms for added persuasion — and not forcing but actually persuading her to come along under her own power and then — still peaceably — extracting the money later at your leisure, using the tender welfare of the infant as a fulcrum for your lever. Or maybe we're both wrong and both should give credit - what little of it - where credit - what little of it - is due, since it was just the money with her too at first, though he was probably still thinking it was just the money at the very time when, having got her own jewelry together and found where her husband kept the key to the strongbox (and I imagine, even opened it one night after her husband was in bed asleep and counted the money in it or at least made sure that there was money in it or anyway that the key would actually open it), she found herself still trying to rationalize why she had not paid over the money and got the letters and destroyed them and be rid herself forever of her Damocles' roof. Which was what she did not do. Because Hemingway - his girl - was quite right: all you have

BANK L7　　　　SLIDE 122
62—REQUIEM FOR A NUN—1329
12 on 13 Bodoni Book (lead 2 pts—x 22; 8 Bod. Bold

If you'll wait until I finish packing, you can even carry the bag.

NANCY

I know. It aint even the letters any more. Maybe it never was. It was already there in whoever could write the kind of letters that even eight years afterward could still make grief and ruin. The letters never did matter. You could have got them back at any time; he even tried to give them to you twice—

TEMPLE

How much spying have you been doing?

NANCY

All of it.—You wouldn't even needed money and diamonds to get them back. A woman dont need it. All she needs is womanishness to get anything she wants from men. You could have done that right here in the house, without even tricking your husband into going off fishing.

TEMPLE

A perfect example of whore morality. But then, if I can say whore, so can you, cant you? Maybe the difference is, I decline to be one in my husband's house.

NANCY

I aint talking about your husband. I aint even talking about you. I'm talking about two little children.

TEMPLE

So am I. Why else do you think I sent Bucky on to his grandmother, except to get him out of a house where the man he has been taught to call his father, may at any moment decide to tell him he has none? As clever a spy as you must surely have heard my husband—

NANCY
(interrupts)

I've heard him. And I heard you too. You fought

back—that time. Not for yourself, but for that little child. But now you have quit.

TEMPLE

Quit?

NANCY

Yes. You gave up. You gave up the child too. Willing to risk never seeing him again maybe.
   (Temple doesn't answer)
That's right. You dont need to make no excuses to me. Just tell me what you must have already strengthened your mind up to telling all the rest of the folks that are going to ask you that. You are willing to risk it. Is that right?
   (Temple doesn't answer)
All right. We'll say you have answered it. So that settles Bucky. Now answer me this one. Who are you going to leave the other one with?

TEMPLE

Leave her with? A six-months-old baby?

NANCY

That's right. Of course you cant leave her. Not with nobody. You cant no more leave a six-months-old baby with nobody while you run away from your husband with another man, than you can take a six-months-old baby with you on that trip. That's what I'm talking about. So maybe you'll just leave it in there in that cradle; it'll cry for a while, but it's too little to cry very loud and so maybe wont nobody hear it and come meddling, especially with the house shut up and locked until Mr Gowan gets back next week, and probably by that time it will have hushed—

TEMPLE

Are you really trying to make me hit you again?

NANCY

Or maybe taking her with you will be just as easy, at least until the first time you write Mr Gowan or your pa for money and they dont send it as quick as your new man thinks they ought to, and he throws you and the baby both out.

BANK L 7   **SLIDE 125**
65—REQUIEM FOR A NUN—1329
12 on 13 Bodoni Book (lead 2 pts—x 22; 8 Bod. Bold

There is no answer. Temple looks a moment longer at the empty door, shrugs, moves, takes up the money Nancy left, glances about, crosses to the littered desk and takes up a paperweight and returns to the table and puts the money beneath the weight; now moving rapidly and with determination, she takes up the blanket from the table and crosses to the nursery door and exits through it. A second or two, then she screams. The lights flicker and begin to dim, fade swiftly into complete

darkness, over the scream.

The stage is in complete darkness.

SCENE III

Same as Scene I. Governor's Office. 3:09 A.M. March twelfth.

The lights go up on upper left. The scene is the same as before, except that the hands of the clock are now at nine minutes past three. The Governor and Stevens are in the same position. Temple is now on her knees facing the desk, her arms on the desk and her face buried in her arms.

TEMPLE
(raises her head)
And that's all. The police came, and the murderess still sitting in a chair in the kitchen in the dark, saying, 'Yes, Lord, I done it,' and then in the cell in the jail—

The Governor makes a slight sign with his hand. Stevens rises, crosses to Temple and takes her arm to raise her up. She resists.

Not yet. It's my cue to stay down here until his honor or excellency grants our plea, isn't it? Or have I already missed my cue forever even if the state should offer me a handkerchief right out of its own elected public suffrage dressing-gown pocket? Because see?
(raising her face still further, into the full glare of

GAL 65A
the lights)

Still no tears.

STEVENS

Get up, Temple.

He starts to lift her again. She is kneeling just beside her own chair, so that with only a turn of her body and without having to stand up, she can sit back into the chair. She evades Stevens' hand and does so, sitting again on the edge of the chair.

TEMPLE

Nor cigarette either; this time it certainly wont take long, since all he has to say is, No.
(to Governor)
Because you aren't going to save her, are you? Because all this was not for the sake of her soul, because her soul doesn't need it, but for mine.

GOVERNOR
(quietly)

Finish first.
(quoting her words)
—and then in the cell in the jail—

TEMPLE

The jail. They had the funeral the next day— Gowan had barely reached New Orleans, so he chartered an airplane back that morning—and in Jefferson, everything going to the graveyard passes the jail, or going anywhere else for that matter, passing right under the upstairs barred windows—the bullpen and the cells where the Negro prisoners—the crapshooters and whiskey-peddlers and vagrants and the murderers and murderesses too—can look down and enjoy it, enjoy the funerals too. Like this. Some white person you know is in a jail or a hospital, and right off you say, How ghastly: not at the shame or the pain, but the walls, the locks, and before you even know it, you have sent them books to read, cards, puzzles to play with. But not Negroes. You dont even think about the cards and puzzles and books. And so all of a sudden you find out with a kind of terror, that they have not

2-3-44

Insert Galley 65

ACT TWO
~~Scene~~ II

~~Same as Scene~~ I. Governor's office. 3:09 A.M. March Twelfth.

The lights go on upper left. The scene is the same as before, Scene I, except that Gowan Stevens now sits in the chair behind the desk where the Governor had been sitting, and the Governor is no longer in the room. Temple now kneels before the desk, facing it, her arms on the desk and her face buried in her arms. Stevens now stands beside and over her. The hands of the clock show nine minutes past three.

Temple does not know that the Governor has gone and that her husband is now in the room.

           TEMPLE
     (her ~~fkx~~ face still hidden)
And that's all. The police came, and the murderess still sitting there in a chair in the kitchen in the dark, saying "Yes, Lord, I done it", and then in the cell at the jail still saying it——
        (Stevens leans and touches her arm, as if to help
        her up. She resists, though still not raising her
        head)
Not yet. It's my cue to stay down here until his honor or excellency grants our plea, isn't it? Or have I already missed my cue forever even if the sovereign state should offer me a handkerchief right out of its own elected public suffrage dressing-gown pocket? Because see?
        (she raises her face, quite blindly, tearless, still
        not looking toward the chair where she could see
        Gowan instead of the Governor, into the full glare
        of the light)
Still no tears.

           STEVENS
Get up, Temple.
        (He starts to lift her again, but before he can do so,
        she rises herself, standing, her face still turned
        away from the desk, still blind; she puts her arm up
        almost in the gesture of a little girl about to cry,
        but instead she merely shields her eyes from the light
        while her pupils readjust)

           TEMPLE
Nor cigarette either; this time it certainly wont take long, since all you have to say is, No.

he has

2 - 3 - 45

TEMPLE (cont)
(still not turning her face to look, even though she
is now speaking directly to the Governor whom she still
thinks is sitting behind the desk)
Because you aren't going to save her, are you? Because all this
was not for the sake of her soul because her soul doesn't need it,
but for mine.

STEVENS (gently)
Why not finish first? Tell the rest of it. You had started to say
something about the jail.

TEMPLE
(still not looking toward the desk)
Oh yes, the jail. They had the funeral the next day -- Gowan had barely
reached New Orleans, so he chartered an airplane back that morning --
and in Jefferson, everything going to the graveyard passes the jail,
or going anywhere else for that matter, passing right under the upstairs
barred windows --- the bullpen and the cells where the Negro prisoners
-- the crap-shooters and whiskey-peddlers and vagrants and the murderers
and murdresses too -- can look down and enjoy it, enjoy the funerals
too. Like this. Some white person you know is in a jail or
a hospital, and right off you say, How ghastly: not at the shame or the
pain, but at the walls, the locks, and before you even know it, you have
sent them books to read, cards, puzzles to play with. But not Negroes.
You dont even think about the cards and puzzles and books. And so all
of a sudden you find out with a kind of terror, that
they have not only escaped having to read, they have escaped having to
escape. So whenever you pass the jail, you can see them -- no, not them,
you dont see them at all, you just see the hands among the bars of the
windows, not tapping or fidgeting or even holding, gripping the bars
like white hands would be, but just lying there among the interstices,
not just as rest, but even restful, already shaped and easy and unanguished to the handles of plows and axes and hoes, and the mops and
brooms and the rockers of white folks' cradles, until even the steel
bars fitted them too without alarm or anguish. You see? not gnarled
and twisted with work at all, but even limbered and suppled by it
it, smoothed and softened, as though with only the penny-change of
simple sweat they had already got the same thing the white ones have
to pay dollars by the ounce jar for. Not immune to work, and in com-
promise with work is not the right word either, but in confederacy with
work and so free from it; in armistice, peace; - the same long supple
hands serene and immune to anguish, so that all the owners of them
need to look out with, to see with -- to look out at the outdoors --
the funerals, the passing, the people, the freedom, the sunlight, the
free air -- are just the hands: not the eyes; just the hands lying
there among the bars and looking out, that can see the shape of the
plow or hoe or axe before daylight comes; and even in the dark, without
even having to turn on the light, can not only find the child, the
baby -- not her child but yours, the white one -- but the trouble and
discomfort too -- the hunger, the wet didy, the unfastened safety-pin
-- and see to remedy it. You see. If I could just cry.

GAL. 66A

a dice game and so at last he could sleep for a little while; which was where the sheriff found him, asleep on the wooden floor of the gallery of the house he had rented for his wife, his marriage, his life, his old age. Only that waked him up, and so in the jail that afternoon, all of a sudden it took the jailer and a deputy and five other Negro prisoners just to throw him down and hold him while they locked the chains on him—lying there on the floor with more than a half dozen men panting to hold him down, and what do you think he said? 'Look like I just cant quit thinking. Look like I just cant quit.'

~~She ceases, sitting motionless on the edge of the chair. Neither Stevens nor the Governor moves, Stevens standing, the Governor behind the desk, his arms folded on the desk before him.~~

(TEMPLE)

But we have passed the jail, haven't we? We're in the courtroom now. It was the same there; Uncle Gavin had rehearsed her, of course, which was easy, since all you can say when they ask you to answer to a murder charge is, Not Guilty. Otherwise, they cant even have a trial; they would have to hurry out and find another murderer before they could take the next official step. So they asked her, all correct and formal among the judges and lawyers and bailiffs and jury and the Scales and the Sword and the flag and the ghosts of Coke upon Littleton upon Bonaparte and Julius Caesar and all the rest of it, not to mention the eyes and the faces which were getting a moving-picture show for free since they had already paid for it in the taxes, and nobody really listening since there was only one thing she could say. Except that she didn't say it: just raising her head enough to be heard plain—not loud: just plain—and said, 'Guilty, Lord'— like that, disrupting and confounding and dispersing and flinging back two thousand years, the whole edifice of corpus juris and rules of evidence we have been working to make stand up by itself ever since Caesar, like when without even watching yourself or even knowing you

(She ceases, blinking, rubs her eyes and then extends one hand blindly toward Stevens, who has already shaken out his handkerchief and hands it to her. There are still no tears on her face; she merely takes the handkerchief and dabs, pats at her eyes with it as if it were a powderpuff, talking again)

BANK L 7 **SLIDE 127**
67—REQUIEM FOR A NUN—1329
12 on 13 Bodoni Book (lead 2 pts—x 22; 8 Bod. Bold

were doing it, you would reach out your hand and turn over a chip and expose to air and light and vision the frantic and aghast turmoil of an antbed. And moved the chip again, when even the ants must have thought there couldn't be another one within her reach: when they finally explained to her that to say she was not guilty, had nothing to do with truth but only with law, and this time she said it right, Not Guilty, and so then the jury could tell her she lied and everything was all correct again and, as everybody thought, even safe, since now she wouldn't be asked to say anything at all any more. Only, they were wrong; the jury said Guilty and the judge said Hang and now everybody was already picking up his hat to go home, when she picked up that chip too: the judge said, 'And may God have mercy on your soul' and Nancy answered: 'Yes, Lord.'

(She rises suddenly, almost briskly)

And that is all, now. And so now you can tell us. I know you're not going to save her, but now you can say so. It wont be difficult. Just one word. Say it.

The Governor rises behind the desk.

GOVERNOR
No.

TEMPLE
Will you tell me why?

GOVERNOR
Yes. I cant.

TEMPLE
The Governor, with all the legal power of pardon or at least reprieve—cant?

GOVERNOR
Yes—cant. We're not talking about law now, any more than the murderess herself was, than her lawyer was, who could have plead insanity for her at the time and so saved her life with-

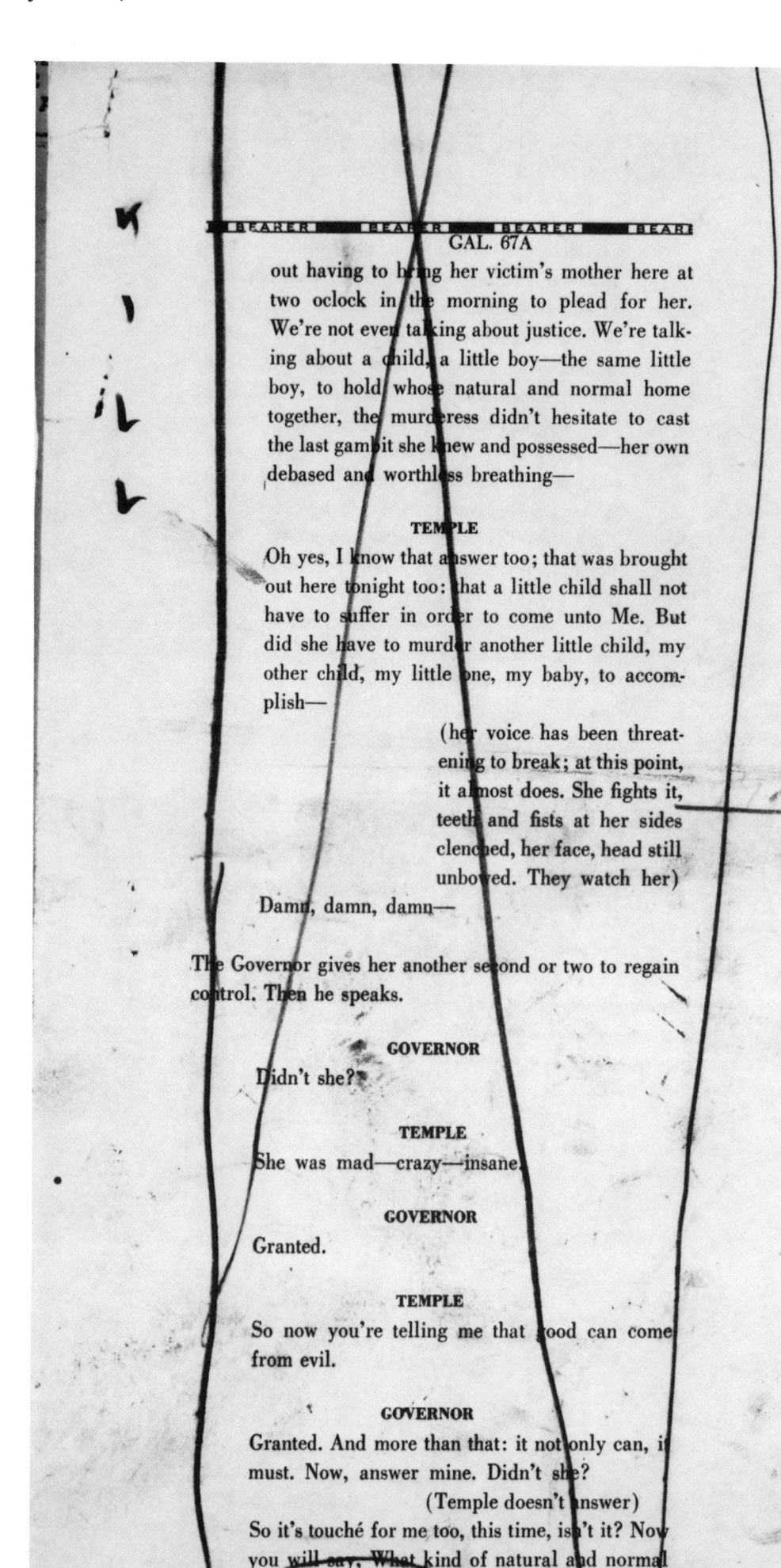

out having to bring her victim's mother here at two oclock in the morning to plead for her. We're not even talking about justice. We're talking about a child, a little boy—the same little boy, to hold whose natural and normal home together, the murderess didn't hesitate to cast the last gambit she knew and possessed—her own debased and worthless breathing—

TEMPLE

Oh yes, I know that answer too; that was brought out here tonight too: that a little child shall not have to suffer in order to come unto Me. But did she have to murder another little child, my other child, my little one, my baby, to accomplish—

> (her voice has been threatening to break; at this point, it almost does. She fights it, teeth and fists at her sides clenched, her face, head still unbowed. They watch her)

Damn, damn, damn—

The Governor gives her another second or two to regain control. Then he speaks.

GOVERNOR

Didn't she?

TEMPLE

She was mad—crazy—insane.

GOVERNOR

Granted.

TEMPLE

So now you're telling me that good can come from evil.

GOVERNOR

Granted. And more than that: it not only can, it must. Now, answer mine. Didn't she?
> (Temple doesn't answer)

So it's touché for me too, this time, isn't it? Now you will say, What kind of natural and normal

BANK L 7   **SLIDE 128**
68—REQUIEM FOR A NUN—1329
12 on 13 Bodoni Book (lead 2 pts—x 22; 8 Bod. Bold

house can that little boy have where his own father may at any time tell him he has none? I dont need to answer that, because you already have, not just six years ago, but constantly during the six years while, as . . . the murderess—

STEVENS

Nancy.

GOVERNOR

(as though to himself)

Nancy. Maingault. Manigault. Mannigoe. Nancy Mannigoe.

(to Temple)

—said, you fought back, not for yourself, but for that little boy. Not to show the father that he was wrong, nor even to prove to the little boy that the father was wrong; but to let the little boy learn with his own eyes that nothing, not even that, which could enter that house, could ever harm him.

TEMPLE

But I quit. Nancy told you that, too.

GOVERNOR

And answered it too. Or will, forever, tomorrow morning.

(to Stevens)

That's right, isn't it? Tomorrow? Friday?

STEVENS

Yes. Tomorrow morning.

GOVERNOR

(to Temple)

Yet you ask me to save her. I cant. Who am I, to have the brazen temerity and hardihood to cope with that, risk the puny appanage of my office in the balance with that simple undeviable aim? Who am I, to render null and abrogate the purchase she made with that poor crazed lost and worthless life?

TEMPLE

Yes. You cant save her. I can see that. Why

GAL. 68A

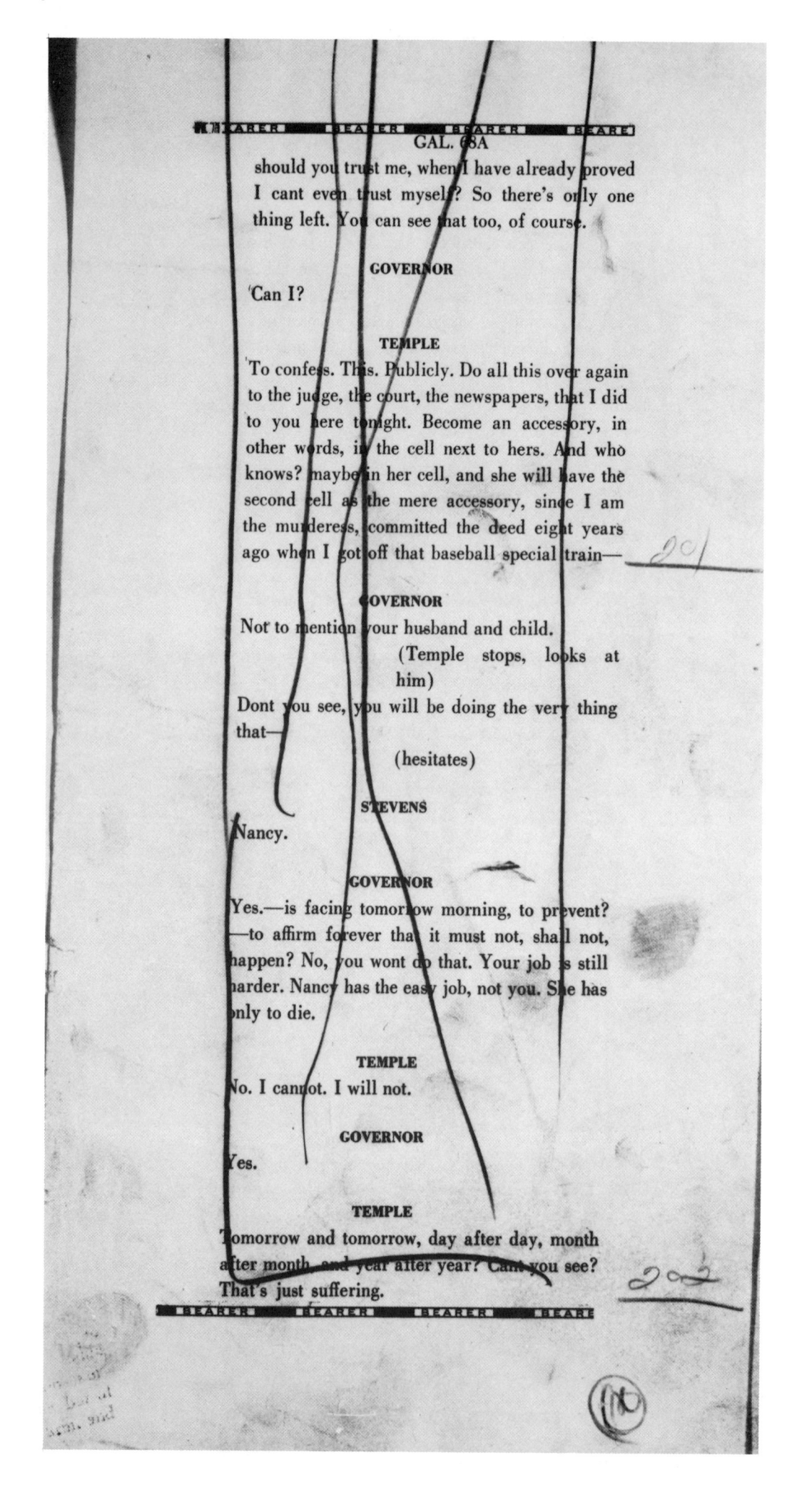

should you trust me, when I have already proved I cant even trust myself? So there's only one thing left. You can see that too, of course.

GOVERNOR

Can I?

TEMPLE

To confess. This. Publicly. Do all this over again to the judge, the court, the newspapers, that I did to you here tonight. Become an accessory, in other words, in the cell next to hers. And who knows? maybe in her cell, and she will have the second cell as the mere accessory, since I am the murderess, committed the deed eight years ago when I got off that baseball special train—

GOVERNOR

Not to mention your husband and child.

(Temple stops, looks at him)

Dont you see, you will be doing the very thing that—

(hesitates)

STEVENS

Nancy.

GOVERNOR

Yes.—is facing tomorrow morning, to prevent? —to affirm forever that it must not, shall not, happen? No, you wont do that. Your job is still harder. Nancy has the easy job, not you. She has only to die.

TEMPLE

No. I cannot. I will not.

GOVERNOR

Yes.

TEMPLE

Tomorrow and tomorrow, day after day, month after month, and year after year? Cant you see? That's just suffering.

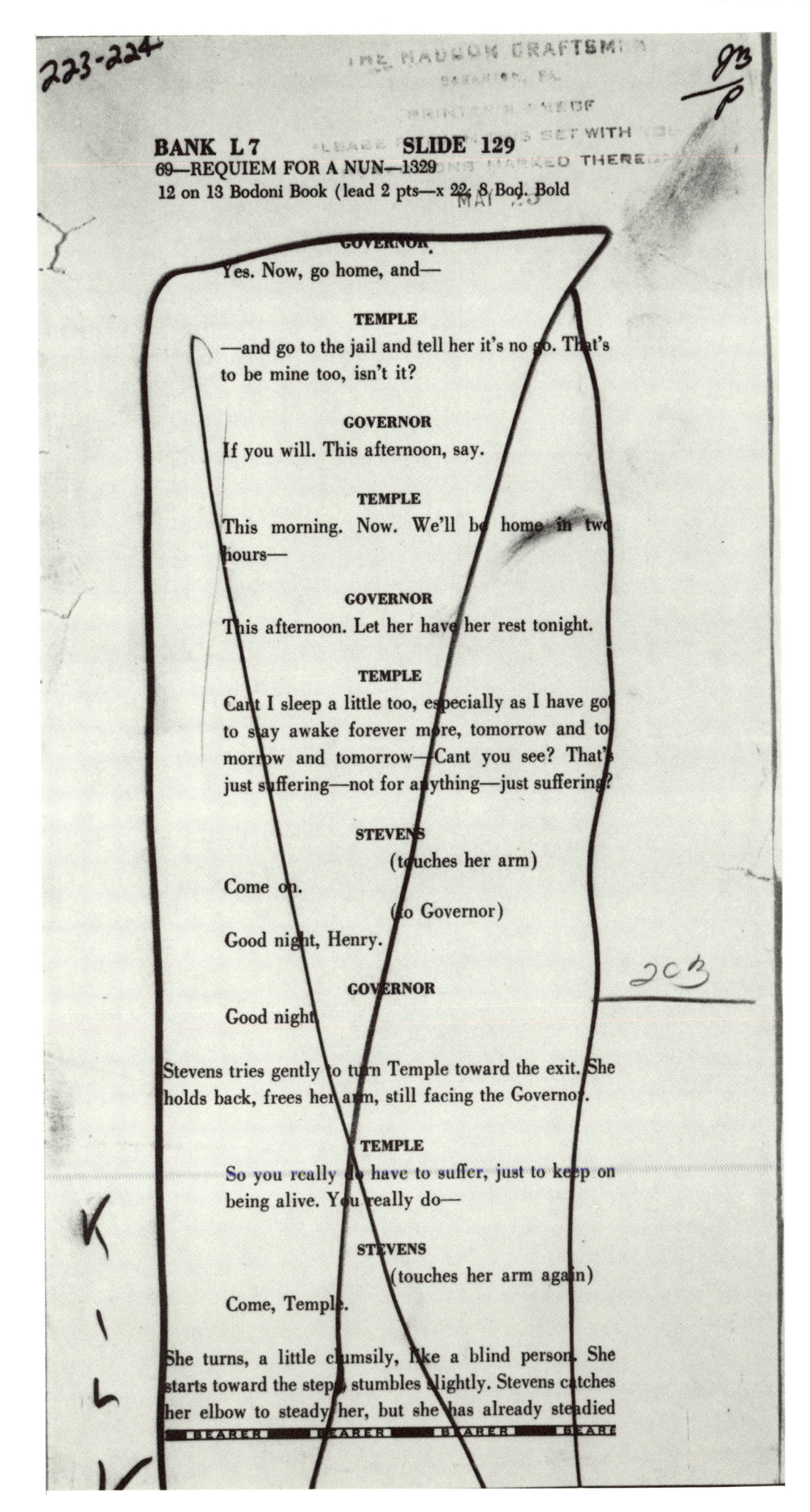

BANK L 7 **SLIDE 129**
69—REQUIEM FOR A NUN—1329
12 on 13 Bodoni Book (lead 2 pts—x 22, 8 Bod. Bold

GOVERNOR
Yes. Now, go home, and—

TEMPLE
—and go to the jail and tell her it's no go. That's to be mine too, isn't it?

GOVERNOR
If you will. This afternoon, say.

TEMPLE
This morning. Now. We'll be home in two hours—

GOVERNOR
This afternoon. Let her have her rest tonight.

TEMPLE
Cant I sleep a little too, especially as I have got to stay awake forever more, tomorrow and tomorrow and tomorrow—Cant you see? That's just suffering—not for anything—just suffering?

STEVENS
(touches her arm)
Come on.
(to Governor)
Good night, Henry.

GOVERNOR
Good night

Stevens tries gently to turn Temple toward the exit. She holds back, frees her arm, still facing the Governor.

TEMPLE
So you really do have to suffer, just to keep on being alive. You really do—

STEVENS
(touches her arm again)
Come, Temple.

She turns, a little clumsily, like a blind person. She starts toward the steps, stumbles slightly. Stevens catches her elbow to steady her, but she has already steadied

GAL. 69A

herself, frees her arm from him, and walks on.

TEMPLE

To save my soul—if I have a soul—If there is a God to save it—a God who wants it—

(Curtain)

2 - 3 - 47

Insert
Galley
67

TEMPLE (Cont)

~~again and, as everybody thought even safe, since now she wouldn't be asked to say anything say at all any more. Only they were wrong; the jury said Guilty and the judge said Hang and now everybody was already picking up his hat to go home, when she picked up that whip too: the judge said, 'And may God have mercy on your soul' and Nancy answered, 'Yes, Lord.'~~

  (She turns suddenly, almost briskly, speaking so
  briskly that her momentum carries her on past the instant
  when she sees and recognises Gowan sitting where she
  had thought all the time that the Governor was sitting
  and listening to her)

And that is all, this time. And so now you can tell us. I know you're not going to save her, but now you can say so. It wont be difficult. Just one word——

  (She stops, arrested, utterly motionless, but even
  then she is first to recover)

Oh God.

  (Gowan rises quickly. Temple whirls to Stevens)

Why is it you must always believe in plants? Do you have to? Is it because you have to? Because you are a lawyer? No, I'm wrong. I'm sorry; I was the one that started us hiding gimmicks on each other, wasn't it?

  (quickly: turning to Gowan)

Of course; you didn't take the sleeping pill at all. Which means you you didn't even need to come here for the Governor to hide you behind the door or under the desk or wherever it was he was trying to tell me you were hiding and listening, because after all the governor of a southern state has got to try to act like he regrets having to aberrate from being a gentleman——

GOWAN

Stop it, Boots. Quit it now.

TEMPLE

I'm sorry. Because it's all right. It doesn't matter. Your heart just has to break, and then it's all right. You can go on. You can forget it.

  (to Gowan)

I would have told you. I ——

  (quickly: to neither of them directly)

But it's all right; it doesn't matter; all that will save until tomorrow or whenever it'll be when we are through with this and ...

  (she stops; a moment; then to Stevens)

You see. I started to say 'Get back to chewing the old hair shirt again.' Then I knew that was wrong, so I started to say 'The new hair shirt.' Then I knew that was wrong too, because it wont last that long now, since you and his honor finally thought about hiding him behind the door or under the desk or wherever it was; it will be quick now, just painful, like a piece of glass or a box of carpet tacks——

2 - 3 - 48

                        GOWAN (to TEMPLE)
I said, stop it.
                        (to Stevens)
Why dont you give her the cigarette now?
                        (Stevens takes up the pack of cigarettes,
                        works the end of one cigarette out slightly,
                        and extends it to Temple. Gowan picks up the
                        lighter from the desk, snaps it on as Temple
                        takes the cigarette from the extended pack
                        and turns as by reflex to the proffered lighter,
                        before she seems to realise that it is Gowan who
                        has snapped it on and now holds it out. She
                        pauses, the cigarette suspended)
                        TEMPLE
Oh God. Again.

                        STEVENS
Unless you mean 'Thank God'. Go on. Say it.

                        TEMPLE (to Gowan)
Thanks.
                        (Then she seems to forget about the unlighted
                        cigarette. She turns back to Stevens; after a
                        moment Gowan closes the lighter and puts it
                        back on the desk)
All right. He said No.

                        GOWAN (before Stevens can answer)
Yes.

                        TEMPLE (to Gowan)
So you were under the desk all the time. But all right. Did he say why?

                        GOWAN
Yes. He cant.

                        TEMPLE
Cant?
                        (to Stevens)
The governor of a state, with all the legal power to pardon or at least reprieve, cant?

                        GOWAN (again before Stevens can answer)
That's law. If it was just law, Uncle Gavin could have plead insanity for her at any time, without bringing you here at two oclock in the morning----

                        TEMPLE (interrupts)
And the other parent too; dont forget that. I dont know yet how he got you here, and besides, it doesn't matter. But just dont forget it.

2 - 3 - 49

STEVENS
He wasn't even talking about justice. He was talking about
a child, a little boy----

TEMPLE (turning on him)
That's right. Make it good: the same little boy, to hold whose
normal and natural home together, the murdress, the nigger dopefiend whore, didn't hesitate to cast the last gambit---and maybe
gambit is wrong too but all right for that too-- she knew and had
her own debased and worthless life.
    (rapidly)
Oh yes, I know that answer too; that was brought out here tonight
too; that a little child shall not suffer in order to come unto
Me.
    (to Stevens again)
So good can come out of evil.

STEVENS (quietly)
It not only can, it must.

TEMPLE
So touché, then. Because what kind of natural and normal home
can that little boy have where his father -- if he still has one
after this -- or maybe it's a mother he wont have after the
court gets through with us -- may at any time tell him he has
no father?

GOWAN (sharper)
Boots.

STEVENS
Haven't you been answering that question yourself every day for
eight years? Didn't Nancy answer it for you when she told you
that you fought back, not for yourself, but for that little boy?
Not to show the father that he was wrong, nor even to prove to
the little boy that the father was wrong, but to let the little
boy learn with his own eyes that nothing, not even that, which
could possibly enter that house, could ever harm him?

TEMPLE
But I quit. Nancy told you that, too.

STEVENS
She doesn't think so now. Isn't that what she's going to
prove Friday morning?

TEMPLE
Friday. The black day. The day you never start on a journey.
Except that Nancy's journey didn't begin at daylight or sunup
or whenever it's polite or tactful to hang people, day after
tomorrow. Her journey began that morning when I got on that train
at the University eight years ago.

2 - 3 - 50

GOWAN
That was Friday too. That baseball game was on Friday too.

TEMPLE (wildly)
You see? Dont you see? It's nowhere near enough yet. Of course he wouldn't save her. If he did that, it would be over, Gowan could throw me out or I could throw Gowan out or the judge would throw both of us out and give Bucky to an orphanage, and it would be all over. But now it can go on, tomorrow and tomorrow and tomorrow, forever and forever and forever.
(to Gowan)
Tell me exactly what he said. You were here; you must have heard it. How long were you here? I mean, before we got here? maybe before we ever left Jefferson even? No, you couldn't have; you were still in bed asleep or at least pretending to, when I brought Bucky in and put him in your bed——
(whirls: to Stevens)
So that was it: the leaking valve, I believe you called it, at the filling station when we changed the wheel: to give him a chance to pass us and get here first, ahead of us——

STEVENS
Maybe a little ahead of us. The Governor said what he had to say about this a week ago.

TEMPLE
Yes; about the same time you sent me that telegram. What did he say?

STEVENS
He said, 'Who am I to have the brazen temerity and hardihood to set the puny appanage of my office in the balance against that simple undeviable aim? Who am I, to render null and abrogate the purchase she made with that poor crazed lost and worthless life?' That's what he said.

TEMPLE
Oh yes, he made it good too, didn't he? Round and ringing too. So it was not even in hopes of saving her life that I came here at two oclock in the morning. It wasn't even to be told that he had already decided not to save her. The reason I came here was not just to confess to my husband, but to do it in the presence of two strangers, something I had spent eight years trying to expiate so that my husband wouldn't have to know about it. Dont you see that that's just suffering? Not for anything; just suffering?

STEVENS
You came here to affirm the very thing which Nancy is going to die tomorrow morning to postulate: that little children, as long as they are little children, shall be intact, unanguished, untorn, unterrified.

2 - 3 - 51

TEMPLE
(after a moment; quietly)
All right. I've done that. Can we go home now? After all,
we've got to get a little sleep, you know.
(quickly)
That is, I presume I'm the one his honor designated to carry
the bad news to the jail tomorrow morning?

STEVENS (moves)
Of course. It is late.
(He takes up his hat, then the pack of cigarettes
and starts to put it into his pocket)

GOWAN
Maybe she wants one now.
(Stevens begins to withdraw the pack of cigarettes
from his pocket; only Gowan seems to remember that
Temple still has an unlighted cigarette in her
hand; even Temple looks at the cigarette stupidly
for a moment as Gowan snaps on the governor's
lighter again and extends it. Temple leans to it
and lights the cigarette)

TEMPLE
Thanks.
(But she puffs only once, then seems to forget the
cigarette again, does not even seem aware when she
puts the burning cigarette into the ashtray and
turns as Gowan comes around the desk, sliding the
lighter across to the middle of it, then picks up he
Temple's gloves and bag from the desk and hands them
to her)

GOWAN (roughly almost)
Here.

TEMPLE (takes the bag and gloves)
Thanks.
(She begins to walk toward the steps up which she
and Stevens entered, Stevens at her side, Gowan slightly
behind them both. As she reaches the first step, she
seems to stumble or falter, a little clumsily, like
a sleep-walker; it is not Stevens beside her, but
Gowan in the rear, who moves in and steadies her by
the elbow for a second before, still in that dazed
sleep-walker fashion, she frees her arm and descends
the first step)

TEMPLE (to no one)
To save my soul - if I have a soul. If there is a God to save it
- a God who wants it------

CURTAIN

Haldon

July 10, 1951

PRINTER:

Herewith new insert copy for the end of Act Two, Scene III, REQUIEM FOR A NUN. You will find old copy attached to galleys at this point. Please remove that copy and replace it by pages 2-3-48 to 2-3-51 herewith.

On page 2-3-47, please find speech

GOWAN

Stop it, Boots. Quit it now.

Please delete this speech and substitute for it the speech at top of new page 2-3-48:

STEVENS
(To Temple)

Stop it.

and continue with new copy attached herewith to the end of Act Two.

PS.

Attached herewith is also new copy for the end of the play, Galley 93 -- ACT Three, Scene I. It replaces the portioned deleted in pencil on that galley.

RJ

This must be done in page proof being sent Random on 7/13.

INSTEAD OF 3 SETS OF PAGE PROOFS THEY WANT 4 SETS. HCW

STEVENS
(to Temple)
Stop it.

GOWAN
Maybe we both didn't start hiding soon enough - by about eight years - not in desk drawers either, but in two abandoned mine shafts, one in Siberia and the other at the South Pole, maybe.

TEMPLE
All right. I didn't mean hiding. I'm sorry.

GOWAN
Dont be. Just draw on your eight years' interest for that.
(to Stevens)
All right, all right; tell me to shut up too.
(to no one directly)
In fact, this may be the time for me to start saying sorry for the next eight-year term. Just give me a little time. Eight years of grattiude might be a habit a little hard to break. So here goes.
(to Temple)
I'm sorry. Forget it.

TEMPLE
I would have told you.

GOWAN
You did. Forget it. You see how easy it is? You could have been doing that yourself for eight years: every time I would say 'Say sorry, please', all you would need would be to answer: 'I did. Forget it.'
(to Stevens)
I guess that's all, isn't it? We can go home now.
(he starts to come around the desk)

TEMPLE
Wait.
(Gowan stops; they look at each other)
Where are you going?

GOWAN
I said home, didn't I? To pick up Bucky and carry him back to his own bed again.
(they look at one another)
You're not even going to ask me where he is now?
(answers himself)
Where we always leave our children when the clutch-----

STEVENS (to Gowan)
Maybe I will say shut up this time.

GOWAN
Only let me finish first. I was going to say, 'with our handiest kinfolks.'
(to Temple)
I carried him to Maggie's.

2 - 3- 49

     STEVENS (moving)
I think we can all go now. Come on.

     GOWAN
So do I.
    (he comes on around the desk, and stops again; to
    Temple)
Make up your mind. Do you want to ride with me, or Gavin?

     STEVENS (to Gowan)
Go on. You can pick up Bucky.

     GOWAN
Right.
    (he turns, starts toward the steps front, where
    Temple and Stevens entered, then stops)
That's right. I'm probably still supposed to use the spy's entrance.
    (He turns back, starts around the desk again, toward
    the door at rear, sees Temple's glove and bag on the
    desk, and takes them up and holds them out to her;
    roughly almost)
Here. This is what they call evidence; dont forget these.
    (Temple takes the bag and gloves. Gowan goes on
    toward the door at rear)

     TEMPLE (after him)
Did you have a hat and coat?
    (He doesn't answer. He goes on, exits)
Oh God. Again.

     STEVENS (touches her arm)
Come on.
     TEMPLE
    (not moving yet)
Tomorrow and tomorrow and tomorrow----

     STEVENS
    (speaking her thought, finishing the sentence)
---he will wreck the car again against the wrong tree, in the wrong
place, and you will have to forgive him again, for the next eight
years until he can wreck the car again in the wrong place, against
the wrong tree----

     TEMPLE
I was driving it too. I was driving some of the time too.

     STEVENS (gently)
Then let that comfort you.
    (He takes her arm again, turns her toward the stairs)
Come on. It's late.

TEMPLE (holds back)

Wait. He said, No.

STEVENS

Yes.

TEMPLE

Did he say why?

STEVENS

Yes. He cant.

TEMPLE

Cant? The Governor of a state, with all the legal power to pardon or at least reprieve, cant?

STEVENS

That's just law. If it was only law, I could have plead insanity for her at any time, without bringing you here at two oclock in the morning----

TEMPLE

And the other parent too; dont forget that. I dont know yet how you did it .... Yes, Gowan was here first; he was just pretending to be asleep when I carried Bucky in and put him in his bed; yes, that was what you called that leaking valve, when we stopped at the filling station to change the wheel: to let him get ahead of us----

STEVENS

All right. He wasn't even talking about justice. He was talking about a child, a little boy-----

TEMPLE

That's right. Make it good: the same little boy to hold whose normal and natural home together, the murderess, the nigger, the dopefiend whore, didn't hesitate to cast the last gambit----and maybe that's the wrong word too, isn't it?---she knew and had: her own debased and worthless life. Oh yes, I know that answer too; that was brought out here tonight too: that a little child shall not suffer in order to come unto Me. So good can come out of evil.

STEVENS

It not only can, it must.

TEMPLE

So touche, then. Because what kind of natural and normal home can that little boy have where his father may at any time tell him he has no father?

STEVENS

STEVENS
Haven't you been answering that question every day for eight years? Didn't Nancy answer it for you when she told you how you had fought back, not for yourself, but for that little boy? Not to show the father that he was wrong, nor even to prove to the little boy that the father was wrong, but to let the little boy learn with his own eyes that nothing, not even that, which could possibly enter that house, could ever harm him?

TEMPLE
But I quit. Nancy told you that too.

STEVENS
She doesn't think so now. Isn't that what she's going to prove Friday morning?

TEMPLE
Friday. The black day. ~~The~~ The day you never start on a journey. Except that Nancy's journey didn't start at daylight or sunup or whever it is polite and tactful to hang people, day after tomorrow. Her journey started that morning eight years ago when I got on the train at the University----
        (she stops: a moment; then quietly)
Oh God, that was Friday too; that baseball game was Friday---
        (rapidly)
You see? Dont you see? It's nowhere near enough yet. Of course he wouldn't save her. If he did that, it would be over: Gowan could just throw me out, which he may do yet, or I could throw Gowan out, which I could have done until it got too late now, too late forever now, or the judge could have thrown us both out and given Bucky to an orphanage, and it would be all over. But now it can go on, tomorrow and tomorrow and tomorrow, forever and forever and forever---

STEVENS
        (gently tries to start her)
Come on.

TEMPLE (holding back)
Tell me exactly what he did say. Not tonight: it couldn't have been tonight - or did he say it over the telephone, and we didn't even need----

STEVENS
He said it a week ago---

TEMPLE
Yes, about the same time when you sent the wire. What did he say?

STEVENS (quotes)
'Who am I, to have the brazen temerity and hardihood to set the puny appanage of my office in the balance against that simple undeviable aim? Who am I, to render null and abrogate the purchase she made with that poor crazed lost and worthless life?'

2 - 3 - 51

TEMPLE (wildly)

And good too - good and mellow too. So it was not even in hopes of saving her life, that I came here at two o'clock in the morning. It wasn't even to be told that he had already decided not to save her. It was not even to confess to my husband, but to do it in the hearing of two strangers, something which I had spent eight years trying to expiate so that my husband wouldn't have to know about it. Dont you see? That's just suffering. Not for anything; just suffering.

STEVENS

You came here to affirm the very thing which Nancy is going to die tomorrow morning to postulate: that little children, as long as they are little children, shall be intact, unanguished, untorn, unterrified.

TEMPLE (quietly)

All right. I have done that. Can we go home now?

STEVENS

Yes.
(She turns, moves toward the steps, Stevens beside her. As she reaches the first step, she falters, seems to stumble slightly, like a sleepwalker. Stevens steadies her, but at once she frees her arm, and begins to descend)

TEMPLE
(on the first step: to no one, still with that sleepwalker air)

To save my soul - if I have a soul. If there is a God to save it - a God who wants it----

CURTAIN

Requiem for a Nun, II

2-3-51

TEMPLE (wildly)
And good too - good and mellow too. So it was not even in hopes of saving her life, that I came here at two o'clock in the morning. It wasn't even to be told that he had already decided not to save her. It was not even to confess to my husband, but to do it in the hearing of two strangers, something which I had spent eight years trying to explate so that my husband wouldn't have to know about it. Dont you see? That's just suffering. Not for anything; just suffering.

STEVENS
You came here to affirm the very thing which Nancy is going to die tomorrow morning to postulate: that little children, as long as they are little children, shall be intact, unanguished, unborn, unterrified.

TEMPLE (quietly)
All right. I have done that. Can we go home now?

STEVENS
Yes. Anxxxxx

(She turns, moves toward the steps. Stevens beside her. As she reaches the first step, she falters, seems to stumble slightly, like a sleepwalker. Stevens steadies her, but at once she frees her arm, and begins to descend)

TEMPLE
On the first step; to no one; still with the sleepwalker air)
To save my soul - if I have a soul. If there is a God to save it - a God who wants it------

CURTAIN

ACT THREE

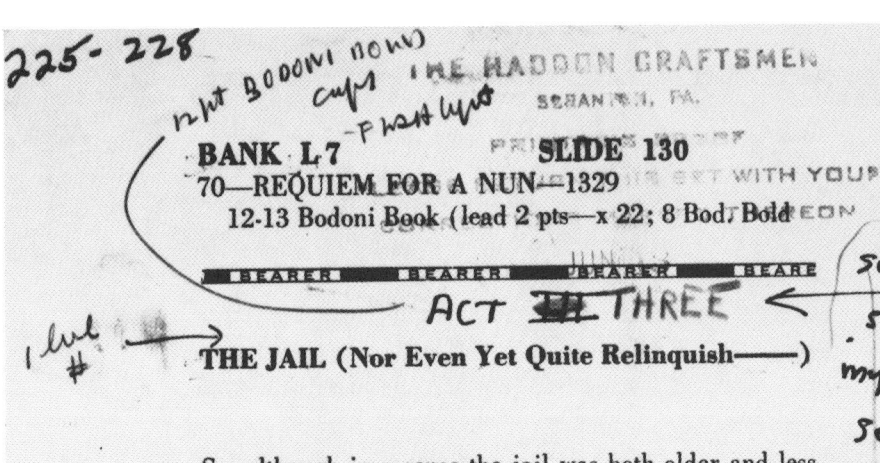

THE JAIL (Nor Even Yet Quite Relinquish———)

So, although in a sense the jail was both older and less old than the courthouse, in actuality, in time, in observation and memory, it was older even than the town itself. Because there was no town until there was a courthouse, and no courthouse until (like some unsentient unweaned creature torn violently from the dug of its dam) the floorless lean-to rabbit-hutch housing the iron chest was reft from the log flank of the jail and transmogrified into a by-neo-Greek-out-of-Georgian-England edifice set in the center of what in time would be the town Square (as a result of which, the town itself had moved one block south—or rather, no town then and yet, the courthouse itself the catalyst: a mere dusty widening of the trace, trail, pathway in a forest of oak and ash and hickory and sycamore and flowering catalpa and dogwood and judas tree and persimmon and wild plum, with on one side old Alec Holston's tavern and coaching-yard, and a little farther along, Ratcliffe's trading-post-store and the blacksmith's, and diagonal to all of them, *en face* and solitary beyond the dust, the log jail; moved—the town—complete and intact, one block southward, so that now, a century and a quarter later, the coaching-yard and Ratcliffe's store were gone and old Alec's tavern and the blacksmith's were a hotel and a garage, on a main thoroughfare true enough but still a business side-street, and the jail across from them, though transformed also now into two storeys of Georgian brick by the hand ((or anyway pocketbooks) of Sartoris and Sutpen and Louis Grenier, faced not even on a side-street but on an alley));

And so, being older than all, it had seen all: the mutation and the change: and, in that sense, had recorded them (indeed, as Gavin Stevens, the town lawyer and the county amateur Cincinnatus, was wont to say, if you would peruse in unbroken—ay, overlapping—continuity the history of a community, look not in the church registers and the courthouse records, but beneath the successive layers of calsomine and creosote and whitewash on the walls of the jail, since only in that forcible carceration

Galley 75-A

panes of it (the window): her frail and workless name, scratched by a diamond ring in her frail and workless hand, and the date: *Cecilia Farmer April 16th 1861;*

At which moment the destiny of the land, the nation, the South, the State, the County, was already whirling into the plunge of its precipice, not that the State and the South knew it, because the first seconds of fall always seem like soar: a weightless deliberation preliminary to a rush not downward but upward, the falling body reversed during that second by transubstantion into the upward rush of earth; a soar, an apex, the South's own apotheosis of its destiny and its pride, Mississippi and Yoknapatawpha County not last in this, Mississippi among the first of the eleven to ratify secession, the regiment of infantry which John Sartoris raised and organised with Jefferson for its headquarters, going to Virginia numbered Two in the roster of Mississippi regiments, the jail watching that too but just by cognizance from a block away: that noon, the regiment not even a regiment yet but merely a voluntary association of untried men who knew they were ignorant and hoped they were brave, the four sides of the Square lined with their fathers or grandfathers and their mothers and wives and sisters and sweethearts, the only uniform present yet that one in which Sartoris stood with his virgin sabre and his pristine colonel's braid on the courthouse balcony, bareheaded too while the Baptist minister prayed and the Richmond mustering officer swore the regiment in; and then (the regiment) gone; and now not only the jail but the town too hung without motion in a tideless backwash: the plunging body advanced far enough now into space as to have lost all sense of motion, weightless and immobile upon the light pressure of invisible air, gone now all diminishment of the precipice's lip, all increment of the vast increaseless earth: a town of old men and women and children and an occasional wounded soldier (John Sartoris himself, deposed from his colonelcy by a regimental election after Second Manassas, came home and oversaw the making and harvesting of a crop on his plantation before he got bored and gathered up a small gang of irregular cavalry and carried it up into Tennessee to join Forrest), static in quo, rumored, murmured of war only as from a great and incredible dreamy distance, like far summer thunder: until the

BANK L 7   SLIDE 138
78—REQUIEM FOR A NUN—1329
12-13 Bodoni Book (lead 2 pts—x 22; 8 Bod. Bold

closed door to a sick-room, Yoknapatawpha County was already nine months gone in reconstruction; by New Year's of '66, the gutted walls (the rain of two winters had washed them clean of the smoke and soot) of the Square had been temporarily roofed and were stores and shops and offices again, and they had begun to restore the courthouse: not temporary, this, but restored, exactly as it had been, between the two columned porticoes, one north and one south, which had been tougher than dynamite and fire, because it was the symbol: the County and the City: and they knew how, who had done it before Colonel Sartoris was home now, and General Compson, the first Jason's son, and though a tragedy had happened to Sutpen and his pride—a failure not of his pride nor even of his own bones and flesh, but of the lesser bones and flesh which he had believed capable of supporting the edifice of his dream—they still had the old plans of his architect and even the architect's molds, and even more: money, (strangely, curiously) Redmond, the town's domesticated carpetbagger, symbol of a blind rapacity almost like a biological instinct, destined to cover the South like a migration of locusts; in the case of this man, arriving a full year before its time and now devoting no small portion of the fruit of his rapacity to restoring the very building the destruction of which had rung up the curtain for his appearance on the stage, had been the formal visa on his passport to pillage; and by New Year's of '76, this same Redmond with his money and Colonel Sartoris and General Compson had built a railroad from Jefferson north into Tennessee to connect with the one from Memphis to the Atlantic Ocean; nor content there either, north or south: another ten years (Sartoris and Redmond and Compson quarreled, and Sartoris and Redmond bought—probably with Redmond's money—Compson's interest in the railroad, and the next year Sartoris and Redmond had quarreled and the year after that, because of simple physical fear, Redmond killed Sartoris from ambush on the Jefferson Square and fled, and at last even Sartoris's supporters—he had no friends: only enemies and frantic admirers—began to understand the result of that regimental election in the fall of '62) and the railroad was a part of that system covering the whole South and East like the veins in an oak leaf and itself mutually adjunctive to the other

Galley 79-A

which would run, and did: crept popping and stinking out of the alley at the exact moment when the banker Bayard Sartoris, the Colonel's son, passed in his carriage: as a result of which, there is on the books of Jefferson today a law prohibiting the operation of any mechanically-propelled vehicle on the streets of the corporate town: who (the same banker Sartoris) died in one (such was progress, that fast, that rapid) lost from control on an icy road by his (the banker's) grandson, who had just returned from (such was progress) two years of service as a combat airman on the Western Front and now the camouflage paint is weathering slowly from a French point-seventy-five field piece squatting on one flank of the base of the Confederate monument, but even before it faded there was neon in the town and A.A.A. and C.C.C. in the county, and W.P.A. ("and XYZ and etc." as "Uncle Pete" Gombault, a lean clean tobacco-chewing old man, incumbent of a political sinecure under the designation of United States marshal —an office held back in reconstruction times, when the State of Mississippi was a United States military district, by a Negro man who was still living in 1925—firemaker, sweeper, janitor and furnace-attendant to five or six lawyers and doctors and one of the banks—and still known as "Mulberry" from the avocation which he had followed before and during and after his incumbency as marshal: peddling illicit whiskey in pint and half-pint bottles from a cache beneath the roots of a big mulberry tree behind the drugstore of his pre-1865 owner—put it) in both; W.P.A. and XYZ marking the town and the county as war itself had not: gone now were the last of the forest trees which had followed the shape of the Square, shading the unbroken second-storey balcony onto which the lawyers' and doctors' offices had opened, which shaded in its turn the fronts of the stores and the walkway beneath; and now was gone even the balcony itself with its wrought-iron balustrade on which in the long summer afternoons the lawyers would prop their feet to talk; and the continuous iron chain looping from wooden post to post along the circumference of the courthouse yard, for the farmers to hitch their teams to; and the public watering trough where they could water them, because gone was the last wagon to stand on the Square during the spring and summer and fall Saturdays and trading-days, and not only the Square but the streets leading into it were paved now, with fixed signs of interdiction and admonition applicable only to something

BANK L 7   SLIDE 141
81—REQUIEM FOR A NUN—1329
12-13 Bodoni Book (lead 2 pts—x 22; 8 Bod. Bold

tawpha County, one last irreconcilable fastness of stronghold from which to enter the United States, because at last even the last old sapless indomitable unvanquished widow or maiden aunt had died and the old deathless Lost Cause had become a faded (though still select) social club or caste, or form of behavior when you remembered to observe it on the occasions when young men from Brooklyn, exchange students at Mississippi or Arkansas or Texas Universities, vended tiny Confederate battle flags among the thronged Saturday afternoon ramps of football stadii; one world: the tank gun: captured from a regiment of Germans in an African desert by a regiment of Japanese in American uniforms, whose mothers and fathers at the time were in a California detention camp for enemy aliens, and carried (the gun) seven thousand miles back to be set halfway between, as a sort of secondary flying buttress to a memento of Shiloh and The Wilderness; one universe, one cosmos: contained in one America: one towering frantic edifice poised like a card-house over the abyss of the mortgaged generations; one boom, one peace: one swirling rocket-roar filling the glittering zenith as with golden feathers, until the vast hollow sphere of his air, the vast and terrible burden beneath which he tries to stand erect and lift his battered and indomitable head—the very substance in which he lives and, lacking which, he would vanish in a matter of seconds—is murmurous with his fears and terrors and disclaimers and repudiations and his aspirations and dreams and his baseless hopes, bouncing back at him in radar waves from the constellations;

And still—the old jail—endured, sitting in its rumorless cul-de-sac, its almost seasonless backwater in the middle of that rush and roar of civic progress and social alteration and change like a colarless (and reasonably clean: merely dingy: with a day's stubble and no garters to his socks) old man sitting in his suspenders and stocking feet, on the back kitchen steps inside a walled courtyard; actually not isolated by location so much as insulated by obsolescence: on the way out of course (to disappear from the surface of the earth along with the rest of the town on the day when all America, after cutting down all the trees and leveling the hills and mountains with

BANK L 7 SLIDE 143
83—REQUIEM FOR A NUN—1329
12-13 Bodoni Book (lead 2 pts—x 22, 8 Bod. Bold

children of that second outland invasion following a war, would also have become not just Mississippians but Jeffersonians and Yoknapatawphians: by which time—who knows?—not merely the pane, but the whole window, perhaps the entire wall, may have been removed and embalmed intact into a museum by an historical, or anyway a cultural, club of ladies—why, by that time, they may not even know, or even need to know: only that the window-pane bearing the girl's name and the date is that old, which is enough; has lasted that long: one small rectangle of wavy, crudely-pressed, almost opaque glass, bearing a few faint scratches apparently no more durable than the thin dried slime left by the passage of a snail, yet which has endured a hundred years) who are capable and willing too to quit whatever they happen to be doing—sitting on the last of the wooden benches beneath the last of the locust and chinaberry trees among the potted conifers of the new age dotting the courthouse yard, or in the chairs along the shady sidewalk before the Holston House, where a breeze always blows—to lead you across the street and into the jail and (with courteous neighborly apologies to the jailor's wife stirring or turning on the stove the peas and grits and side-meat—purchased in bargain-lot quantities by shrewd and indefatigable peditation from store to store—which she will serve to the prisoners for dinner or supper at so much a head (plate) payable by the County, which is no mean factor in the sinecure of her husband's incumbency) into the kitchen and so to the cloudy pane bearing the faint scratches which, after a moment, you will descry to be a name and a date;

Not at first, of course, but after a moment, a second, because at first you would be a little puzzled, a little impatient because of your illness-at-ease from having been dragged without warning or preparation into the private kitchen of a strange woman cooking a meal; you would think merely *What? So what?* annoyed and even a little outraged, until suddenly, even while you were thinking it, something has already happened: the faint frail illegible meaningless even inference-less scratching on the ancient poor-quality glass you stare at, has moved, under your eyes, even while you stared at it, coalesced, seeming actually to have entered into another sense than vision: a scent, a whisper, filling that hot cramped

BANK L 7   SLIDE 146
86—REQUIEM FOR A NUN—1329
12-13 Bodoni Book (lead 2 pts—x 22; 8 Bod. Bold

Begin new right-hand page

~~ACT THREE~~ *delete see my note.*

SCENE I

Interior, the Jail. 10:30 A.M. March twelfth.

The common room, or 'bull-pen'. It is on the second floor. A heavy barred door at left is the entrance to it, to the entire cell-block, which—the cells—are indicated by a row of steel doors, each with its own individual small barred window, lining the right wall. A narrow passage at the far end of the right wall leads to more cells. A single big heavily barred window in the rear wall looks down into the street. It is mid-morning of a sunny day.

The door, left, opens with a heavy clashing of the steel lock, and swings back and outward. Temple enters, followed by Stevens and the Jailor. Temple has changed her dress, but wears the fur coat and the same hat. Stevens is dressed exactly as he was in Act Two. The Jailor is a typical small-town turnkey, in shirt-sleeves and no necktie, carrying the heavy keys on a big iron ring against his leg as a farmer carries a lantern, say. He is drawing the door to behind him as he enters.

Temple stops just inside the room. Stevens perforce stops also. The Jailor closes the door and locks it on the inside with another clash and clang of steel, and turns.

JAILOR

Well, Lawyer, singing school will be over after tonight, huh?
   (to Temple)
You been away, you see. You don't know about this, you aint up with what's—
   (he stops himself quickly; he is about to commit what he would call a very bad impoliteness, what in the tenets of his class and kind would be the most grave of gaucherie and bad taste: referring directly to a recent bereavement in the presence

more suffering simply because there was a little more time left for a little more of it, and we might as well use it since we were already paying for it; and that would be all; it would be finished then. But we were wrong again. That was all, only for you. You wouldn't be any worse off if I had never come back from California. You wouldn't even be any worse off. And this time tomorrow, you wont be anything at all. But not me. Because there's tomorrow, and tomorrow. All you've got to do is, just to die. But let Him tell me what to do. No: that's wrong; I know what to do, what I'm going to do; I found that out that same night in the nursery too. But let Him tell me how. How? Tomorrow, and tomorrow, and still tomorrow. How?

NANCY

Trust in Him.

TEMPLE

Trust in Him. Look what He has already done to me. Which is all right; maybe I deserved it; at least I'm not the one to criticise or dictate to Him. But look what He did to you. Yet you can still say that. Why? Why? Is it because there isn't any thing else?

NANCY

I dont know. But you got to trust Him. Maybe that's your pay for the suffering.

STEVENS

Whose suffering, and whose pay? Just each one's for his own?

NANCY

Everybody's. All suffering. All poor sinning man's.

STEVENS

The salvation of the world is in man's suffering. Is that it?

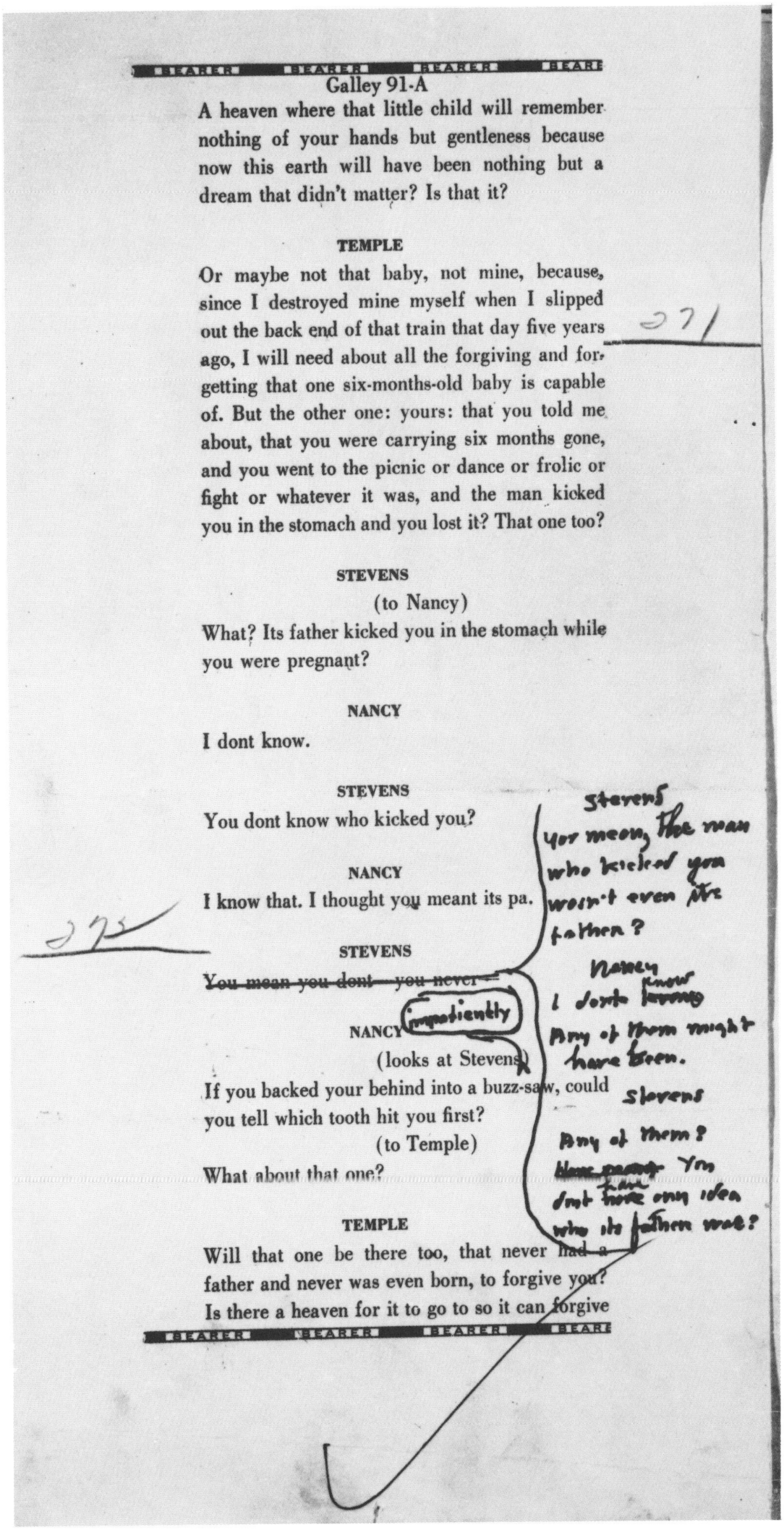

Galley 91-A
A heaven where that little child will remember nothing of your hands but gentleness because now this earth will have been nothing but a dream that didn't matter? Is that it?

TEMPLE

Or maybe not that baby, not mine, because, since I destroyed mine myself when I slipped out the back end of that train that day five years ago, I will need about all the forgiving and forgetting that one six-months-old baby is capable of. But the other one: yours: that you told me about, that you were carrying six months gone, and you went to the picnic or dance or frolic or fight or whatever it was, and the man kicked you in the stomach and you lost it? That one too?

STEVENS
(to Nancy)
What? Its father kicked you in the stomach while you were pregnant?

NANCY
I dont know.

STEVENS
You dont know who kicked you?

NANCY
I know that. I thought you meant its pa.

STEVENS
~~You mean you dont—you never—~~

NANCY *impatiently*
(looks at Stevens)
If you backed your behind into a buzz-saw, could you tell which tooth hit you first?
(to Temple)
What about that one?

TEMPLE
Will that one be there too, that never had a father and never was even born, to forgive you? Is there a heaven for it to go to so it can forgive

[handwritten marginalia:]

Stevens
You mean the man who kicked you wasn't even its father?

Nancy
I dont know. Any of them might have been.

Stevens
Any of them? You dont have any idea who its father was?

BANK L 6   **SLIDE 143**
93—REQUIEM FOR A NUN—1329
12-13 Bodoni Book (lead 2 pts—x 22; 8 Bod. Bold

> that the Jailor has barely time to react to it, though he does so: with quick concern, with that quality about him almost gentle, almost articulate, turning from the door, even leaving it open as he starts quickly toward her)

Here; you set down on the bench; I'll get you a glass of water.

> (to Stevens)

Durn it, Lawyer, why did you have to bring her—

TEMPLE
> (recovered)

I'm all right.

She walks steadily toward the door. The Jailor watches her.

JAILOR

You sure?

TEMPLE
> (walking steadily and rapidly toward him and the door now)

Yes. Sure.

JAILOR
> (turning back toward the door)

Okay. I sure dont blame you. Durned if I see how even a murdering nigger can stand this smell.

He passes on out the door and exits, invisible though still holding the door and waiting to lock it.

TEMPLE
> (walking: at the door)

Anyone to save it. Anyone who wants it. If there is none, I'm sunk. We all are. Doomed. Damned.

Corrected Galleys 211

Galley 93-A

Finished.

(she exits)

STEVENS
(follows through the door)
Of course we are. Hasn't He been telling us that for going on two thousand years?

They exit. ~~He exits~~. The door closes in, clashes, the clash and clang of the key as the Jailor locks it again; the three pairs of footsteps sound and begin to fade in the outer corridor.

~~Curtain~~ Stevens,

Temple, followed by ~~Gowan~~, approaches the door.

JAILOR'S VOICE
(off-stage: surprised)

Howdy, Gowan, here's your wife now.

TEMPLE
(walking)

Anyone to save it. Anyone who wants it. If there is none, I'm sunk. We all are. Doomed. Damned.

STEVENS
(walking)

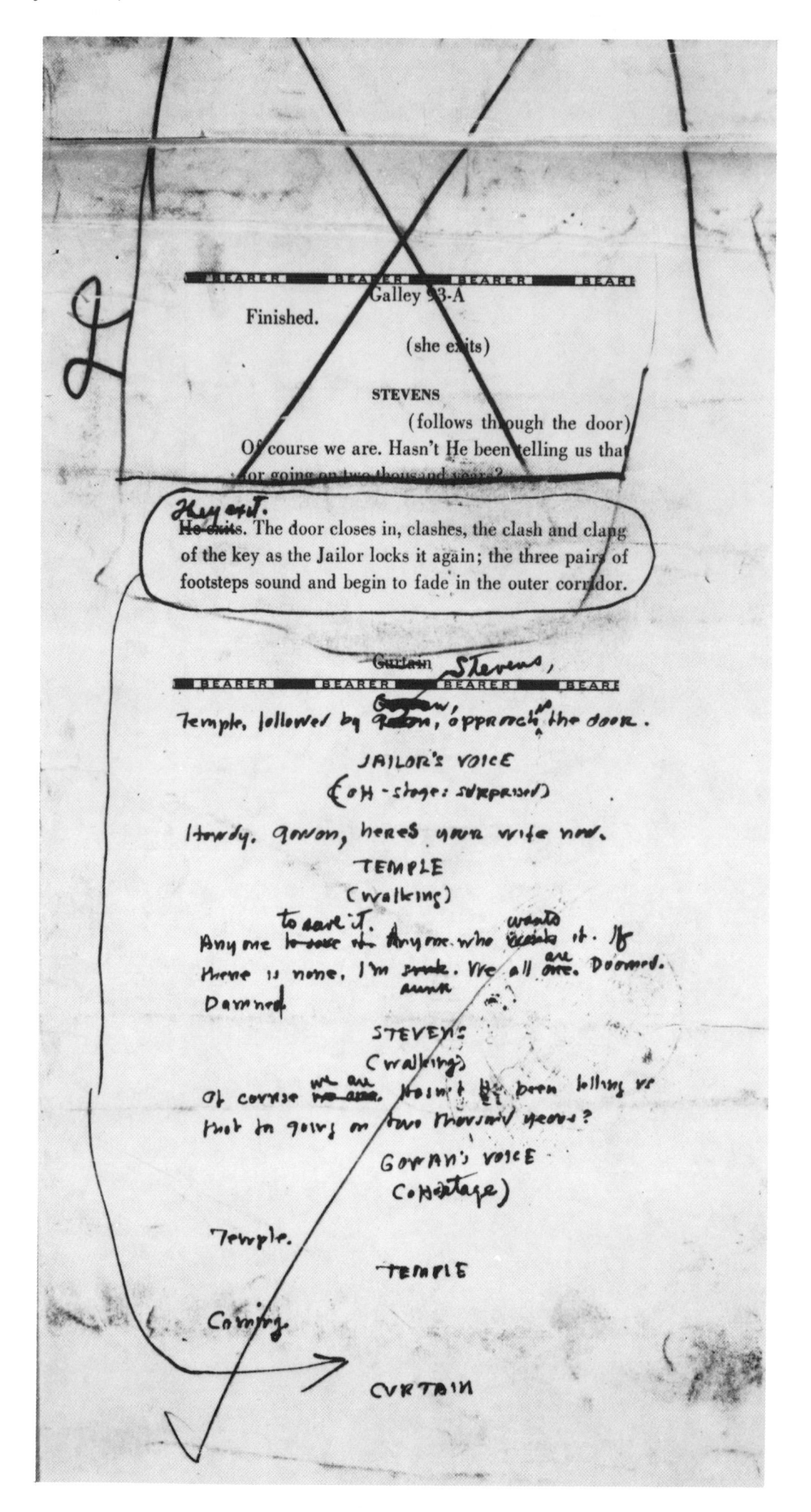

Of course we are. Hasn't He been telling us that for going on two thousand years?

GOWAN'S VOICE
(offstage)

Temple.

TEMPLE

Coming.

CURTAIN

Corrected Galleys 213

70 | REQUIEM FOR A NUN

GOWAN

I dont. I had nothing to do with it. I wasn't even the plaintiff. I didn't even instigate—that's the word, isn't it?—the suit. My only connection with it was, I happened by chance to be the father of the child she— Who in hell ever called that a drink?

He dashes the whiskey, glass and all, into the ice bowl, quickly catches up one of the empty tumblers in one hand and, at the same time, tilts the whiskey bottle over it, pouring. At first he makes no sound, but at once it is obvious that he is laughing: laughter which begins normally enough, but almost immediately it is out of hand, just on hysteria, while he still pours whiskey into the glass, which in a moment now will overflow, except that Stevens reaches his hand and grasps the bottle and stops it.

STEVENS

Stop it. Stop it, now. Here.

He takes the bottle from Gowan, sets it down, takes the tumbler and tilts part of its contents into the other empty one, leaving at least a reasonable, a believable, drink, and hands it to Gowan. Gowan takes it, stopping the crazy laughter, gets hold of himself again.

GOWAN

(holding the glass untasted)

~~Six~~ years, ~~Six~~ years on the wagon—and this is

[margin note: Correct *Eight* it]

71 | REQUIEM FOR A NUN

what I got for it: my child murdered by a dope-fiend nigger whore that wouldn't even run so that a cop or somebody could have shot her down like the mad-dog— You see? ~~Six~~ years without the drink, and so I got whatever it was I was buying by not drinking, and now I've got whatever it was I was paying for and it's paid for and so I can drink again. And now I dont want the drink. You see? Like whatever it was I was buying I not only didn't want, but what I was paying for it wasn't worth anything, wasn't even any loss. So I have a laugh coming. That's triumph. Because I got a bargain even in what I didn't want. I got a cut rate. I had two children. I had to pay only one of them to find out it wasn't really costing me anything— Half price: a child, and a dope-fiend nigger whore on a public gallows: that's all I had to pay for immunity.

STEVENS
There's no such thing.

GOWAN
From the past. From my folly. My drunkenness. My cowardice, if you like—

STEVENS
There's no such thing as past either.

GOWAN
That is a laugh, that one. Only, not so loud, huh? to disturb the ladies—disturb Miss Drake—Miss

88 | REQUIEM FOR A NUN

TEMPLE

Truth? We're trying to save a condemned murderess whose lawyer has already admitted that he has failed. What has truth got to do with that?
(rapid, harsh)
We? I, *I*, the mother of the baby she murdered; not you, Gavin Stevens, the lawyer, but I, Mrs Gowan Stevens, the mother. Cant you get it through your head that I will do anything, *anything?*

STEVENS

Except one. Which is all. We're not concerned with death. That's nothing: any handful of petty facts and sworn documents can cope with that. That's all finished now; we can forget it. What we are trying to deal with now is injustice. Only truth can cope with that. Or love.

TEMPLE
(harshly)
Love. Oh, God. Love.

STEVENS

Call it pity then. Or courage. Or simple honor, honesty, or a simple desire for the right to sleep at night.

TEMPLE

You prate of sleep, to me, who learned six years

STEVENS

I did. I said, so you can sleep at night.

91 | REQUIEM FOR A NUN

TEMPLE

And I told you I forgot six years ago even what it was to miss the sleep.

She stares at him. He doesn't answer, looking at her. Still watching him, she reaches her hand to the table, toward the cigarette box, then stops, is motionless, her hand suspended, staring at him.

TEMPLE

There is something else, then. We're even going to get the true one this time. All right. Shoot.

He doesn't answer, makes no sign, watching her. A moment: then she turns her head and looks toward the sofa and the sleeping child. Still looking at the child, she rises and crosses to the sofa and stands looking down at the child; her voice is quiet.

TEMPLE

So it was a plant, after all; I just didn't seem to know for who.

(she looks down at the child)

I threw my remaining child at you. Now you threw him back.

STEVENS

But I didn't wake him.

TEMPLE

Then I've got you, lawyer. What would be better

BANK 5   **Slide 90**

93 | REQUIEM FOR A NUN

STEVENS
Nothing.

TEMPLE
Swear.

STEVENS
Would you believe me?

TEMPLE
No. But swear anyway.

STEVENS
All right. I swear.

TEMPLE
        (crushes cigarette into tray)
Then listen. Listen carefully.
        (she stands, tense, rigid,
        facing him, staring at him)
Temple Drake is dead. Temple Drake will have been dead six years longer than Nancy Mannigoe will ever be. If all Nancy Mannigoe has to save her is Temple Drake, then God help Nancy Mannigoe. Now get out of here.

She stares at him; another moment. Then he rises, still watching her; she stares steadily and implacably back. Then he moves.

TEMPLE
Good night.

BANK 7   **Slide 19**

166 | REQUIEM FOR A NUN

knows? because of that fragility, a kind of pride, triumph: you have waited for destruction: you endured; it was inevitable, inescapable, you had no hope. Nevertheless, you did not merely cringe, crouching, your head, vision, buried in your arms; you were not watching that poised arrestment all the time, true enough, but that was not because you feared it but because you were too busy putting one foot before the other, never for one instant really flagging, faltering, even though you knew it was in vain—triumph in the very fragility which no longer need concern you now, for the reason that the all, the very worst, which catastrophe can do to you, is crush and obliterate the fragility; you were the better man, you outfaced even catastrophe, outlasted it, compelled it to move first; you did not even defy it, not even contemptuous: with no other tool or implement but that worthless fragility, you held disaster off as with one hand you might support the weightless silken canopy of a bed, for (six) long years while it, with all its weight and power, could not possibly prolong the obliteration of your fragility over five or six seconds; and even during that five or six seconds you would still be the better man, since all that it—the catastrophe —could deprive you of, you yourself had already written off (six) years ago as being, inherently of and because of its own fragile self, worthless.

BANK 7   Slide 33
208 | REQUIEM FOR A NUN

TEMPLE

That's right. Make it good: the same little boy to hold whose normal and natural home together, the murderess, the nigger, the dopefiend whore, didn't hesitate to cast the last gambit—and maybe that's the wrong word too, isn't it?—she knew and had: her own debased and worthless life. Oh yes, I know that answer too; that was brought out here tonight too: that a little child shall not suffer in order to come unto Me. So good can come out of evil.

It not only can, it must.

TEMPLE

So *touché*, then. Because what kind of natural and normal home can that little boy have where his father may at any time tell him he has no father?

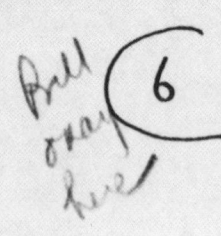

STEVENS

Haven't you been answering that question every day for eight years? Didn't Nancy answer it for you when she told you how you had fought back, not for yourself, but for that little boy? Not to show the father that he was wrong, nor even to prove to the little boy that the father was wrong, but to let the little boy learn with his own eyes